MAGICAE: POWER DAWNING

MAGICAE: POWER DAWNING
CHRONICLES OF AN URBAN ELEMENTAL™ BOOK 2

AUBURN TEMPEST
MICHAEL ANDERLE

DISRUPTIVE IMAGINATION®

This book is a work of fiction. All of the characters, organizations, and events portrayed in this novel are either products of the author's imagination or are used fictitiously. Sometimes both.

Copyright © 2023 LMBPN Publishing
Cover by Fantasy Book Design
Cover copyright © LMBPN Publishing
A Michael Anderle Production

LMBPN Publishing supports the right to free expression and the value of copyright. The purpose of copyright is to encourage writers and artists to produce the creative works that enrich our culture.

The distribution of this book without permission is a theft of the author's intellectual property. If you would like permission to use material from the book (other than for review purposes), please contact support@lmbpn.com. Thank you for your support of the author's rights.

LMBPN Publishing
PMB 196, 2540 South Maryland Pkwy
Las Vegas, NV 89109

Version 1.01, February 2023
eBook ISBN: 979-8-88541-326-8
Print ISBN: 979-8-88878-225-5

THE MAGICAE: POWER DAWNING TEAM

Thanks to our JIT Team:

Daryl McDaniel
Jim Caplan
Dave Hicks
Christopher Gilliard
Dorothy Lloyd
Diane L. Smith
John Ashmore
Jan Hunnicutt

Editor
SkyFyre Editing Team

CHAPTER ONE

Turns out that killing a hella powerful fae prince hybrid and getting your ass kicked in the process doesn't excuse you from door duty at the annual Gagne family Canada Day party. Even though I've never played the part of a traffic cop while on the job, I got elected to do so today.

The silver fox striding up the driveway has always reminded me of Pierce Brosnan but without a British accent. He has aged well over the twenty-seven years I've known him, and I can only imagine how many hearts would break in Montréal if he ever decided to settle down. "Hey, Jules. I hope I'm not late."

That makes me laugh because *he's totally late*.

The party is already raging in the backyard. Papa always said Uncle Leon would be late for his own funeral, and we've learned to joke about it.

"Not at all, Uncle Leon. Come on in." I greet our father's closest friend in the open bay of the fire station where we live and point straight back at the door leading to the yard. "Everyone's out back."

He hands me a grocery store fruit tray in a plastic shopping bag, and I set it on the munchies table next to the brass fireman pole. Hitting the power button on the bay door, I get that rolling closed before following him toward the back.

"Help yourself to anything." I flip open the lids so he can scan the selection. "We've got beer, cider, coolers, sodas, and anything else you could think of."

He reaches into one of the two ice bins flanking the back door and grabs a can as we join the rest of the guests. Briar is grilling, Charlie is fussing over the food tables under the tent, and Kenzie is keeping the slip-and-slide strip slick with water.

With the hose in her hand, it might look like she's simply watering it down, but with her water powers, she's secretly amping up the game so our friends and family can get some speed.

Add to that, our friends from near and far have gathered to drink, play some music, and celebrate a long weekend and it's exactly the stress relief we all need.

Zephyr comes up beside me and hands me a cooler. "Is it just me or does all this seem surreal?"

"It's not just you, bro." I snap the tab of my can open and take a long drink, watching people mill around. These are people we've known for years—our whole lives in some cases—but now that the truth has come out about our fae powers, it feels a little like we're strangers.

Or at least like we live in a different world.

"Zephyr, come here, my man," a buddy calls.

My brother *clinks* drinks with me and pushes off to join whatever conversation his buddy is drawing him into.

Leon finishes saying hello to Charlie and doubles back to me. "How are you doing, *ma belle?*"

The worry in his warm, hazel eyes tugs at my heartstrings. Although the four of us decided not to come out to everyone about our fae transition, Leon is a fire chief and was part of the response team at the warehouse explosion. There no denying the ten-foot-tall, green-scaled mass of fucked up fae monster lying dead in the parking lot or the fact that we put him there.

Thankfully, with the veil between the human and fae realms currently down, Leon has seen a lot of crazy shit over the past seven months. He's taking it pretty well.

At least he seems to be.

"We're doing okay. Everything is still sinking in. It's taking a lot of getting used to. The good thing is we have each other, so we've got the support we all need."

A chorus of cheers rings out, and Danny climbs onto a picnic table. He's one of Zephyr's friends. He's drunk and nearly steps into a bowl of Charlie's potato salad.

I pity him and Zephyr if he can't rein him in.

Charlie's very protective of her potato salad.

"I was thinking about your father this morning," Leon continues. "He was one of the best-damned firefighters I ever worked with. He had a magical touch, I tell you. Like...fires seemed to bend to his will. Like he could tame them or something. It got me wondering if maybe he had some fire fae in him too."

The praise is something I've heard all my life. Papa's firefighter buddies insisted he was a flame whisperer and had some mystical power to keep them safe while they got a blaze tamed down.

As a kid, I figured they were exaggerating for our benefit. Now, though, I don't know.

Charlie says he was wholly human, but I thought I was too until a week and a half ago.

Zephyr and Briar get Drunk Danny off our picnic table. He's one Jägerbomb from being trashed, but this is a "you do you" and call an Uber crowd. Everyone is rowdy and raucous, and as long as no food is lost during the drunken debauchery, s'all good.

One of the paralegal "Aceys" from the firm where Kenzie works taps me on the shoulder. "Hey, do you know if there are any more of those brownies?"

"Sure, let me check." I'm pretty sure that was Casey, but it could've been Macy or Tracey. I can never keep them straight. The three are sleek brunettes with a fetish for pencil skirts and heels.

It's a thing.

The party is going strong in the garage bay where the firetrucks used to park. A handful of our longtime firefighter family and their other halves are hovering around Charlie's sandwich spread.

They're arguing about ingredients.

"There's some extra spice in it," Braydon insists. "I'm telling you. Like chili peppers or something."

"It's not spice," his wife Ainsley argues. "It's a tanginess I can't place."

"It's caper juice," I tell them. "She dips the lettuce in it before she lays it down on the bread. Says it keeps it crunchy and adds a bit of flavor."

"Capers!" Braydon snaps his fingers. "I knew it!"

His wife laughs. "You did not. You thought it was chili peppers."

"Yeah, but I was going to guess capers next."

"You're such a liar, Braydon." One of his buddies punches his arm and laughs.

I scan the table and the counter and jog upstairs to check inside the oven. Sure enough, there's a fresh batch of brownies staying warm inside. I pull them out, cut them up, and head back to the party.

"Oh, yum," one of the wives downstairs gushes.

"I've always loved Charlie's cooking," Braydon tells the group. "When we were teenagers, she kept a tight leash on these guys, so we usually ended up at their house for the weekend. When she brought in snacks, everyone would stop whatever they were doing to rush over and grab some before they were gone."

"Yeah, we were lucky. It could've gone much worse for us

when our parents died." I flash them a big smile and carry the brownies outside, where a chorus of cheers and a crowd of my cop coworkers jostling to grab their share meet them.

"Charlie's baking is a thing of legend," Marx claims.

Morin nods and stuffs his mouth with a brownie. "Normally, I'd say you're exaggerating for effect, but in dis case, you're right."

The two men have been a fixture at the station since before I was born, but thankfully, they took me under their wing when I was a rookie and have taught me so much about the kind of cop I want to be.

After letting them each snag another chocolate treat, I make my way over to where Uncle Leon is telling Anna and Micah about our adoptive father.

"One summer, during a particularly nasty wildfire season, they asked a bunch of us to take a seasonal gig at a forestry station way up at the edge of Terrebonne. Eight of us bunked up north, but Marcel couldn't bear to be away from Laurette and the kids. He made that terrible commute every morning for a month."

Micah laughs and arches a brow. "I'd think he'd have embraced the chance to get away from you guys. From what I've heard, you were monsters. He probably didn't want to leave all the headaches to your *Maman*."

My mouth drops open. "Rude. We weren't monsters. We were spirited young orphans who needed a loving, guiding hand."

Leon chuckles. "Whatever the reason, he trekked back and forth for weeks. Anyway, one morning he gets to the forestry station, all bleary-eyed from the drive. He mentions his little sister stopped by to make donuts the night before with the kids, and he brought a box up for us."

Micah grins. "Charlie's donuts are epic good."

"We knew that, but there he was with no box of donuts. He said he must've left them in the truck, so naturally, we go out to get them. But the back seat of his truck is empty."

I laugh. "This is a sad story, Uncle Leon."

He makes eyes at me and chuckles. "Your Papa says, 'Shit, I must've left them back at home.' It wasn't easy for him to get out the door on those mornings with little goblins running around."

I might protest if I didn't remember that summer. We hated him being gone so much. It wasn't uncommon for Zephyr to hide Papa's work boots or for Kenzie to be mysteriously stricken ill in an attempt to keep him home with us.

"Anyway, Marcel shrugs and says he'll try to bring them tomorrow. We all sigh and grumble, but then, as we all head back to the station, the most wonderful thing happens! It starts to rain!"

Micah laughs. "Which meant there'd be no wildfire raging that morning."

Leon waggles his brows. "With the danger of a fire outbreak low, we make it our mission to get those donuts up to the forestry station where they belonged."

Anna giggles. "What did you do?"

"What any devoted firefighter would do. A few of us piled into the biggest fire engine at the station and went on a rescue mission. We peeled down the street, lights flashing and sirens blaring."

I snack on a brownie as he winds up his story.

"When we got to your house, the four goblins ran out in their pajamas, and sure enough, there was a big box of delicious home-baked donuts with our name on them."

"I remember that morning." I laugh. "You guys drove us to school in the big pumper truck, and our friends talked about it for days. It was the highlight of our school year."

Leon winks at me. "Cops aren't the only heroes that go above and beyond for donuts...especially Charlie's donuts."

I help myself to one more brownie, then return to circulating.

Briar has finished with the burgers and turned the grill over to Kenzie. My sister from another mister is grilling up her famous marinated veggie kabobs. Well, she thinks they're famous, anyway.

Briar is leaning against the big oak in the back corner of the yard, nursing a beer and watching the festivities. I set the near-empty brownie tray on the table under the tent, grab another cooler, and join him in the shade.

"Having fun?" I *clink* my bottle against his.

"Yeah, I am." His response seems stiff, and I follow his gaze to where he's watching a large black raven perched on the square tower on the attic of our roof. "It's weird, but I'd swear that bird is watching us."

It takes a moment, but it clicks almost instantly. "I'm sure you're right. That's Bakkali's raven. I'm not sure if it's his familiar or friend or what, but that's him."

"Why is he here staring at us? It's freaking me out."

I chuckle. "I would guess that Bakkali is surveying his city and ensuring all is well. He seems to know what is going on with the empowered members of his guild. Maybe the raven helps him to do that."

In that vein of thought, I raise my arm and give the bird a thumbs-up. "S'all good here, Kevin."

Briar snorts. "The Viking's raven is named Kevin?"

"I have no idea, but that was the Sandman's raven's name, so I'm going with it."

Briar laughs and raises his beer. "We're good, Kevin. Thanks for checking in."

When the bird pushes off and soars into the pink sky, flapping its wings, I marvel at how strange our life has become.

"It's weird, don't you think?" Briar absently notes. "Our family and friends are the same people we've loved for years and years. They look the same, we have shared pasts, yet everything feels different and slightly out of sync."

I lean against his muscle-banded arm and lay my head against his shoulder. "I was thinking the same thing, but it's not them that changed. It's us."

"For sure." Briar and I sip our drinks in companionable silence, watching the party. Eventually, some of the guys wave Briar over to complete their volleyball team, and he wanders off to play.

I sit at one of the picnic tables next to Uncle Leon. He slings an arm around my shoulder and pulls me in with a proud smile. "He'd be so proud of you guys if he were here. You know that right?"

"I hope so. I hope they both would be."

"They would, but Marcel always held an especially tender spot in his heart for the little babe who brought his family to life. He was in love from the moment he found you that day."

"You were there, right?"

Uncle Leon meets my gaze, the golden flecks in his eyes warm and soft. "I sure was."

"I heard the story a dozen times from Papa and *Maman*, but I don't know if I've ever heard your account of things."

Leon shifts a couple of feet down the bench and straddles the wood plank to face me. "It was a nasty blaze, hotter and bigger than it should have been for the time it had been burning. A shop owner from across the road told us he thought there were people inside, but the chief says until we assess the structure and the spread, no one was to go in."

I chuckle. "It's hard to imagine the man who cautioned me to be safe my whole life charging into a blaze against orders."

Leon presses the mouth of his beer bottle to his lips and tips it back. After he swallows, he chuckles. "That was AKM—After Kids Marcel. Before Kids Marcel was a thrill-seeker. He fancied himself a warrior for those who needed a champion."

"Sounds like Papa."

"Anyway, the minute Chief walked off to check the status of things, Marcel pulled his mask down and slipped into the side entrance. I was still cursing when he came out a few moments later, singed and streaked with soot, holding the tiniest little infant in his arms."

"I wasn't that small."

He makes a face and stares at his cupped hand. "You were a wee lima bean blinking up at us. Perfectly calm. No burns. No screaming or squalling. You looked around with big eyes like you were ready for the next adventure."

"I guess my state makes more sense now."

He shrugs. "I suppose. Still, you being a fire elemental takes nothing away from how he claimed you and fell in love with Laurette in the process."

No. I suppose not.

Uncle Leon, aka Fire Chief Leonide Côté, might not be related to us by blood, but he's one of our parents' friends who's been there our whole lives.

He's a good guy, even if he's chronically late...well, for anything except a fire.

Having a long weekend gives us an extra day to work on our training. While the four of us have grown comfortable calling our element to the fore, Azland isn't convinced we are one with our weapons: my whip, Zephyr's Storm Staff, Kenzie's bracelet, and Briar's sledgehammer.

Extra training practice is his answer.

While all other Canadians are sleeping it off, enjoying a quiet summer day, or continuing the long weekend celebrations, we're battling conjured enemies in the back yard of our fire station.

Azland has used his magic to produce an injured victim flopped unconscious beneath a pile of stone rubble he directed Briar to create.

"Ye've got to get him out of there without makin' any noise," Tad reminds us. "In this scenario, there are enemies all around."

"Then why shout so many instructions at us?" Zephyr asks.

"Because he's not part of the simulation," Azland snaps. "Focus and stop being difficult."

Zephyr rolls his eyes. "Touchy."

After Briar carefully moves enough of the stones to get to the fake victim, Zephyr bends and tries to pick the guy up.

The injured person lets out a loud wail.

"Quietly!" Azland yells.

"He's hurt," Briar says rather uselessly. "We can't move him without him making noise."

"Dude, we have to try to be quiet," Zephyr whispers to the nondescript magically projected injured guy. "Shh." Zephyr tries picking him up again, but the guy cries out, this time louder than the last.

Azland throws up his hands. "Enemies have now found you, and you're dead."

"We're *not* dead," Zephyr grouses.

"Fine, then try again. If you're not quiet, enemies will be at your location any moment," Azland says.

Zephyr glances at me. "Should we gag him or something?"

I snort. "This is a rescue operation, not a kidnapping."

"Then what?" Zephyr asks.

"Kenzie needs to heal him," Briar says.

"Kenzie isn't with you in this scenario," Azland states. "It's only you two, boys, so think."

Briar looks at where Kenzie and I are sitting on the sidelines awaiting our turn and frowns. "We need to find a way to move him without hurting him."

Zephyr throws his hands up. "I thought training was about practicing cool fighting moves."

"How many times have you needed to rescue someone from a hostile area recently?" Azland asks.

Zephyr opens his mouth to argue, then lets it fall shut without a word. Stepping back, he assesses the fake situation with a fresh outlook. "Okay, let's try something."

Zephyr crouches, then slides his staff under the guy's shoulder blades. He focuses his gaze on the end of his staff. "B, raise the ground under him a bit so I can get some air under him."

Briar kneels beside him and uses his powers to raise him off the ground gently. At the same time, Zephyr creates a cushion of air to ease the man's limp body up and floats him away, holding him aloft.

Zephyr and Briar get the victim away from the rubble, then the guy disappears. Kenzie and I clap our hands for their success.

"Excellent job," Tad praises.

Azland doesn't appear to agree. "Had that been real, you would have taken way too long, made too much noise, and most likely lost your target in addition to provoking a battle."

"I didn't hear him complaining," Zephyr points out.

Azland narrows his eyes, but he's learned better than to get into an argument with a petulant Zephyr.

Tad waves, cutting through the tension. "All right, I think we've made ye eat enough vegetables fer one day. Who wants to try an all-out brawl?"

Yee-fucking-haw.

Everyone does.

Azland sets up the battlefield, casting a colorful, shimmering target at three points in our yard: one green, one blue, and one red.

Then he hands each of us a crystal roughly the size of our palms. Kenzie and I have blue crystals, Zephyr and Briar have red, and Azland and Tad take the green.

"Carrying your crystal through the correctly colored target will earn you points. Forcing another person's crystal through your target will earn you double points. Each hit you take will cause you to lose points."

Briar grunts. "So we want to hold onto our crystals and take them through our targets as often as possible, while also trying to take other people's crystals through and prevent them from going through their own?"

I blink. "While also avoiding taking damage."

"Exactly."

Zephyr curses. "And Tad and Azland are on the same team? They've all got years of experience on us."

Azland rolls his shoulders and grins. "So will most of the folks you'll find yourselves fighting."

"We don't have a healer on our team," Zephyr protests. "Jules and Kenzie will heal themselves no matter who plows through their targets."

Azland shrugs. "You won't always have Kenzie with you during a battle. Besides, Jules needs to practice getting to the healer before throwing herself back into the fray."

Rude. I toss my crystal into the air, flipping it end over end while the sunlight catches it, sending reflected light off it like a kaleidoscope. "Are we going to stand around whining and pointing fingers all day, or are we going to get this game started?"

It turns out to be a lot more fun and difficult than expected. Kenzie positions herself at our blue portal for a while, running our crystals through it as many times as she can while I try to keep the others from getting to their targets.

Before long, Briar presses a hand against the ground and raises a stone wall in front of our target, ending that strategy and forcing Kenzie to engage.

I spend time guarding the red portal, preventing Zephyr from getting through. Briar is trying to build another stone wall in front of Tad's and Azland's green target, but Tad isn't having it.

"It's a battle between druid and earth elemental!" I shout in a cheesy announcer voice, and Kenzie laughs.

Snapping my fire whip, I manage to keep Zephyr from scoring for a while before he assaults me with a gust of wind, knocking me on my ass.

When I *thud* onto the ground, a second gust hits me and steals my crystal out of my hand. He runs it through the red target twice before I tackle him.

We go down in a tangle of limbs, wrestling and elbowing each other in a series of "Oofs" and "Ouches."

In the end, I tear it out of his hands and reclaim my crystal. "That's how you do it, wind boy."

Zephyr laughs, rolls to his feet, and brushes off his shirt. "Yeah, yeah. You fight like a girl."

When I reassess, I realize Azland has staged an assault on Briar, stealing his red crystal and carrying it through his green target a few times.

Zephyr rushes over to help his partner. Kenzie and I decide to gang up on Azland and Tad to keep them from getting too far ahead of us.

After that, Kenzie and I retake our portal but not before Kenzie loses her crystal to a sneaky maneuver from Tad and Aurora.

Green Team's experienced warriors dominate the field, forcing us to join forces against them with some frequency. Kenzie and I come up with a few clutch moves. One involves her using a jet stream of water to shoot Briar's captured crystal out of his hand and over everyone's heads.

With a running leap, I snatch it out of the air and run it through our blue portal to gain double points.

We play for almost an hour, shouting, forming and un-forming alliances, racing and chasing each other around the yard, and building our stamina.

Eventually, Azland calls the game. We flop on the grass, laughing and trying to pull oxygen into our tired lungs.

"You four are getting better." Azland sounds surprised and

superior.

Zephyr laughs. "What's that? A compliment from the taciturn dog wizard?"

"Not really. You still have a long way to go."

Briar sighs. "Seriously, dude. Can't you say anything nice without following it up?"

"Prince of the backhanded compliment," I add.

Azland grunts. "Briar is the only prince here. I'm the guy trying to keep you four alive."

CHAPTER TWO

The next morning, I lay in bed and watch Jack and Jack make lazy laps around their bowl. When the craziness of fae awakenings, half-demon enemies, and drug-induced division in my city gets too much, it's soothing to chill and watch my goldfish.

Life is good in fish-landia.

They swim, darting around the sunken ship and the greenery, and occasionally they venture up to the surface to check for food flakes.

Living the dream.

I roll out of bed, shuffle my bare feet over to my dresser, and shake some food onto the water's surface. As it floats there, they nibble excitedly and wiggle their fins. "There's nothing wrong with being content with a simple life, little dudes. It keeps things in perspective."

I watch them swim for a while before getting dressed for work and making my way out to our home's common area. "Morning, girlfriend."

"Morning." Kenzie lowers her coffee mug. She's glamored her blue skin to its original rich brown for work.

No, wait—since she was born the daughter of a magical healer from the water empire of Uisce, I suppose her *original* skin tone is ice blue. She only grew up black because *Maman* glamored her true appearance.

It's mind-bendy.

Still, Kenzie looks like Kenzie, and her raging sea of an identity crisis calmed when Tad taught her how to glamor her awakened self to blend in.

Now, she looks the same as she always did growing up, and we're eternally grateful to Tad for fielding that tsunami. It'll take time for her to adjust to being a different kind of person of color.

"Where are the boys?" I ask.

"Zephyr's sleeping it off. Briar went out last night and texted around three that he was going home with a random from the club. He'll go to work from wherever he ended up."

I grab a pie plate from the fridge, cut a fat wedge of tourtière, and stick it into the microwave. Then I slide a mug under the spout of the Keurig and select my flavor for the morning.

What goes with meat pie?

Peppermint tea?

I go with that and get things started. "I know Briar's a big boy, but I don't like him going home with randos from an illegal fight club. The type of people hanging around down there is a bad element."

Kenzie arches a brow. "He's a very big boy and can take care of himself. Besides, he's part of that bad element. He's a fighter at that illegal fight club."

I know. I don't like to think about it.

My breakfast *beeps* in the microwave, and I pull it out and grab a fork. "Do you think it's fair? Now that his powers have awakened, isn't it like cheating?"

Kenzie tosses me a placemat, and I set my plate down before going back for my tea. "You're assuming he's the only fae-awakened fighter. From what he's told me, there are more and more awakened fighters on the roster. Lots of them don't know how to vent the sudden aggression or life chaos that comes with a fae transition, so they go there."

"To pound opponents to a pulp. That's healthy."

Kenzie chuckles. "You're cranky this morning. What's bugging you?"

"Nothing. I'm good." I dig into my breakfast and try to lose myself in the savory delight of meat, onion, spices, and fluffy pastry.

"No, you're not. You need to get laid."

"There's one problem with that."

"Which is?"

"The only guy I've liked in ages is sexing my sister."

She blinks at me. "You like Tad?"

"What's not to like? He puts Abercrombie models to shame. He's one helluva fighter. He's fit, smart, magically gifted, and has a wicked sense of humor."

Kenzie's brow tightens more with each thing I say. "Careful, now. You're rhyming off the shopping list of sexy for the guy I'm currently sleeping with."

"My point exactly." I chuckle inwardly and keep chewing.

"Are you interested in Tad? I thought you two were hitting it off as friends." Unlike most women, when Kenzie is facing something she's not enjoying, her lawyer mode kicks in, and instead of getting frazzled, she gets focused and calm.

Like now.

"Are you fucking with me?"

I snort and take a sip of my tea. "Of course I am. I love Tad, no question. He's all those things and more, but he's totally into you, and he and I hit it off as friends. My point is, me liking people is rare, and I don't often like people enough to want to date them."

"Who says you have to like them?"

I roll my eyes. "I'm not wired the same way as you, Kenz. I see the worst of humanity all day at work. When I'm contemplating going home with someone, I have to know who they are and what they stand for. I'm not good at anonymous. I don't let my guard down well."

"Then what about the hottie guy from the park? He's attractive, you know he has a construction business, and you know he spends his downtime helping fae kids fit in and have a little fun. What was his name again?"

"Gareth, but you already know that. You never forget a name." I finish my breakfast and take my plate over to the dishwasher. "It's a moot point. He's not interested. I gave him my card two weeks ago, and he hasn't called."

"Maybe he's shy."

I laugh. "You were there when he dissed me at Casse Croûte, right? Did he seem shy? No…I didn't think so."

"He teased you about raising the bar from battery-operated dildos. I think that shows interest."

I take a last sip of tea and pour the rest down the sink. "You keep thinking that. I've gotta go to work."

Before she can come back at me about Gareth, I shrug into my backpack, wrap my ankle around the brass pole, and slide down to the garage bay to say good morning to Scarlett.

Most people who work outside the home wish their commute were shorter. I'm the outlier. As the pull of wind tugs at my leather jacket and the buildings of the city blur past, I wish I had another half-hour to ride before I pull into the station's parking lot.

Scarlett, my Ducati Multistrada V4S motorcycle is the bomb. She's sleek, fast as fuck, and has enough of a throaty growl to turn heads but not so much that she's pretentious and disturbing the peace.

The world and all its problems melt away when I'm on her.

She is my great escape, and I take time to appreciate her every chance I get.

Rue Notre-Dame is my favorite way to cross the city. It's the historic east-west street of old Montréal and follows the contours of the St. Lawrence River. Through Hochelaga, past the Old Port, and the Notre-Dame Basilica. Downtown Montréal is a beautiful thing.

Unfortunately, I don't go even that far.

Too soon, I'm turning off the westbound lanes and winding through the side streets. Dickson to Hochelaga, then I'm gearing down to pull into the parking lot of Montréal's Twenty-Third Precinct.

After pulling off my helmet, I kick my leg over the seat and leave my girl to gather attention for another day.

"Morning, Stanton." I open one of the Tupperware containers in my backpack to offer the desk sergeant a treat as I pass.

"Morning, Gagne." He makes his selection with a nod of appreciation. "Have a good one."

"You too."

I unload my backpack on the scratched-up table next to the copier and head into the locker room. After setting my helmet on the shelf of my locker, I hook my backpack, finger-comb my helmet hair, and head out.

"Morning, fellas." I drop into my office chair and power up my computer for the day. "Help yourself to the treat table. I brought some brownies, a bunch of cookies, and some tamale casserole from yesterday's festivities."

Tremblay stands in his cubicle and salutes me with a brownie in hand. He already made himself a plate.

Likewise with Morin. He has a mitt full of cookies.

"No moss grows on you, boys."

Marx laughs and rises from his desk. "Some of us have the manners to wait until we're invited to partake. Some don't."

Morin waggles his pinky in the air as he scarfs down a cookie. "Well, la-tee-da."

Marx gives Morin a middle-finger salute and forks in a mouthful of tamale casserole. "Delicious as always. Please tell Charlie we appreciate her."

"Finally, something we agree on," Morin adds. "She does more to serve de citizens of de city than de brass. Having cops in a good mood after filling up on home cooking is de best thing for Montréal."

"He's not lying." Reese chuckles. "I've seen Marx when he's hangry. It's not a pretty sight."

Tremblay teases, "To be fair, a well-fed Marx isn't a pretty sight, either."

I laugh, scrolling my mouse awake. I love these guys. Even since finding out about my awakening, they've been the same old goofy friends I count on.

Although it's possible that without me, they know they'd be eating noodles out of Styrofoam cups and stale donuts every day.

I haven't told them everything. They don't know the whole long story about the elemental children being spirited away to keep our essences from being consumed by the six Poreskoro children. Or that *Maman* was a Scaith Warrior. Or that there's an invisible tower in the middle of Boucherville National Park that acts as fae headquarters.

I don't think they need to hear everything.

They know I had an awakening of fae genes and have fiery powers. They understand they might give me an advantage in certain situations or a disadvantage in others.

At least we figured out why I like my shower water so hot.

The banter and jibes die after everyone fills their plates and settles back at their desks. Then it's back to business.

I spend most of the morning with my mind thoroughly focused on a string of armed robberies where the criminals only take infant formula and baby items. Desperate times. It's sad.

The phone rings, startling me out of my daze. "Hello? Inspector Gagne."

"Yo, Firestar! Burning the candle from both ends? Blazing your trail? Sparking any good leads lately?"

I chuckle at my bestie's attempt at humor. He thinks he's much funnier than he is. "Hey, Luc. To what do I owe the pleasure?"

"I see dead people."

"I'm aware."

"I have something I need to talk to you about. Can you come down to the morgue?"

I glance at the tall stack of cases that got away from me while I was out of commission during my awakening, adjustment, and Lamech Poreskoro targeting me.

I haven't gotten halfway through them.

The responsible thing would be to focus and see Luc at the morgue on my lunch break.

Except…I can guarantee whatever Luc has for me will be much more interesting than itemizing stolen organic washcloths and chemical-free baby bottles.

The mystery of what he wants to show me is too compelling to resist. "Yep. I'm on my way."

Luc's lab is the second to last on the left, in the basement of the medical examiners' building a few blocks from my precinct. It's a newer, fancier municipal building than my station house, but a faint chemical smell permeates everything. Hard pass.

I'll take my cracked ceiling tiles and chipped paint, thank you very much.

Luc is sitting at his desk and beating out an erratic rhythm to whatever electronic music he's pumping into his massive, LED-lit headphones. He smiles, bops his head for whatever big finale he hears, and after a wild but impressive silent drum solo, he takes off his headphones and joins me.

"And the crowd goes wild." I wave excited jazz hands.

"Thank you, thank you very much," he acknowledges with his best Elvis lip curl.

Luc kinda looks like Elvis—a skinny young Elvis with shaggy, spiky hair and inappropriate slogan T-shirts. This one says Everyone was excited at Autopsy Club... It's open Mike night.

I snort. "I like the shirt."

He grins and presses a hand down the front. "Thanks. I got my sister a heat press for her birthday so I can get her to make me better shirts."

"Oh, man. You mean you took out the filter of marketable good taste."

"Something like that." He waggles his brows. "Any new powers I should know about? Can Briar turn himself entirely into stone yet?"

"Not entirely, no. Let's see...Kenzie is still blue but learned to cast a glamor to appear human. Briar's using his super strength to clean up in illegal cage-fighting matches. Zephyr is finally sleeping through the night. Turns out he isn't as volatile and hot-headed as we always thought. He had a hurricane inside him and hadn't slept for fifteen years."

"That would do it. I get homicidal after one night of my cat trying to sleep on my face. Good for him. I'm glad for the updates."

"Don't forget you're inside the vault. Everything about my siblings is still hush-hush. The captain and the guys on my squad know about me, but that's for safety and full disclosure. The fact that my brothers and sister are fae is private."

"Of course. My lips are sealed. You can trust me with your awesome new fae magic secrets."

By the expectant way he's looking at me, he's waiting for

some big reveal. "Sorry to disappoint. I *am* getting stronger, though. Bigger flames. Hotter. More control."

"Are you still ending up naked?"

"Yep. Tad *poofed* back to Toronto last night to check in with the head of his Guild of Governors. He said he'll continue to work on getting me a new wardrobe."

"Or even a onesie under your clothes that doesn't burn up. Like Superman." His enthusiasm is endearing.

Honestly, if there were a Fae Elemental Fan Club, Luc would be the president.

I'm ready to change the subject. "Anyway, why did you call me down here?"

"What do you think?" Luc rifles through a stack of files on his desk and comes away with a folder in hand. "This is a morgue. When a pathologist calls you, it's about bodies—it's always about bodies."

I figured. "What's so unique about today's body that I had to rush over here and kill a bunch of brain cells breathing in the eau de death?"

Luc grunts. "If this place killed brain cells, would I still be as wondrously intelligent as I am today?"

"Maybe not, but you're the number one case study of how this job makes people weird."

He considers that. "Fine. Weird, I will accept. Dumb, absolutely not. You will agree once you see what I've got for you."

I follow Luc to one of the two autopsy tables. A thin white sheet covers a body. He pulls back the drape far enough to reveal the hand.

It's feminine, with slender, filthy fingers. This woman was living rough.

"Take a look at this." He lifts the hand, and I bend for a closer look at what he's showing me.

Weird. There's some magenta veining, like blood vessel spider webs or the roots of a plant spreading under her fingernails.

"What is that?"

"Not sure, but look at this." He tucks the woman's hand back under the sheet and leads me to his desk. After taking off his gloves, he pitches them into the bin and pulls up a screen on his computer.

There's a picture of a pale green circle with a bunch of squiggles inside it. It's a cell or something he's seen in his microscope, but I've got nothing. "Luc, I don't speak geek. What am I looking at?"

"Teresa captured this last night." He pats a huge, beige machine. "She's the best microscopic examiner I've ever had the pleasure of working with."

"You named your microscope Teresa? Dude, this is what I'm talking about. You've gotta get more fresh air."

Luc feigns insult. "Teresa and I are very happy down here, fuck you very much. Look what she found. These are the cells from under her fingernails. What do you notice?"

The squiggles in the center of the cells have three distinct shapes. Some are round with soft edges, some are jagged, and some are smooth in the center and jagged around their borders.

"There are different shapes?"

Luc grins, apparently pleased with my deductive observation. "These cells are in the process of changing. Specifically, the change from human to fae."

"She died because of an awakening gone wrong?"

"Not exactly. See the center of the cells? That's the nucleus, where the DNA is stored. Check out those strange protrusions."

"Luc, you are a strange protrusion. Can you explain, in plain English, what's going on?"

"Boring, but fine." Luc points at the screen as he continues. "Up until now, I've seen people with human cells, fae cells, and cells in the process of changing. That process doesn't cause irregularities in the nucleus. It's a smoother, more natural process."

"Trust me. It didn't feel natural when it happened to me. I bet my cells were jagged like these."

"No, they weren't. I checked."

Figures. He's so weird.

"Okay, so what do you mean by a smoother, more natural process?" I rub my head, wondering if the headache coming on is from the chemicals in the lab or this conversation.

"A magical awakening is a natural thing." Luc holds up a finger to stop me from arguing. "It might feel like a truck hit you, but on a microscopic level, the magic is doing its work. These cells aren't undergoing a natural magic awakening. They're mutating."

"Mutating? Like Ninja Turtles?"

"Yeah, like Ninja Turtles. Only I don't think it was radiation in the sewers that caused it."

"Then what?"

He grins as if I asked the right question. "In every cadaver where we've seen this bizarre veining, the tox screen has come back positive for Second Sight."

"Great. Even though we destroyed the factory, it's still killing people."

"Seems so."

"What are we looking at? Has the chemistry of the drug changed to trigger this? Is it contaminated? Are they designing it as a two-point-oh variant version?"

"No idea. I see dead people. I don't hear from them."

"Let's be thankful for that. The world is fucked up enough without zombies and resurrections."

"True, but here's what I can give you in the meantime." He hands me a thick file folder with glossy color printouts of the cellular slides. Luc's handwriting is scribbled on them in red marker, circling and pointing out where the DNA is visibly mutating.

There are also three headshots of three victims who exhibited the same markers: magenta veining under their fingernails, Second Sight in their systems at the time of death, and mutations on a cellular level.

Unfortunately, that's all that links the three dead.

Otherwise, they seem to have nothing in common. One is a respected Black businessman who worked in an office downtown, one is a First Nations student at McGill University, and one is the homeless woman whose hand I inspected. Her file says she was living in a flophouse down near the Jacques Cartier Bridge.

"All different ages, ethnicities, and social settings."

Luc nods. "And all died while using Second Sight and exhibiting unnatural mutations."

I tuck the file folder under my arm and lift my fist for a bump. "One day, I wish you would call me down here and say hey, Jules, I've got a case all neatly solved and wrapped up for you."

Luc laughs. "I don't believe that for a second. If there were no mystery to solve, you'd lose your mind, not to mention your job security."

He meets my fist with a bump and I turn on my heel. "Thanks for the good times."

"That's what *she* said."

I laugh. "I'm sure she did."

Outside the building, I draw a deep breath of fresh air, take out my phone, and scroll through my contacts. When I find the name I'm looking for, I select it and strike off toward the parking lot. "Hey, Rene? Are you around?"

"I checked the obits this morning, and my name wasn't in them. So, yeah, I'm still kicking."

"Great. Can we meet? I have something that needs your eyes."

"Same place?"

"Hells yeah, best lunch in Montréal."

CHAPTER THREE

The best lunch place in Montréal is Poutine Centrale. I park Scarlett at the curb and head inside to find Rene Michaud standing at the door waiting for me. Rene and I go way back, far enough for us to know each other's favorite lunch restaurants and for them to be the same.

We both have a penchant for talking out the worst cases on the streets of Montréal while eating the city's best fries, gravy, and cheese curd specialties.

"It's been a while. How are things?" He pushes off the wall to join me in line, and I swing my backpack around to grab my wallet.

"Good. You know...a lot of changes."

He nods but won't make me elaborate because he knows what kind of changes I'm talking about—the fae powers kind.

I order a medium pulled pork poutine with a Sprite and he orders a Sloppy Joe poutine special with a Coke. It's my treat because I asked him here.

Inside, there's one long table that stretches to the back or the bar seating along the side wall and front. Neither offer much privacy for the types of conversations we tend to have, so we go out back and claim one of the wooden picnic tables by the back fence.

"What's new with the fae outreach squad?" I set the folder to the side for the moment, take a sip of my soda, and get ready to dig in.

"Things have been pretty crazy for the task force." Rene tucks into his poutine.

"No doubt." It's been rough, but it's also incredibly important work. For the last few months, Rene has been building a task force of cops dedicated to protecting the rights of the fae.

They act as liaisons between the community of magical beings, humans, and the police departments that are trying to best serve everyone.

They invited me to join when Rene got the appointment and again when my powers woke, but it didn't sound like the right move for me.

I wish them well, but I'm more of a frontline fighter and less of a diplomat.

"How about you?" Rene asks. "How are things going with your recent life changes?"

I glance around the small outdoor patio, checking for any familiar faces. This is a known haunt of Montréal's finest, and I want to ensure our conversation is private. "I'm keeping it as quiet as I can for now."

"That's fine, but there are things we need to talk about. You and your siblings aren't the only elementals to awaken over the past month."

"No?"

"No. It seems the awakenings often come in clusters with elementals. You four were adopted as siblings, but we're seeing close friends or coworkers who gravitate to one another. From what we've seen, the four elements seek out the others magically...four elements and thus, elemental quartets."

That blows my mind.

"Technically, there are five elemental kingdoms," I correct. "The fifth one is often called spirit magic. It deals with spatial energy, portals, and a dozen things I don't understand, but it's classified as one of the five."

"I thought Azland said they were extinct."

"He thinks he's the last of them, but he doesn't know for sure."

Rene sits back and thinks about that. "I guess if our cluster theory is right, we'll find out."

I guess so.

As we eat our lunch, I think about that. Kenzie, Briar, Zephyr, and I are all together because *Maman* and Papa rescued and raised us. It's cool that even without the actions of those in the know, elementals in the wild have gravitated to close groups. "I had no idea."

Rene takes a drink through his straw and swallows. "This whole thing is one giant learning curve. We're doing our best to plot it all out so we can support and understand the fae population."

"That brings me to why I called. I have information pointing to a Second Sight two-point-oh death wave coming our way."

Rene pauses with his fork in front of his mouth and scowls at me. "Now you've ruined our perfectly delicious lunch date. Why couldn't that shit show have ended when you decapitated the green fucker and blew up his warehouse?"

I hold up my hands. "Technically, Briar decapitated Lamech, and the warehouse blew up because of an unstable buildup of contained fae energy. I'm innocent."

He laughs. "Yeah, sure. Do you know how many times a day I hear that claim?"

I chuckle and pull the photos out of the file Luc gave me. "Either the dicks in charge added a new ingredient to the Second Sight secret sauce, or we're getting to the long-term side effects. Either way, bodies are dropping with magically altered genetics."

As Rene scans through the photos, I explain the three bodies in the morgue and Luc's theory that Second Sight is causing fae mutations on a cellular level. "Have you come across anything like this?"

Rene shakes his head and sighs. "No, but if it's true, it's horrifying and really bad news. You said there are three bodies?"

"So far. With so much of the shit still on the street, there are bound to be more."

Rene gets back to his poutine. "Then I guess we better finish our lunch. What's the plan?"

I swallow and take a sip of Sprite. The lemon-lime bubbles tickle and bite down my throat. "Other than the drug in their system and their cell mutations, there are no obvious similarities between the three. Maybe that's all there is or maybe not. I need to find out."

Rene finishes his meal and wipes his fingers and mouth. "Well, if someone is doping humans to convert them into fae or kill them, that's my department. I'm in."

I thought so. I flip open the cover of the folder and let him peruse the notes on the victims.

"Stanley Everson was found dead in the washroom of his office building. He missed a meeting and was found collapsed on the floor." Rene scans down the page. "Any history of drug use?"

"None we know of, but the officer only talked to his coworkers."

"Okay." Rene turns the page, pulling the file closer to himself. "What about victim number two?"

"His name is Deganawida Brant. Friends knew him as Degan. First Nations, belongs to the Iroquois Nation."

"Student?"

"Sophomore at McGill University. Music major."

"Where was he found?"

"In his dorm on campus."

Rene rubs his forehead as he turns to the next page. "And this one?"

"Alison Ida. Homeless. She collapsed outside the Old Port shelter right after dinner."

"Was she dealing or just taking?"

"Not sure. When the cops got there, the locals had already taken her belongings."

"So, we hardly have any leads."

"What, you don't like a challenge?"

Rene stands and gathers his garbage onto his tray. "Just like old times. Let's go beat the streets, Gagne."

The first place Rene and I stop is the shelter down by the water in Old Port. It has a full-service soup kitchen for lunch and dinner. The lunch crowd is milling around, and after a few inquiries, we find the woman in charge.

"Liza?" I pull my leather jacket back to expose my badge hanging on a lanyard around my neck. "Could we ask you a couple of quick questions about the woman who died here the day before yesterday?"

The woman holds up one finger, calls a volunteer over to finish what she's doing, and gestures at one of the long lunch tables used as part of the soup kitchen. "If you don't mind, I'll take any excuse to get off my feet for a few minutes."

"Not a problem at all." I take a seat opposite her. "Were you here when the woman died?"

"Alison, yes. It's sad. She was a nice woman. Kept to herself mostly. Never caused any problems. Around here, that's all you can ask for."

"Had she been here long?"

"Off and on over the past couple of years. She'd fall on hard times, stay a while, and move out. Every time she left, she said it would be for good, but then she'd get kicked out or miss a payment or something and end up right back here."

"How long had she been here this time?"

"A couple of weeks."

"Do you know where she was before that?"

"Sorry."

"What about visitors you saw her with or anyone who came asking for her?"

She frowns. "Sorry."

"We know from the coroner's report that Alison was doing Second Sight when she died. We think it killed her. Do you know anything about local connections or who we might be able to track down on that front? Maybe someone else in the shelter that does Second Sight?"

The woman chuckles. "I'd guess half of the people in this room are on one drug or another, but we make it our business not to get into theirs. We're here for a hot meal and a safe place to lay their heads at night. That's it. We don't judge, and we don't get involved."

That's unfortunate.

"Could we examine her locker?" Rene asks.

"You could, but it was empty when the police were here yesterday, and we've already sanitized it and assigned it to someone else."

I sigh. "All right. Thanks for your help. Here's my card in case you think of anything else."

Rene and I step outside and stop at the top of the entrance stairs. He gestures at the food truck at the curb. "How about I buy a couple of beaver tails to cheer us up? Cinnamon or icing sugar?"

I look at him. "Seriously?"

"Cinnamon it is."

While we wait for our sugary goodness to be deep-fried and coated in cinnamon wonder, I grab a flyer from a hawker and check out what he's peddling.

"So, on to the next victim?" Rene hands me my plate.

I consider that and return my attention to the hawker. "Hey, buddy, can I ask you something?"

The kid is in his early twenties, likely a street kid or a dropout picking up cheap labor jobs. "Do you give out your flyers in this area often?"

"Yep. This is my block."

"Were you around when the woman from the shelter died out here?"

"No, but I heard about it."

"It looks like she had a bad reaction to Second Sight."

He leans into a line of oncoming pedestrians and hands out some flyers. "And?"

"Seeing as how you're milling around on the street, I thought maybe you might've seen something."

He chuckles. "Definitely not."

"What about hearsay hypotheticals? Do you have any idea what it's going for right now? Are there different kinds, maybe a stronger version that costs more?"

"I couldn't tell you."

"Couldn't or—"

"Hey!" Rene's voice jerks me out of my thoughts. He's pointing toward the water, where something is splashing around.

Not something...some*one*.

It looks like a shirtless teenage boy with his blond hair soaked and matted to his forehead.

Rene starts to unbutton his shirt and take his service radio off his belt, but I throw an arm out to stop him from running off to save the kid. "He's not drowning. He's a merman."

Sure enough, as the boy dives under the water, we get a flash of shiny silvery scales and the long graceful curl of a tail.

"Seriously?" Rene grumbles as he straps his radio back on. "It's too damn cold in the St. Lawrence for merpeople, isn't it?"

"You're asking the wrong person. Even before my awakening,

I didn't dip in any water that wasn't warmer than my body temperature. I'm more of a hot tub girl."

Rene chuckles. "I know. I've been in the locker room during your showers. You being a fire fae shouldn't have been that surprising."

I laugh. "Yet it was."

After not-saving the not-drowning kid, Rene drives us downtown to the gleaming skyscraper that houses Marcus, Bell, & Kellen. The receptionist is a long-necked, very efficient-looking brunette with high gloss, polished nails, and purple contact lenses.

"Good afternoon, Rae." I read her name off the silver plate on the counter. "We have a few follow-up questions about the death of Stanley Everson. Is there someone who could speak with us?" I flash the receptionist my badge and Rene does the same.

"Anyone in particular or will I do? The senior staff is in a meeting."

"Then we'd be happy to have your help."

She gestures at the registration book open on the desk's raised surface. "Please sign in, and I'll get you visitor badges."

I pick up the pen and do my thing. Rene follows suit.

"We're all still in shock." She hands us shiny plastic visitor badges before walking around her desk to let us into the main office behind.

I clip the badge to my shirt and follow her inside. "We're very sorry for your loss. If you could point us toward his desk and the washroom where he was found, that would be helpful."

She walks through a maze of desk groupings, stopping at a tidy cubicle with a decent view of the city. "This was Stanley's station."

A sleek laptop is plugged into its charger, and next to it is a cell phone with a dead battery. "Is someone supposed to pick up his personal effects?"

"I'm not sure. His parents were deceased, and he was single. He came out with us socially on a few occasions, but no one seems to know much about his personal life or whom to call."

"Do you mind if we look in his drawers?"

"Look—no. I don't think you should take anything, though."

"Not a problem. Just a look."

I take a moment to scan through things, check his drawers and credenza cabinet for anything interesting, and find nothing except some greasy food wrappers and a printout of some meeting agenda.

I hand Rene the printout. "What does 'sync with Matt re: Objectives & Key Results for quarterly metrics presentation' mean?"

Rene makes a face. "It means his job would make my head explode."

Mine too. "Is Matt in the senior staff meeting?" I ask.

Rae shakes her head. "No, he's there." She points a few desks over to a rakish man in his mid-thirties wearing wire-rimmed glasses. "Matt, these officers are following up on what happened to Stanley."

"He died in the shitter." Matt's brow pinches. "What is there to follow up on?"

Rae rolls her eyes and waves away his comment. "Forgive Matt. He has his own way of looking at the world. He doesn't mean anything by it."

"It's fine," I assure her. "What can you tell us about Stanley, Matt?"

"I can tell you Stanley was an MVP when it came to OKRs and that he was two PROs away from a BJU. We were working on the QRP the day he died. One minute he was here. Then he stepped AFK and never came back."

"I'm not fluent in acronyms, but did anything you say have anything to do with drugs?"

Matt blinks. "Drugs? Absolutely not. Not in these halls, anyway. We know better."

"What does that mean?"

He frowns. "A few years ago some intern got caught selling Adderall to the finance guys. It was a big shit storm. No one will make that mistake again."

I weigh that info and come up with nothing. "Does your company ever do business with Julian Street Crating & Moving?"

Matt opens his laptop and searches. "Not that I'm aware of, no."

"Can you point us toward the drug-buying finance guys?"

Rae frowns. "Maybe you should come back when one of the partners is available. This is more than a follow-up on Stanley. Now you're fishing for something."

I shake my head. "No. Not really. We know Stanley died from taking Second Sight. We're simply looking for the entry point of how that drug got into his life."

"You think the finance boys know that?"

Rene holds his hands up. "No one is accusing anyone of anything, Miss. We're simply asking a few questions. This isn't a witch hunt. You want us to find out what happened to Stanley, don't you?"

"Of course, but…"

"But nothing," I say. "Everyone seems to be aware of Second Sight. Plenty of people will even admit to using it, but as soon as we ask where it's being sourced, suddenly no one knows anything about anybody."

Rae snatches the visitor's badge off my shirt and grabs Rene's too. "I'm sorry. I'm going to have to ask you to leave and make an appointment with one of the partners if you have more questions."

I sigh. "All righty then. We'll do that."

CHAPTER FOUR

"Uh-oh." Kenzie frowns at me when I get home. "I know that look. You spent the day spinning your wheels, didn't you?"

I grunt, toss my backpack toward my bedroom door, and shuck off my jacket. "Is it that obvious?"

"To me? Yes. I happen to pay attention."

I know she does. It's why she makes a great lawyer. She watches people and reads them. She has good instincts. If she wasn't such a girlie girl, she could've been a decent cop.

I frown at her sitting cross-legged with a Ouija board. "What are you doing?"

"What do you think? I'm trying to commune with the dead. I have questions."

I shake my head. "Seriously? After everything we've learned about how our parents—both sets of our parents—were murdered, you think it's a good idea to play with something like that?"

She scrunches up her face at me. "It's pressed cardboard with some letters printed on it."

"No, it's not." Azland storms in and grabs the board off the floor. "How many times have I told you magic is as much about intention as it is the spells we cast?"

Kenzie frowns. "Why is everyone so cranky today?"

Azland sighs, ignoring her rant. "If you ask for the dead to come through, they will. With something like this, there are no parameters or safeguards to control who or what comes through. Don't fuck around with things you don't understand."

Kenzie gives him the finger. "First off, I wasn't fucking around. I was genuinely trying to make contact with either *Maman* and Papa or my birth parents.

"I want to know more about them. Are we sure they're dead? Surely The Six and their skoro army couldn't have killed everyone. There had to be survivors. Hell, *you* are a survivor."

I see the flash of pain in his gaze as she brings up his survival from the kingdom of Draíocht. "As one of the only survivors from the lost magic kingdom, I know more about magic than you. This isn't me being prickly, Kenzie. This is a genuine warning of dire consequences. The Ouija board is a hard no. Learn to read Tarot. Become a master at scrying. I will support you reaching across the magical plane in several ways, but not with this."

That dampens the fire in Kenzie's fight. "Okay, fine. I hear you. Consider me properly schooled."

Man, the tension in here is palpable.

I force a grin and clap my hands together. "On that note, I'm going to get changed and go for a long jog. Does anyone want to join me?"

"I do." Azland stretches his neck from side to side. "I'll meet you downstairs as Backup. FYI, I bought a chest halter you can put on me. I always hated having a collar around my neck."

"Fair enough. Give me two minutes."

I change quickly from my work clothes into my jogging outfit and catch sight of Zephyr working out in the backyard with his staff.

Of the four of us, he seems the most intent on practicing, deepening his skills, and connecting with his inner magic. I'm proud of him. He's risen to the challenge of being an elemental warrior.

I suppose after feeling like he was battling his body for the past decade, learning his biological father ran the elemental training academy for an entire kingdom is something to aspire to.

"Good for you, Z."

"You sure you don't want to jog, Kenz?"

She snorts. "If there's no one chasing me, what's the point? Sweat? Breathlessness? I can think of a much better pursuit of those things."

"When does the Celt return from Toronto so you can get back to being sweaty and breathless?"

"He didn't say."

I check that I've got my phone, wrap my ankle around the pole, and drop to the garage bay. "Laters."

"Have a good run."

I smile at the bull mastiff sitting beside an expensive black leather harness and matching leash. "Wow, you went all out on yourself."

Knowing our overly critical wizard is in there, I hold the straps and let him step into them.

"That was a shit ton easier than the wrestling match we've been participating in for the past decade. Another reason you should've told us who you are sooner."

The dog gives me a droll stare and growls.

"Yeah, yeah, I know."

We weave through the neighborhood, quickly hooking up with my favorite riverside trail. From there, we jog toward the bridge and over to Boucherville National Park on the island.

As Backup runs beside me, it occurs to me that to anyone else out here, we look entirely normal—a girl and her dog out for an evening jog.

Not a fire freak and a fae magic man in animal form.

It's weird. I'm still not sure why our parents were so chill with having a grown man living in our house without us knowing. Then again, he came through for us when we needed it.

As annoying as Azland is, I am thankful for all his help releasing my powers and helping me and my siblings train.

As my rhythmic footfalls beat a steady pace and drain the day's frustrations, my endorphins kick in, and my cells begin to hum.

The sun is setting, and I soak in the view.

Since I got my powers, the sky seems pinker and buzzes with ambient fae energy. Fiona told me that the source power for fae is called prana, and when it's visible, it's hot pink.

It can be found in the air and the earth but flows most strongly through water and tributaries.

That's why Montréal is one of the epicenters of magical awakenings. Many tributaries converge in the St. Lawrence River, which means it's highly charged with fae power.

People without magical powers don't notice it, but now that my fae side is flowing freely, I can't miss it.

Backup slips behind me when the pathway narrows and forces us to run in single file between the bushes. They, too, are humming with fae magic.

Tad and Briar feel that the most.

It's cool how the druid can help Briar with his earth connection. Maybe there's someone out there who could help me with mine.

I'm lost in my thoughts. My mind drifts from the beauty of the sunset to the magic in our lives to our foster parents. *Laurette and Marcel Gagne.*

How lucky were we to—

Two skinheads jump out of the bushes and into my path. I

skid to a stop and pat my chest. "Shit, guys. You can't close in on people like that. Personal space is real."

I try not to judge, but my instincts are flaring.

They've got a vibe, and it's not good.

When they don't move, I draw a deep breath and square off. "Is there a problem?"

They shore up, standing shoulder to shoulder. "Yeah. People like you are overrunning the city."

I feign confusion. "Women joggers?"

"No. Fae freaks." His words are sharp with impotent rage, and it takes all my self-control not to lay into him.

The other guy scowls. "You've got your dogs in on it now too? Your mutt lights up as much as you."

They take a few steps toward me, their posture menacing. Two more brutes appear from out of the bushes.

Backup growls.

I turn as four more move onto the trail behind us.

Well...shit. Even with a warrior like Azland at my side, eight against two isn't good.

Being careful not to make any sudden movements, I pull my badge out from under my shirt and let it hang visibly around my neck. "Be very sure you want to go down this road, boys. First off, I'm a cop and trained to take down your asses."

The lead man scoffs. "Eight against one and you're warning us? That's hilarious."

I don't take the bait. "Second, you'd only know I had an awakening by taking an illegal drug. Maybe I call it in and have you all charged."

"You could try."

"Finally, yeah, I *am* fae, but you have no idea what kind or what my strengths are. Trust me. You don't want to find out."

Unfortunately, these guys are too stupid to recognize a clear invitation to leave. Shifting closer, they box us in.

"All right, boys, don't say I didn't warn you." Broadening my stance, I get ready for the inevitable.

They come at me, and the fight is on.

I light up my palms and fight hand-to-hand with only my fists flaming. As much as I'd like to wreath my skin in flame and let my full-fire flag fly, I'd burn off all my clothes and end up naked in the middle of the park.

That falls under the last resort category.

Backup snarls, lunges, and bites the bicep of one skinhead. The guy arches back, bellowing as Azland's fangs sink through flesh.

Tad's teleportation powers would be handy right about now.

I grapple with one of the guys, burning his clothes and the side of his face. He bellows and stumbles backward, holding his cheek.

I whirl with fire licking up my wrists. "Anyone else feeling a little undercooked?"

The hit comes hard and fast from behind and throws me forward to the ground. My palms take the brunt of the fall. Before I can push to my feet, men drag me toward the riverbank.

Arms flailing, I singe one's shoulder, but he doesn't let go. The crashing water silences as they plunge me under the surface, the chaos muted by the distortion of being submerged.

My flame fizzles out as I splash and struggle to breach the surface. My mouth stays sealed, but I'm screaming with everything inside me.

The water around me pulses with incredible power, and I try to call that strength to me.

It's no use.

The water is freezing, and my fire is extinguished now that I'm soaked.

A lucky strike to someone's balls gives me a moment to push my head above the water, and I gulp for air.

Pure panic has me fighting like a berserker and I manage to stagger a couple of feet to collapse onto the grassy bank.

The *thumping* of heavy footfalls surrounds me.

I can't fight a whole pack of violent idiots.

Bruising fingers drag me up the bank and drop me into the dirt. The first boot to my ribs connects with incredible force, and I curl into a ball as my screams ring out into the park.

Bile and filthy river water burn my throat.

Shielding my face with my forearms is my only defense. The beating is brutal. My chance of walking away from this is getting worse by the moment.

A booming roar sounds close to my ears.

Then everything stops.

CHAPTER FIVE

One minute I'm getting beaten to a pulp by a gang of anti-magic morons, and the next…nothing. Nothing except the pain bombarding me from all angles. The roaring bellow of fury isn't human. It isn't anything I recognize.

Trembling on the ground by the river, my hair matted with mud and river water and my body aching, I'm not sure if I'm freezing or going into shock.

Likely both.

My mind tells me to get up and get the hell away from there. My body isn't speaking the same language.

I have no idea how long it takes me to uncurl from my fetal position, but when I do, my mind struggles to understand what's happening around me.

My attackers are strewn around like broken twigs. Their faces are bloody, and their limbs point at odd angles.

I'd like to think it's because I wore them down first, but I can't claim credit for anything I see.

It's not an army that's come to my rescue. It's one man. My savior lands a solid roundhouse kick to the chest of a gang leader, and I see his face.

His chiseled, beautiful, rage-crazed face.

Gareth.

It's the DJ from the fae rave I discovered in the park a few weeks ago. I knew when I met him he was some kind of magical being, but I never guessed...

Shit, he's strong. He's also possessed and brutal, and his eyes glow a bright scarlet. I swear rage is coming off him like steam from a boiling kettle.

He grips the shirt of one skinhead, and a *whooshing* rush of fire ignites from his fist. He curls the long, talon-sharp claws of his fingers around the ball of flame and rams it against the skinhead's chest.

The guy's shirt ignites like a torch doused in gasoline, and this sends him shrieking and flailing into the river.

Gareth has fire powers like me.

No. Not like me. He is something else.

Huge shivers rack me, and I realize I'm lying in the sloppy muck, damp and freezing instead of trying to get out of this situation.

My limbs are heavy and spear me with agony as I crawl over to Azland. He's given up his dog persona and is in human form. Still, he doesn't seem to have fared any better than I have.

He's lying on his side with rage in his eyes as he struggles to get to his feet.

I know what he's thinking because I'm thinking the same thing. I want to help, to rejoin the fight, but I've taken some serious hits.

So has he.

Police training teaches that egos don't help people survive. Sometimes, the best thing to do is to stay down and out of the action, even when it sucks.

I watch.

Gareth has some scary violent skills. When I met him in the

park, he was doing his best to create a pocket of joy for the city's fae youth. I found him annoying yet endearing.

This is something else.

This lethal vibe is badass.

A cop shouldn't support violence in the streets, but I make an exception considering he's pulping the assholes who were trying to kill me.

When my ambush party mobilizes their wounded to bug out, Gareth hurries over to me. He kneels to check on me, and I'm relieved to see he's the man and not the beast.

His fingers are incredibly warm against my skin as he checks my pulse. Then he inches my shirt up my belly a bit and grimaces. "Fuck. You need an emergency room and your jogging buddy isn't doing much better."

He pulls out a phone and begins to dial for emergency services.

I grab his arm to stop him. "No. I'm a cop, and people in the ER know me. My awakening is new, and if what I am gets out, it will put people in danger. I can't expose my fae side."

He frowns. "You've likely got internal bleeding."

I wouldn't be surprised. "My sister is a healer. Just take me home."

He looks skeptical, but he puts the phone away. "Where's home?"

I give him the address.

When he lifts me, the movement shifts something inside me that doesn't appreciate the movement. I cry out, and the world recedes into a black void.

I wake to soothing water washing over me and the rich smell of Briar's lasagna filling the air. It's one of our favorite Charlie recipes, and he's mastered it over the years.

I start to sit up, but Kenzie presses a gentle blue hand against my shoulder and holds me in place. Damn, her true fae self is so stunningly exotic.

The *swish* and *slosh* of water have me assessing my surroundings. I'm in the bathtub. I'm still wearing my running clothes, the faucet is open, and Kenzie's infusing the water with healing magic.

I relax back into the tub as she guides her power over my battered body. "Where's Gareth? And Azland?"

"They're both fine," Kenzie reassures me. She sits back on her heels and captures the magical orb she uses to focus her powers. When it shrinks in size, it settles against her wrist and takes its place in her bracelet. "Can you stand to change out of those nasty clothes or should I have Briar come help?"

The big guy could do the heavy lifting, but I'd rather not involve my brother in the changing duties if I can help it. "My muscles are stiff, and I might sleep for a week, but you fixed the worst of it. I'm good."

Kenzie arches a brow. "You're better, but I'm no miracle worker. You're lucky none of the damage was done magically. It would've been much worse."

"Then let's be thankful it was a standard-issue beat down and not a fae freak beat down."

Kenzie turns off the water flow and pushes up to her feet. After setting a towel on the floor at the bathtub's base, she hooks under my elbow and helps pull me until I sit on the edge. "Take it slow. Your comfy clothes are on the counter. Call if you need me."

"Thanks, Kenz."

She nods. "Thanks for not getting dead."

"You're welcome." When she leaves, I peel off my jogging clothes and realize the silt and filth are still clinging to my skin despite the tub healing.

Turning the hot water on, I open the shower nozzle and step under the spray.

Standing under the piping hot stream does more to restore my equilibrium than anything else I can think of, so I stay there longer than is technically necessary.

After drying off and changing into my comfy sweatpants and a soft old T-shirt, I pad barefoot out to the shared area of our home. Briar is pulling the lasagna out of the oven and Gareth is sitting at the kitchen table looking all kinds of uncomfortable.

"Where's Azland?" I ask as Briar sets the lasagna down on a woven trivet.

Briar glances around. "He was here. Kenzie healed him, and he disappeared. He'll either be tracking down the ones that attacked you or curling up in his doggy bed. It's a tough call."

"I swear, that guy is so weird."

"Dog bed?" Gareth asks.

"It's complicated." I join him at the table, easing into an empty chair. "He's sort of our family dog, but he's also our fae guardian."

What does it say about Gareth that he doesn't seem thrown by that? Maybe living in the fae world, things like dogs turning into warriors aren't that bizarre.

"I was lucky Azland was there, but even luckier you were. Thanks for saving my ass."

Gareth drops his chin. "Don't mention it."

"I'd say I owe you one, but if you're staying for dinner, we'll be even. Briar's lasagna is world-altering."

Gareth chuckles. "Then it worked out all around. The part where I found you and brought you home. Not the part where you were targeted and jumped by assholes."

"Still, I appreciate your intervention." Zephyr emerges at the top of the stairs, carrying the leftover drinks from the fridge in the parking bay. He sets them on the center of the table, and I reach for my pick. "Have you been introduced?"

Gareth glances at Kenzie and Zephyr, then at Briar, who's

setting plates out on the table. "Not so much introduced as interrogated." His tone is friendly and defensive.

I peg them with a look and Zephyr waves his fingers dismissively at me. "Don't give us that look. When a guy shows up with our sister beaten to a bloody pulp and unconscious, what should we do if not ask questions?"

"It's exactly what you would have done if the situation was reversed," Kenzie points out.

True story. "It's hard to know whom to trust these days. Weird things are afoot."

Gareth gratefully accepts the offer to grab a beer from the ones left to choose from. "Don't worry about it. I did my best to explain the situation as I understood it. I don't blame them for not trusting me."

"It's nothing personal," Zephyr claims.

"Except our sister's safety is very personal," Kenzie adds, holding up a finger.

Briar brings over a stack of plates and a loaf of French bread. With everything at the table, he cuts and serves. "So, Gareth. Jules mentioned she met you working with fae kids before this fae craziness took hold of our lives. What was that about? Do you work for a community outreach?"

Gareth frowns. "Wait…before the fae craziness? Did you not know you were fae when we met in the park?"

I shake my head. "Nope. It's been a mind-blowing couple of weeks. Why? Did you know?"

He nods. "Well, sure. I knew there was something. I could feel it in you. That's why I asked what you were."

I remember that, but at the time, I thought he was being difficult. "Do you think you could feel it because you're a fire guy too?"

"A fire guy?"

"Yeah. I saw you fighting. You flame up too. What are you? Are you like me?" There's too much neediness in my voice, and I grimace inwardly. "Sorry. I'm not that girl—*I'm not*—but I'd love to learn more about my powers from someone who knows."

Gareth cuts a bite of lasagna with his fork and pauses before eating it. "You're new to this, so let me teach you all an important lesson. Telling people who and what you are gives them knowledge you don't want to share. They can glean your weaknesses and use them against you. Keep your details close to the vest. And give others the privacy to do the same."

Gareth's attitude strikes me as sad and lonely.

I'd hate to be so cynical that I kept myself from connecting with other magical people. I don't know what I would have done if I didn't have my siblings, Tad, Fiona, and Azland to talk me through things.

Then again, I get his point.

The way he fought off those skinheads in the park was brutal and telling. I might not know much about Gareth's powers or history, but it's clear there's some gnarly shit in his past.

"Okay. Sorry."

Gareth forks in his bite and chews. "No apology necessary. I do think it's funny that you're a fire fae and live in a fire station. That's ironic."

Briar points out, "To be fair, we all live here and have since way before the awakenings started, and we found out we have powers."

Zephyr glares at him. "Did you not hear the man tell us not to announce our powers to people?"

Briar shrugs. "He knew. Don't get all crusty."

Gareth holds up his hand. "He's right. There's no need for secrecy with me. The four of you are obviously an elemental quartet."

Briar's cheeks go a bit pink.

Zephyr's gaze narrows with irritation, but Gareth either doesn't care or doesn't notice.

"As I said, there's no need for secrecy. I have no interest in exposing or exploiting you. Considering you're only a couple of weeks into your awakenings, have you got your enrichment stations set up yet?"

"I'm sorry. Our what?"

He turns to answer my question. "Enrichment stations. The place where you bask in your element and rejuvenate."

"Do you have one?" Kenzie asks.

"I do. I have a massive stone fireplace. I turn on the gas, crank the flames, and climb in to bake. It's like ten trips to the spa. You guys should think about that."

I glance around, wondering where I could put a fireplace big enough to crawl into. "How big would that need to be?"

Gareth lowers the bottle pressed to his lips and swallows. "You have plenty of space out back. You could install a pool, a mud bath, and a magma pool."

"What about me?" Zephyr asks. "What does a wind regeneration spa look like?"

"I'm not sure, but I'll think about it."

Zephyr looks disappointed, but Briar is interested. "You're in construction, right?"

Now it's Gareth who looks suspicious.

I chuckle and wipe my mouth. "When we ran into you at Casse Croûte, you mentioned you were quoting a job in the area. Then, we saw you unloading lumber a few days later when we were heading there to pick up a lunch order."

That settles his issue, and he goes back to eating. "Yes, I run a small construction business. Why do you ask?"

"Because I work in construction too. If you can help me plan these spa rejuvenation stations, I can build them."

Gareth nods. "I can do that."

CHAPTER SIX

When morning light creeps across my bedroom wall, I can no longer avoid getting out of bed. I'm sore, and my bed is amazing, but my hesitation to emerge into sibling-landia is a futile attempt to avoid the Gareth twenty-question routine waiting for me.

After all, I'm the one who asks the questions. I'm not the one sitting in the interrogation chair.

I don't think my captain would accept that as a reason for being late, though.

With a groan, I flip back my sheets, get dressed, and feed the goldfish. The moment I open my door, I smell the sweet succulence of French toast, complete with cinnamon, powdered sugar, and fresh berries.

There goes my plan to go straight out to work. They know I can't resist. "You guys are playing dirty."

Briar flashes me a smug smile and winks at Kenzie sitting at the table in her robe sipping coffee.

"You both suck, by the way."

Kenzie snorts. "Me? How'd I get dragged into your grump?"

I reach for the maple syrup. "Don't even try to play the innocent card with me."

Briar laughs and sets a plate of back bacon on the table in front of me. "Like a rabbit in a snare. Jules can't resist my brunch offerings."

I'd argue if he wasn't right. "All right, fine. Open the floodgates but know I'm meeting Rene in half an hour."

"So. Gareth." Kenzie sets her mug down to start in on the bacon and French toast. "He's fit, hot AF, not only has a job but has his own business…"

"Is there a question in there somewhere?"

"All right. When are you seeing him again?"

"Who says I am?"

Kenzie snorts. "Please. He's got a 'bad boy for a great night' vibe written all over him. He's exactly your type."

"I don't have a type."

Briar busts up laughing. "Then why have three of your exes called you from lockup, hoping you can post bail or get them out of trouble?"

"No comment."

Kenzie bites the end of her bacon strip and grins. "Add to that, he shows up out of nowhere and rescues you. That's sexy."

I dust my breakfast with sugar and berries and shovel a forkful into my mouth, earning me a brief reprieve. As soon as I swallow, the questions restart.

"He's like you," Briar remarks. "A fire guy."

I chuckle at how much alike the four of us are. See, "fire guy" made perfect sense.

"Maybe he'll invite you to get naked and join him in his fireplace," Kenzie adds.

Zephyr snorts as he comes in to join us. "Most people think making out *in front* of a fire is sexy. Of course, Jules would take that a step further by climbing into the flames."

"Yeah, baby." Kenzie waggles her eyebrows.

"I still don't trust him," Zephyr points out. "Am I the only one who thinks it's weird he happened to show up when Jules was getting attacked? And he happened to go to Casse Croûte for the first time the week she got her powers?"

I love Zephyr's protective instinct, but I think he's off-base in this case. "I harassed Gareth at the fae rave, and he was already sitting at a booth eating when we ran into him at Casse Croûte. I don't think there's anything nefarious going on."

Zephyr sits, claims a plate, and heaps on his choices. "I'm just sayin' we don't know him, and he's not telling us what kind of fae he is, so maybe we shouldn't encourage him to hop in Jules' bed."

I laugh. "No one is hopping in my bed. Hello? Don't I get to be the one who decides things like that?"

Briar rolls his eyes. "Please. With the way that boy is ripped, the tats, and his sexy, deep voice, your girl bits have already placed their order and paid extra for express delivery."

Kenzie and Zephyr both get a good laugh at that.

"You guys suck."

Zephyr shrugs. "I'm just suggestin' you use some of that cop mojo you channel to think objectively. As he said, we have to be careful. Havin' people know too much about us exposes our weaknesses."

I hear the subtext of what he's saying and blink. "You want me to investigate him?"

"Why not? You investigate our prospective lovers all the time."

Okay, so I might have run a few background checks to ensure no bunnies ended up in boiling pots. "You guys are getting way ahead of yourselves. I don't even know the guy's last name. I can't exactly look up guys named Gareth and hope to find anything."

Kenzie shrugs. "Then I guess you need to see him again to get more dirt on him."

"At the same time, keep your virtue intact."

I stop with a forkful of French toast berry bliss poised in front of my mouth. "You're late to the play there, bro. My virtue hasn't been intact since backseat sex in Timmy Renaux's Kia."

Briar makes a face. "You are so annoyingly literal. Anyway, you get our point."

"I do. You get to hook up with randos after a cage fight, but I'm supposed to work up a full background check on the guy who has shown no interest in me except to save me from being killed. Hey, what was the name of the girl you stayed out with the other night?"

He gives me the finger. "The next time you see your badass boyfriend, make sure to ask him more about building those elemental retreats in the backyard."

"Or we could talk to Azland about that," Kenzie counters.

I finish my French toast and rinse the syrup off my plate in the sink. Kenzie joins me, yelping as she sticks her hands under the hot water.

"Jules! That's boiling!"

"My bad." I turn the faucet temperature back toward something safe for the non-fire fae.

Kenzie pouts as she cradles her hand. Her healing signature builds in the air and tingles against my skin. "If you're not working late, join us at Casse Croûte tonight."

"Yeah, my first set is at nine," Zephyr adds.

Kenzie grins. "You could invite Gareth, and we could all get to know him better."

I decide not to dignify that with a response. I finish the dishes, grab my backpack, and slide down the brass pole. "Laters."

Rene is waiting for me at the station when I arrive. He still has his desk here, but since he's been heading up the fae liaison task force, he's mostly been working out of Montréal City Hall.

Although, if he was at the mayor's office, I don't think he'd have his feet up on the desk, flipping through my case files.

"Make yourself at home, why don't you," I quip as I shoo him out of my chair and take my seat.

He leans over my shoulder, pointing at an underlined section of Stanley Everson's file. "I was thinking about the toxicology linking these deaths to Second Sight. We need to learn more about how it's killing folks."

"My guy at the morgue says it's altering existing cells, mutating them. He's not sure if it's a designed intention or a side effect from prolonged use."

"Then maybe that's our angle. We track down people we know have been using based on the dates of their arrests and see if we can get an idea of what's happening from the drug side of things."

I pull up a case file and copy down the address. "I know just the guy we can talk to."

Nakey Kid is partly an informant and partly a running joke in the commentary of my policing career. There's something to be said about wrestling a naked guy to the ground and bringing him in as a night's collar.

It creates a strange kind of bond.

Although he makes lifestyle choices that baffle and concern me, he was helpful when I needed intel on some of Montréal's shadier characters.

Since Rene is driving, I navigate and get us where we need to be. "This is the place."

"Looks like the party started without us."

It does.

As we pass the Old Brewery Mission, I eye the police cruisers parked on the street with lights flashing.

A crowd has gathered on the patchy, dried-out lawn of the rundown apartment building. Sadly, it's the kind of complex where seeing cruisers and red and blue strobing lights would happen daily.

Rene parks and he and I flash our badges, ducking under the police tape. The plan is to pass through the commotion and continue focusing on our case. Still, out of professional courtesy—and no small amount of personal curiosity—we pull aside a uni and ask what's going on.

"We have a body on the side lawn." She gestures at the location. "Looks young, too. A neighbor found him shirtless, lounging in the shade. Looks like an OD."

I meet Rene's gaze. "It can't hurt to take a look."

Around the side of the building, the scene is swarming with cops, a couple of EMS, and some resident looky-loos.

I have a sinking feeling even before the guy on the scene tugs back the sheet to let me take a look. "Well, shit. I guess Nakey Kid won't be helping us after all."

Rene frowns at the body. "Such a waste."

I blow out a long breath and go back to the body. "Can you show me his fingers?"

The crime scene tech grips Nakey Kid's wrist and lifts his hand free for me to examine. There is magenta spider veining under his fingernails.

"All right, this kid is part of our ongoing investigation. Can you make sure Luc Leclerc gets flagged as the coroner on point for this one?"

The guy in the blue gloves nods. "It's fine with me. You'll have to clear it through them, though."

Rene nods and strikes off to speak to the primary working the scene.

"Was there any Second Sight on the scene?" I ask.

The tech lifts two packages the size of sugar packets and waves them in the air.

"Excellent. Make sure the coroner gets a sample of that too."

Once we're back in the car, I text Luc.

Sending you another body with pink fingernail veins plus a sample of the drug on scene. Told them to make sure you caught this one. Let me know what you find.

He sends back a single thumbs-up emoji.

The drive back to the station is a quiet one. I hate that the kid is dead. He was too young.

Drugs suck.

I thought I had more time to turn things around for him. Maybe if I'd tried to get him into a program…

To his credit, Rene says nothing.

He's been on the job long enough to know where I am in this, and he knows enough to leave it be.

Once we're back, I go straight to evidence and pull the processing kit from the night I first arrested Nakey Kid. After signing that out, I'm on the move again.

Maybe Nakey Kid can help us figure out what's going on after all.

Turning the corner, I nearly run smack into Reese coming the other way. He steps back, raising his hands. "Shit, Gagne, where's the fire?"

I glare at him. "What's that supposed to mean?"

He blinks, and I realize it meant nothing more than the fact that I nearly bowled him over.

"Sorry, man. I'm just touchy. Do you remember the naked kid I brought in a couple of weeks ago?"

"My retinas are still burning."

"Yeah, well, he was DOA this morning outside his piece of shit apartment."

"That sucks." Reese's sympathetic look quickly turns into confusion. "If he's dead, why do you need the kit?"

"I want Luc to run a latent cell test on him."

"You think he died because he was having an awakening?"

"No. I think he was wholly human and Second Sight is causing fae mutations and killing people."

Reese frowns. "Seriously? Is that a thing now?"

"Seems to be."

"Fuck. The shit keeps getting more twisted."

"That's about it."

I tuck the evidence kit into my bag, then find Rene back at my desk. He's in my seat again but doesn't have his feet up like he owns the place.

He hands me a folded piece of paper.

I unfold it and glance down. It's a bunch of scribbled letters and numbers. "What's this?"

"Do you remember when I said there were other elementals awakening in the area?"

"Yes."

"That's the login and access information to my files. I figured, knowing you, there's a good chance you'll want to learn more and maybe touch base with them."

I flash him a grin that shows my teeth. "You know me so well."

CHAPTER SEVEN

As much as I want to dive into Rene's information about the other elementals, Kenzie will have my head if I skip out on a night at Casse Croûte to hover over my computer.

The roads are fairly empty and gearing up and zipping between cars feels good. A fast motorcycle ride usually clears my head after a rough day.

Tonight, my mind won't settle. I can't get the sight of Nakey Kid out of my head.

It sucks.

It's not that I haven't seen death before. As a cop, I see it all the time. It's usually senseless, but this—the idea that someone might've done this on purpose—it's horrible.

Did he suffer? I know how horrible I felt when my cells were awakening. What did it feel like to have his cells turn against him?

I study the sunset of the Montréal sky.

Since fae magic started pouring into our city, the sky has been candy-floss pink. It makes for a lovely sunset but also stands as a constant reminder that things are not as they once were.

When I lean into the turn and gear down to stop, I study the pickup parked outside the fire station and the guy sitting behind the wheel.

Why is Gareth here? Dammit. I can't deal with him tonight. If Kenzie invited him, she's so fucking dead.

I ride past his tailgate and drive into the garage bay. After parking Scarlett and taking off my helmet, I shake out my hair and try to calm myself.

Having him here makes my skin tingle, and not in a good way. Something about his fiery side enflames mine, and I don't have the energy to control it.

Gareth hops out of the truck as I approach and looks me over with a crooked smile. "Good evening, Inspector Gagne."

"What are you doing here? Did my sister put you up to this?"

"I assure you. No one puts me up to anything."

"Then what are you doing here?"

Gareth runs a hand through his hair, looking chastened. "I didn't realize it would piss you off this much to see me. My mistake. I'll go."

Fuckety-fuck. I draw a deep breath and close my eyes. "It doesn't. I'm not pissed off at you. I didn't mean to be rude."

"Rough day?"

"A kid I know wound up dead in front of me today, and I keep running into brick walls with my investigation. I'm tired and frustrated and don't know how to deal with all this pent-up fire inside me. You happened to be standing within firing range."

Gareth's expression softens. "That's why I came. Here." He hands me a thumb drive in the shape of a cheap lighter with rubbery flames down the side.

"What's this?"

"Your brother—the big one—asked about blueprints for elemental enrichment stations. The place where you bask in your element and rejuvenate."

I turn the thumb drive over in my hand. "That's thoughtful of you."

He lifts a shoulder. "Most of my plans are for fire fae, but I did my best to find a few ideas for earth, water, and wind."

"Thank you. I appreciate it."

Gareth shrugs. "My pleasure. I honestly can't imagine what you're all going through right now. First, to not know who and what you are for so long, then for it to all get thrust at you at once. It's insanity."

"Well, it certainly hasn't been easy."

He chuckles. "Maybe I was a bad seed, but I had a lot of negative energy to burn. Without guidance and outlets to let off steam, I would've burned down half the fae realm."

My mind spins out on that one. "You've been to the fae realm?"

His smile falters. "In a different lifetime, yeah. Now I live here and have for a long time. Montréal's my home and I'd rather you not burn it to the ground because you're having a bad day."

I chuckle. "I think Montréal's safe. I might be struggling, but I have outlets too."

He leans back against his truck. "Yeah? Like what?"

"I go for runs—"

"And get mugged."

"I also go on long, fast, dangerous motorcycle rides."

"I get that. I was a thrill junkie too, but eventually, that won't cut it. Elemental energy builds and sooner or later, you'll need an outlet for it."

I turn the thumb drive over in my palm. Now I have two things tempting me to bail on the evening and hang out with my laptop.

I can't.

"Unfortunately, my simmering energy will have to wait. My brother's playing at Casse Croûte tonight, so instead of researching an elemental oasis or making progress on my cases, I'll have to settle with getting shit-faced."

Gareth's grin is knowing. "I'm very familiar with that tactic for tamping down the fire as well. Enjoy your evening, Inspector."

He moves to leave, but I reach out and grab his wrist. "You wouldn't want to come, would you? I really should buy you a burger and a beer. Between the rescue and the building plans, you deserve at least that much."

Gareth bites his bottom lip. "Probably not the best idea. I don't do well in crowds."

I get the sense that he's bowing out in an attempt to do me a favor rather than because he doesn't want to go. "You do eat, right?"

"Yes. I have been known to eat."

"Well, the place won't get busy until after the second set. By then you'll have a full stomach and a couple of beers in you."

He considers that for a moment before he relents. "Fine, I could eat...but you're not buying."

Ha! I'll let him think that. "Excellent. It's settled."

The two of us head inside and up the stairs. When I see who's sitting in the living room with Kenzie, I jog over to hug him. "Tad. I've missed your face!"

"Aye, well, I've missed yer face too." Tad returns my hug and eases back with a sweet smile and a flirty Irish wink. "Fi sends her love."

"Make sure to send mine back. She's been amazing."

Tad glances at Gareth standing behind me and extends his hand. "Tad McNiff."

"Gareth." He gives him a friendly, two-finger wave but doesn't accept the handshake. "Sorry. I appreciate the welcome, but I don't touch strangers."

"Fair enough. No offense taken." Tad reclaims his spot on the sofa and stretches his arm across the back of the cushion behind Kenzie's shoulders.

Am I the only one who thinks it's weird he refused Tad's handshake?

Nope. By the wrinkling of Kenzie's nose, she's weirded out by that too.

"Don't get yer knickers in a bunch, ladies." Tad chuckles. "Yer new to the empowered world. There are a great many social nuances to be learned. The fact that yer man there doesn't make physical contact with other magical beings he doesn't know isn't a slight—it's self-preservation in a dangerous world."

I twist to meet Gareth's gaze, and he shrugs. "I told you I don't do well in crowds."

"I thought you meant you were claustrophobic or something."

"Nope. Just not a people person."

I have a hard time reconciling that with the DJ of a fae rave for a bunch of empowered fae kids.

"Jules, it's fine," Tad assures me. "Ye'll get used to people of different sects havin' different ways about them. S'all good."

I shake off the niggling of my instincts and let it go. If Tad's not concerned, why should I be? He knows a thousand times more about this world than I do. "Sorry. It's been a day. I need a drink. Want one?"

Gareth nods. "Sure."

I point for him to have a seat while I shrug out of my leather slicker and head to the fridge. I grab him the same brand of beer he chose during dinner the other night, and I grab a cooler.

The water is running in Briar's suite. I check my watch. He must've just gotten home from work and is taking a shower before we leave.

Returning to the living room, I hand Gareth the beer and take the chair opposite him and the couch.

It's nice to see Tad with Kenzie.

The two of them hit it off from the start, and it's obvious to everyone where that's going. She deserves a good guy, one as handsome, talented, and honorable as Tad. The fact that he finds her blue skin gorgeous and knows about the magical world means they've started with no secrets and being open with one another.

I can't help but frown inwardly as my attention moves to Gareth. There's nothing open about this guy. He's one big twisted ball of secrets and red flags.

Unfortunately, mysteries are my weak spot.

"Och, I recognize ye now." Tad grins at Gareth. "Yer the tall, dark drink of whiskey the girls were fannin' themselves over a few weeks back. They were watchin' ye handle yer lumber in ripped jeans and steel-toed boots."

Okay, shoot me now.

I blink at the blond hottie that has officially mortified me and send him a look of promised retribution. "You wait, druid. Payback is a bitch, and so am I."

Tad busts up laughing. The bastard isn't the slightest bit concerned.

"You won't be busting a gut when I fry your balls in training tomorrow."

Kenzie frowns and points at me. "You leave his balls alone, missy."

Briar joins us. "All righty then." His sandy blond hair is still damp from the shower and curling over his ears. "I feel like I missed something worth witnessing."

Tad chuckles. "I was takin' the piss. Yer sister is too easy to stir into a frenzy."

"Which one?"

I stick my tongue out at him, but before I can say anything more, a rush of air *whooshes* past me. Something smacks the side of my head. "What the hell?"

I lift my hands to shield my face as a stunning bird of prey soars past. My brain shorts out as I watch the rich brown and sterling silver of feathers glide through the air.

The bird lands on Tad's shoulder, squawks at me once, and starts to preen its wings.

"What just happened?" I rub the sore spot on the side of my head.

"Ye pissed off Aurora." Tad smiles at the bird adoringly. "Aurora, ye shouldn't have cracked Jules. She's a friend. We were teasin'. Now, go on, say yer sorry."

The bird makes a short squawking noise and fluffs up her feathers. I don't speak attack bird, but I'm fairly sure it wasn't an apology.

"Come now." Tad reaches up and strokes the silky feathers on her head. "Mind yer manners."

Aurora glances around the room with irritation in her small, round eyes.

Tad arches a brow, but by the smile curving his mouth, it's obvious he thinks the sun rises and sets around this bird. "Aurora is my animal companion. She's a kestrel, and unfortunately, she's a bit impassioned about bein' here."

"And taking it out on me." I down a few hearty gulps of my cooler.

"Aye, well, I'll be stayin' on fer a bit to help train ye, and she belongs with me and not alone in Toronto."

She squawks and snaps her beak, interrupting him as he's talking.

Tad sends her a scolding look. "Cheeky girl."

She ruffles her feathers and vocalizes again.

Briar chuckles behind me. "Why is she mad at you?"

"Because she misses Ireland. She wasn't any happier about movin' to Toronto. Thing is, sometimes ye gotta go where life takes ye."

She makes a high-pitched shriek.

"Just give it a chance."

"She's speaking to you?" Briar asks.

"Aye, of course. She's very eloquently telling me I'm a stubborn prat and we should go home, where the sky is clear to soar under, and rodents run free in the grasses."

Briar chuckles. "There are rodents in the city too, beautiful, but they're likely bigger than field mice."

I laugh, thinking about the last rat I saw climbing into a dumpster. Yeah, it was bigger than a field mouse by a large margin.

"Och, don't mind her. She'll come and go with the window open up there, and ye'll hardly realize she's here."

"As long as you don't threaten Tad's junk." Briar laughs at me.

"Lesson learned." I upend my cooler, ready to move along. "Give me two minutes to change, and we'll get going."

I don't have a ton of bar outfits in my wardrobe, and most of what I do have was gifted to me by Kenzie so it's either too tight, too skimpy, or too colorful. Opening my closet, I rifle through the various shades of gray and black to come up with something that might be good for hanging out with the crew at Casse Croûte.

"No yoga pants," Kenzie says behind me.

I drop the pair of black stretch pants and pretend that wasn't my intention.

"You're tragic." Kenzie pushes me out of the way and dives into my closet.

I huff and sit on the edge of my bed. "No. I have a different style."

"Lazy isn't a style. It's a commentary on your expectations."

"What's wrong with my expectations?"

"You don't have any."

"Rude."

She rolls her chestnut eyes and points at the shared area of our home. "That man out there is smoking hot, and for some reason, he accepts your abrasive, anti-social tendencies without comment. He also has his own business, a running vehicle that came off the production line this decade, and scooped you out of the muck, bleeding and broken after destroying a half-dozen bully assholes. Fate has thrown him in your path, and if I leave it to you, you'll fuck it up."

"Very rude."

She shoves a few hangers at me. "Put that on."

I take the selection of clothes and growl. "Your bossy bitch lawyer is showing."

"For once, don't argue."

It would be no good if I did. When Kenzie gets like this, there's no refusing. I pull on the tight black leather pants and a burnt orange metallic sequin top with a halter neck.

"I look like a shiny tangerine."

Kenzie grunts. "You look like a girl with fire powers. Trust me. It's a key thing you have in common. He'll make the connection, and it'll turn him on."

"What if I don't want to turn him on? I barely know the man."

Kenzie snorts, pushing me toward the bathroom. "What does that have to do with anything?" When we get inside, she drops the lid for the toilet and points. "Sit. I'll do your hair and makeup."

Normally, I'd protest. I'm not nearly as girly as Kenzie, and I don't have the patience for fussing that she does. Still, she's been so moody since her skin turned blue and it's nice to see the fire in her eyes again.

"Fine. I'll play the part of your pet project this once."

The excited surprise in her expression hits me right in the feels. I have to try harder to make the people around me happy.

"All right." Kenzie examines me. "Close your eyes, relax, and leave everything to me."

I draw a deep breath and exhale to show her I'm playing nice. In truth, after the day I had, it helps.

"So, Gareth."

I chuckle. "You didn't last one minute."

"I'm seizing the moment. It's not often I get you cornered and unable to avoid me."

"You're making me regret this makeup party."

"Back to the man with the tats. When I say Gareth, what's the first thing that comes to your mind?"

"Closed off."

She laughs. "Right. Not like you, of course."

"I'm a cop. We're taught to put our emotions to the side. I need to be guarded, but when it comes to guys, I'm an open book."

"Saying the words doesn't make them true." There's a rustle of pencils, and she grips my chin and starts lining my eyes. "You really could do with a few more liner colors."

"Christmas is coming."

Kenzie clucks her tongue as she traces the pencil along my eyelids. "I'm going with bronze and silver smoky eyes with some sparkle that matches your shirt. It's super cute, by the way."

"I have never doubted your skills."

After a dozen different applicators, sponges, and brushes the masterpiece is as good as it will get.

Kenzie steps back and assesses her artwork.

"I think darker lips with some shine." At this point, she's mostly talking to herself. She dabs dark, wine-red lipstick onto my lips, then follows up with a tiny brush dipped in a lightly glittering gloss.

"Will I still look like myself after all this?"

"Of course. Just, you know, a more attractive version of yourself."

"Rude."

"How about some detail braids for tonight?"

I do not know what a detail braid is, but I agree. It turns out to be two small tight and close braids running down the side of my head behind one ear.

Tilting my head to catch the angles in the mirror, I take it all in. Damn, she's done a great job. As promised, I still look like myself, but also like I might belong in a bar, flirting with guys and having fun with friends.

"Moment of truth." I grip the doorknob of my bedroom tighter than necessary.

Tad, Briar, and Gareth are deeply involved in a conversation about the current state of the city and its prejudices.

"That's why we met," I interject by way of announcing our arrival.

I have the distinct pleasure of catching Gareth's visceral response to my appearance before he regains his composure and locks down his appreciation.

He tips back the rest of his second beer and swallows. "I'm certainly not the only one out there rooting for the kids, but yeah, it's important for the fae youth not to be shamed or shunned because of being different."

There's no mistaking the conviction behind his words, and it makes me even more determined to discover what in his past created that kind of devotion to kids finding their way.

Was he ostracized? Was someone he cared about hurt because of being different? Did someone he knows hurt themselves because they felt alone and unwanted?

"What you do is such a good thing." I give him all the credit he deserves. "There was an incident a month or two back when someone threw a meet-and-greet party for the newly awakened, but it was a setup, and they all got robbed and roughed up."

Tad spouts a colorful string of Irish cursing. "That's deplorable. It's one thing to be confused and concerned when the world changes around ye, but to be violent against perfect strangers because their magic woke? I don't get it."

"People can be nasty." Gareth swigs the last of his beer and stands, picking up his cans. "Where can I put these?"

"On the kitchen counter is fine," I answer.

Kenzie grins. "Shall we get going?"

"Is Aurora coming with us?" Briar asks.

Tad shakes his head. "She doesn't like loud music. She'll stay here and probably head out for a snack or two. If this neighborhood had a rat problem before, it certainly won't anymore."

Kenzie glances at the open skylight above. "You're sure that will work for her?"

"Och, aye. She's a wee thing. She'll have no issue comin' and goin'."

With that settled, Tad stands and puts his hand between us. Kenzie and Briar pile their hands on top, and I do the same. As crazy as it sounds, we're getting used to the idea of portaling.

Gareth stares at our hands, and his reticence is obvious. "It's fine. You can touch my shirt or something, and the circuit will pick you up for transport."

He mutters a soft curse as his jaw flexes. Then he slips his hand around my hip to rest against the small of my back.

CHAPTER EIGHT

Since Zephyr is playing tonight, he and Camile made sure we have a "VIP table" up near the front. Plus, our first round of drinks is free, which gives me a reprieve from arguing with Gareth about which one of us is paying for the other tonight.

Zephyr joins us when we get settled. He's finished tuning his guitar and is ready to start playing the minute the last of his band members arrives.

In the meantime, we can hang out.

Tad hears there is an injured pigeon out back and wanders off with one of the bussers to help it.

Unfortunately for Gareth, that leaves him as the only non-Gagne at the table, which lands him squarely in the hot seat.

Zephyr runs his fingers through his hair. His silver rings run a real risk of catching on the dark strands. "I'm impressed. I wasn't sure Jules would ask you to come."

Gareth shrugs. "It seems I dropped by at the right time. People gotta eat, right?"

"Right." I shoot Zephyr a warning look. "Don't you need to check your microphone or your amp or something?"

"Nope. I'm good." Zephyr chuckles and tips back his bottle of beer. "So, you dropped by? What was that about? What are your intentions with our sister?"

I groan. "*Tabarnak*, Zephyr. Don't."

He chuckles. "It's in the bro code. Sorry, Jules. It's gotta be done."

I roll my eyes. "I'm going to light your mattress on fire while you're sleeping."

He chuckles. "I'll blow it out."

"It's fine." Gareth waves away my ire. "I stopped by to drop off some building plans for elemental enrichment stations."

"For his trouble, I offered to bring him for a burger and a beer as a thank you."

Briar blinks. "I can't remember the last time you bought me dinner."

"Right?" Zephyr makes a face. "I was thinking the same thing."

"You can buy your dinners. I'm living off a civil servant's salary over here."

Briar laughs. "I'm not exactly rolling in it."

Gareth turns his attention toward Briar. "You and Jules both mentioned you work construction. What kind?"

"New builds. Large scale subdivisions mostly."

I tap the dry patch on his arm. "Which is why when his awakening started, we all thought he was spending too much time around freshly poured concrete."

Gareth shakes his head and leans in. "I still can't believe you four went your entire lives without knowing what you were or having any access to your powers."

"You always knew?" Briar asks.

Gareth nods.

"How long did it take you to learn and control your powers?" Zephyr asks.

Gareth glances around. Even though the bar speakers are blasting music and no one else seems interested in eavesdropping on us, he doesn't want to discuss his magical status and personal history in this public place.

I change the subject. "Briar, speaking of your construction expertise, now that Gareth gave us some designs, when can we go over them and start planning for the backyard?"

"You want me to build during my downtime? I doubt you can afford my hourly rate."

Kenzie rolls her eyes. "Isn't it worth any amount of money to have a more relaxed and happier Jules?"

Seriously? "How did this become about me? I'm not that miserable."

Zephyr holds his hand flat and tilts it back and forth. "Meh... that's debatable."

Briar chuckles. "I suppose we could write it off as a public service to the citizens of Montréal. You know, keeping a cop in a good mood."

I shake my head. "You all suck."

Zephyr slings an arm around my shoulders and shakes me playfully. "Ah, don't get bent outta shape, sista. Most days you're a goddamn delight."

"A fucking ray of sunshine," Briar adds.

"One that can burn you to a crisp," I finish. "So you better be careful when describing my personality."

The manager, Ashlynn, steps up to the microphone and taps it a few times. "Live music in five, folks. If you need a refill before the show, now is the time to get it."

That's Zephyr's cue.

He throws back the rest of his beer and saunters up on stage. His drummer, a shaggy-haired guy who never seems entirely sober, has arrived and is settling in behind the drum kit.

"Oh, Harlan is playing bass tonight." I wave at Zephyr's buddy.

"Yeah, Drake's ex-wife screwed him at the last minute and wouldn't take the kids. He had to cancel."

"In the long run, he's better off without that bitch, but I doubt it'll feel like that for a long time."

Kenzie's eyes widen as she nods. "Sally is a bitch with a capital B."

Tad returns from his wildlife quest and reclaims his seat next to my sister.

"How's the pigeon?" I ask.

"Och, she'll be fine. I healed her wing and took her back to her nest to rest fer the night. She'll be right as rain by mornin'."

I giggle, sitting back in my chair. How weird is it that Kenzie's boyfriend healed a pigeon and escorted it home to its nest?

Amazing...but still weird.

Zephyr steps up to the mic, holding his guitar. "We're gonna open with a few of our favorites. If you know the words, sing along. If you don't, get your asses onto the dance floor and have a good time."

Energized by the beat, people jump up to dance.

"Wanna dance?" Kenzie asks.

"Hells yeah," I jump up.

Tad, Briar, and Gareth all shake their heads.

"Your loss." I wave over my head, giving a little extra swagger to my hips.

Kenzie and I hit the dance floor, bopping and rocking along to the beat. We've both had a few drinks, not enough to be drunk, but pleasantly buzzed.

The metallic sequins on my shirt catch the light, glinting and sparkling in the stage lights as I dance.

It was a great choice for tonight.

I glance at Gareth, and our eyes lock. He's been watching me dance, but not in a creepy way. He gives me a friendly smile. I motion for him to come to join me.

He declines but lifts his drink as if cheering my willingness to get my groove on.

I turn back to Kenzie, but she's not there. I look around,

noticing that the crowd has shifted, and now Kenzie and I are separated.

I think I see her toward the back of the crowd and I stand on my tiptoes. Craning my neck, I recognize her hair and blouse.

Swaying to the rhythm, I sashay toward her.

Lost in the chaos of the crowd and the rocking beat of Zephyr working his magic on stage, I miss the arrival of several big bouncer dudes.

Four burly brutes muscle between Kenzie and me. With my path blocked, I crane my neck to the side to keep an eye on her.

Nope. I can't even see the top of her hair.

"Excuse me." I try to navigate around them.

They straighten, making a muscled wall blocking my path. Wait. These guys aren't standard-issue drunken goobers acting like assholes on the dance floor.

When they stare down at me, all my survival instinct fire to life.

"Excuse me." I lace my words with intention, ready to get aggressive in my attempts to get Kenzie.

They don't respond. Two stay focused on me and two break off behind them, corralling Kenzie toward the back hall.

"Oh, hell no."

I spin, trying to assess my surroundings. Maybe I can catch Gareth's eye again, or maybe Zephyr will notice me from up on stage…

I twist to see if I can wave down Zephyr, but as soon as I raise my arm, I feel a sharp prick in my side.

Shit la marde. This is so not good.

I try to cry out, to get someone's attention as my legs go rubbery, and my vision recedes to darkness…

Galump-bump. Lying curled on my side, I blink awake and push at the fog smothering my brain. I'm in an enclosed space...it's dark...and I'm moving. The gentle bump and sway of the world around me, mixed with the rough carpet under my cheek and the scents of grease and gas tell me I'm in the trunk of a car.

I exhale, test my limbs, and remember the bite of an injection into my side.

As my situation focuses into more clarity, I realize a few key points of alarm. Cable ties bind my hands and feet, I have no idea if they got Kenzie too, and on top of the smell of grease and gas, there's also a strong whiff of burned cookies.

Dammit. Another spark of fire floods my system and threatens to break past my control. I close my eyes and focus on reining in the chaos trying to explode.

Deep breaths, Jules. In and out.

These guys are skoro, demon minions of the powerful demon-fae hybrid siblings of the Poreskoro family.

I thought we rid the city of these assholes when Briar ripped Lamech Poreskoro's head off. The tie of a skoro to their maker means when we kill one of The Six, we also take down their begotten.

Maman and Papa took down Draven and their ilk.

We took down Lamech and his.

According to Azland, that leaves us with Rance, Razgarath, Zissa, and Sasobek to worry about.

I draw another deep breath, but after the day I've had, I don't know that I'll be able to tamp down my fire.

My blood is running hot. My skin itches. My heart is pounding. I need to know my sister is safe. I need out of this fucking trunk.

My hands ignite, and the warm, orange glow is a comfort in the dark space. Cops are trained to remain calm in stressful situations. I can handle this.

Breathe. Think. Focus on a plan.

The first thing that comes to mind is that with my hands on fire, maybe I can—*Snap!*

Yay me. The tie binding my wrists was no match for a fire elemental. It takes a bit of wriggling in such a cramped space to work my arms to my front so I can reach down to my feet.

Seriously, burning my leather pants to melt the bindings pisses me off almost as much as getting kidnapped by essence-sucking d-holes.

Once I have my hands and legs free, I feel around, searching for something I can use as a weapon. Yes, I can flame up, but if anything happens like at the river and I get extinguished, I'm powerless, weaponless, and naked.

Until I have better control over things, I prefer to flame up as a last resort.

Besides, as a cop, I know something these idiots probably don't. A safety mandate requires all cars to feature a glow-in-the-dark trunk release lever.

If pulled from the inside, it will open the trunk.

My hands are still aflame. I search the tail light area of the trunk, looking for the dark lever.

There isn't one.

That's a serious violation, not to mention dangerous. Then again, drugging and kidnapping someone is also seriously illegal. When I get out of here, automobile citations will be the least of their worries.

I scoot around on the scratchy carpet and position myself with my head near the back seat and my feet near the latch.

Maybe I don't escape.

Maybe I try to learn their plan and who's involved.

Since Lamech is no longer with us, one of the other four Poreskoro siblings must be behind the skoro still in the city. I need to figure out where they're taking me and what their plan is.

Falling still, I press my ear to the thin wall separating the trunk from the rest of the car and listen.

"—elemental is fine dining."

"Cute too. Looks like she'll put up a good fight."

They have no idea. Disgust and outrage overrule my control and my fire surges to the fore. Heat builds in me along with anger. They won't lay a hand on me.

What about Kenzie? Is she in this car? Did the other brutes take her to a different skoro party? I need to get out of here. If they took Kenzie to consume her energy, I need time to track her.

I need out of here!

If I can't get out of the trunk, maybe I can make my way through the back of the seats into the car. That way, I can plan my attack and find out if Kenzie is in the car.

My instincts say she's not.

After all, this is a spacious trunk with plenty of luggage space. If they wanted both of us in one car, why not pile her in with me?

With that in mind, I find the release latch for the split seats in the back and yank it. Then, with my finger in the strap's loop, I ease it forward, hoping there's no one sitting in this seat or beside it.

There isn't.

The seat pushes forward, and I see there's no one in the back and only skoro assholes up front. Excellent.

That's all I needed to know.

My breathing has grown ragged, and I've fought to tether my flames. Now that I know who the collateral damage will involve, why tether it?

Fuck it. Fuck them.

Closing my eyes, I tune into the rage coursing through my cells and focus all my energy, heat, and anger on a fiery body sheath.

Here's hoping these assholes filled the gas tank before their kidnapping plans.

Kaboom.

CHAPTER NINE

The heat is incredible, the scream of twisting metal buffered by the explosion's *whooshing* roar. Everything around me detonates into a flaming inferno as heat that warms me to the marrow of my bones engulfs me.

If this is what having an elemental enrichment station is like, sign me up.

I climb out of the fiery ball of metal feeling like my entire being is alive and vibrating power.

It's more than empowering. It's intoxicating.

As a cop, it pisses me off that it destroyed the entire scene. Any evidence is gone. Any tie to the Poreskoro on the scene is lost. The skoro thugs that kidnapped me might have been hellborn, but they didn't survive.

I'm safe, but that doesn't help me find Kenzie.

The wall of flame I sent reaching for the stars settles, and I step out onto the street. We're in a remote area. Warehouses mostly. Metal grates and wide garage doors line the street, but everything is closed.

The road is cratered beneath my bare feet. Dammit. I loved those boots.

I let my flames burn freely.

I'd rather be a human torch than a naked chick trotting down the streets of Montréal.

After stepping around the bonfire, I scan the two black luxury sedans stopped in the roadway facing me. I recognize the driver of the first one as one of the thugs from the dance floor.

Interesting.

The car I obliterated was part of a caravan of evil.

"Surprise. I did not go gentle into that good night."

When the men in the sedans realize what's happened, they bail out and run at me.

"Bring it, assholes." I laugh as two of them shoot at me. In this form, raging as I am, bullets melt long before they hit. "Sucks to be you, boys. You're going to have to play with fire."

Their confused looks make me laugh.

Were they expecting me to run? Not bloody likely.

I slide my dominant foot back, drop into a fighting stance, and blast hot air at them. The force of the wall pushes them staggering back. One of them trips backward on a chunk of asphalt and lands sprawled on his ass.

I jump onto him, bashing my blazing fist into his stupid face. One of his buddies grabs me, cursing as he yanks me off the guy.

I whirl and shove him hard with both flaming hands. His shirt singes and smokes, but it doesn't slow him down. The stench of his skin burning is gratifying and gross, but he keeps coming.

Gripping the shoulders of his shirt, I pull him forward and knee him solidly in the nuts.

He doubles over, his breath escaping in a grunt. I shove him back, letting him slump to the ground.

A flash of pain flares and I spin. Two guys swing chunks of twisted metal at me, and I lift my hand to block. Whatever they hit me with drew a dull ache, but I'm not bleeding. My skin self-cauterizes.

Handy.

Another vehicle races around the corner. Its headlights swing in a wild arc as its tires screech in protest.

It's Briar.

Zephyr borrowed our brother's truck to get his gear to the bar, and now the cavalry is here.

The tires screech as the doors fly open. Briar, Zephyr, and Gareth jump out. My brothers rush the other vehicles, Gareth is booking it toward me, and Tad *poofs* beside me and joins the fight.

Flames surge and crackle off my body and newfound confidence fills me. I'm not alone. When it comes to my family and friends, I'll never be alone.

My kidnappers realize this too.

Turning tail, they beat feet in the opposite direction, trying to get away from me. "No way, dickwad. You don't get off that easily."

One tucks behind the burning wreck and crouches low.

Does he not think I can find him? I circle the fire one way as Gareth rounds the vehicle from the opposite side. I grab his arm, and his shirt bursts into flames.

He screams, skitters back, and stumbles into the burning wreck. More screams peal through the night sky as the flames from the mangled car envelop him.

I strike off to deal with his equally doomed buddies.

Tad is a marvel to watch in a fight. With his portal powers, he flashes around in a blink—on their left, behind them, coming at them from the front—disorienting his opponents.

"Jules, focus!" Gareth shouts.

My distraction breaks. In an instant, I realize my flames have died down. My skin still simmers enough to hide my more private bits, but it's more lit fireplace than a raging inferno.

I follow Gareth's gaze and turn.

Shit. Three skoro are almost upon me. They're grinning their too-wide smiles, implying they think they'll take me down.

"Think again, boys." Gareth sends a massive ball of fire in our direction. It's a weird kind of flame that seems to have a mind of its own. As it blows past me, I hunker down, enjoying the rush of heat.

The guys surrounding me don't.

The fireball explodes as it hits them, wrapping them in crimson tendrils and squeezing them into the core of the molten ball. All three disintegrate into ash and drop.

What. The. Hell?

Holy hell, whatever Gareth is, it's badass.

It feels good to let off steam, but we run out of opponents too soon. Two or three in each vehicle means the fight is over as we're getting into the swing of things.

When all is said and done, I'm disappointed there aren't more to battle. It's also concerning that I'm anxious for more.

I've never been one to actively look for a fight but ever since my elemental side awoke... It feels damn good to crack heads and flame up.

Sadly, that's over for now.

"Briar, do you still have that fireproof blanket in your truck? I'm about to be really freaking naked."

"Got you covered, sista." He jogs back to the truck and a moment later wraps me in a heavy blanket lined with silver foil like the world's largest and angriest baked potato.

I tug the ends around myself, a little embarrassed. "I don't generally end up naked on the first date."

Gareth grins. "The fire blanket is quick thinking. I had to settle with eyes up and chin out while I strutted home in the buff when I first started flaming up."

Well now, doesn't that conjure all kinds of images?

"How's Kenzie?" Briar jogs to where Tad is standing at the open door of one of the other cars.

"She'll be fine," Tad assures him. "Just unconscious."

Zephyr advises, "There are two more in the other truck. Also unconscious."

"If they jabbed us with the same drug, why did I wake up so much earlier?"

"It's your metabolism," Gareth informs me. "Our systems burn hotter than a human or any other magical being without a fire gene. It makes perfect sense that you'd burn through the sedative quickly. It works with booze too. Now that your elemental side is unlocked, it'll be tough to get your buzz on."

"I'll be the queen of drinking contests."

Gareth makes a face and laughs. "Not even remotely where I was going with that."

Doesn't matter. The point is, I did wake up, and we took down the bad guys of the night. "How many of us did they grab?"

Zephyr points at the trucks. "One in with Kenzie and two in the last vehicle. I can't be sure, but I think they took them from the bar."

Gareth curses and shakes his head. "This shouldn't have happened."

"No, but this isn't our first run-in with the skoro or The Six."

"The Four," Briar corrects.

"Four?" Gareth asks.

Briar grins. "Yeah. Two attempts on our family and two fewer Poreskoro assholes alive to torment the innocents of the fae world."

I nod. "Draven found us when we hit puberty. He killed our parents, but they took him down with the help of a group of warriors so we'd be safe."

"Fuck. I didn't know."

"Neither did we until a couple of weeks ago. Still, their sacrifice meant that we grew up to live a fairly safe and normal life until now."

Gareth shifts on his feet and exhales. "I'm so sorry."

I shrug. "Not your fault. Besides, I'm sorry too. I'm sure the

Gagne baggage is daunting. I never meant for you to get caught up in our family drama."

Gareth frowns. "Yeah, me too. More than you know."

There's an edge of defeat in his tone that I've heard more than once. That disappointed but determined subtext to his words tells me he's looking for the door. He glares at the burned car and sets his hands on his hips. "Jules…as much as I like you…this was a mistake. I can't get involved."

Ouch.

I force a nonchalant smile and shrug. "No fault. No foul. Thanks for your help."

He looks at me with a storm brewing in his gaze and the muscles in his jaw flexing. "I'm sorry."

"Understood. *Sayonara*, fire guy."

Gareth curses, turns, and storms off, throwing small fireballs off himself as he goes.

"Well, that was fun while it lasted." I sigh and lean against the truck.

Briar checks his watch. "Twenty-seven hours. That might be a new record for you."

Zephyr chuckles. "Is the record that it blew up in twenty-seven hours or that it lasted that long?"

I flip them both off with a middle-fingered salute, then cross my arms and stomp off to where Tad sits next to an unconscious Kenzie in the back of one of the black sedans. "Tad, I'm done with this shit. *Poof* me and Kenzie home, please. She needs to be somewhere safe, and I need new clothes."

Tad nods and reaches for my hand. We're home in a minute, and I go straight to my room to pull on some yoga pants and a hoodie. I pick old and ratty ones that I wouldn't mind incinerating if my skin isn't cool enough yet for the fabric to survive.

I think I'm okay. Although, wouldn't it be nice if I could go back to coming home wearing the same clothes I had on when I left?

Is that too much to ask?

I find Tad sitting on the edge of Kenzie's bed. He has her all tucked in and is holding one of her hands.

Damn, he's one of the good ones.

I thought Gareth might be a good guy too. As usual, I'm a horrible judge of male character. Whatevs. Kenzie can live and love for both of us.

Joining the two of them, I study my sister's sleeping form. Either the drug or her being unconscious has broken the glamor that keeps her looking human. Now that I'm getting used to her blue skin, I'd be hard-pressed to decide in which form she's more stunning.

Tad saw her for the beauty she was from the beginning. Huge points for him. Setting my hand on his shoulder, I stand at his side. "Hey, thanks for the assist tonight."

He shakes his head. "It shouldn't have happened. Maybe if I had joined ye on the dance floor—"

"Nah, don't play that game. They could've grabbed us if we went to the bathroom, stepped outside for fresh air, or in a half-dozen other scenarios. If someone intends to do something, they'll find a way to try."

He sighs. "Aye, I suppose that's true."

"It is. The important thing is that you and the boys found us and we whupped some serious skoro ass. All's well that ends well."

He nods. "If ye say so."

"I do. While I don't want to disturb you from standing vigil, do you think you could *poof* me back to the scene? I'm still wound up, and I'll be more use there than I will here."

Tad looks at Kenzie, his expression telling me he is hesitant to leave her, but he stands and extends his hand. "Sure."

Back at the scene of the skoro attack, Briar is piling the bodies and removing all wallets and personal effects before taking a picture of each dead guy. A few of them burned too badly to make a useful ID, but hey, they shouldn't have kidnapped a fire elemental.

Zephyr stares at the security cameras affixed to the closest buildings and frowns. "The last thing we need is some business owner calling the cops on us and making this an even bigger mess."

Yeah, that would be bad. "I'll text Bakkali. I bet the Guild of the Laurentians has a team that responds to clean up things like this."

"Sounds like a plan."

I finish with the text and frown at the scene. No doubt those cameras already recorded quite a show. I pull out my phone and snap an image of the license plates for the two sedans.

"What should we do with the cars?" Briar asks.

"If Bakkali's people don't take them, I'll call them into the precinct as abandoned. Some uniforms will come out and tow them to the impound lot."

Briar surveys the damage we've done to the street and sidewalks. "In the meantime, I might as well do my civic duty and ensure the folks who work here can make it to work tomorrow morning."

I chuckle. "Are you a part of the roadwork department now?"

"Seems so." Briar uses his powers and construction skills to flatten the potholes and cracks.

When he finishes, I widen my eyes and make a face. "Uh-oh, this might be a problem."

"What, uh-oh? It's perfect."

I chuckle. "Yeah. That's the problem. When has any street maintenance in Montréal been perfect?"

Briar laughs. "Yeah, good point."

When Bakkali's team arrives, I let Zephyr and Briar run the scene with them. I head over to the people in the kidnappers' vehicles. They're finally coming around and will no doubt be freaked out and disoriented.

A girl with electric blue hair appears to be a couple of years younger than Kenzie. She sits up and takes in the scene with eyes glistening with emotion. I don't know much about the different fae sects, but if I were a betting person, I'd guess she's a sprite of some kind.

I hold my hands up as I approach the car's open door. "Hey, there. I'm Inspector Gagne of the SPVM. You're safe now. Are you feeling okay?"

She reaches up to touch her forehead. "A headache."

"Me too. We were drugged. Do you remember anything from before? Where is the last place you remember being?"

"Dancing at a bar."

"Casse Croûte?"

Her gaze narrows on me. "Yeah. How'd you know?"

"Because that's where I was when they grabbed me."

Briar comes over. "Bakkali's team has everything in hand. We're supposed to take these two home."

A groan from the other seat brings the second person to consciousness. They are androgynous with long, lithe limbs, nut brown skin, and silky chestnut hair.

"What? Where am I?" They cast a frantic gaze around the car's interior. "What's going on?"

"You were taken." I keep my voice calm. "You're safe now. The men who took you drugged you. You might be rocking the after-effects hangover, yeah?"

They wince and rub their temple. "Who are you?"

"Inspector Jules Gagne. They made the mistake of grabbing me too. That's been taken care of. You're safe, and my brothers and I will take each of you home now."

"Who are 'they?' Why did they do this?"

"We don't know." It's mostly the truth. It won't do any good to have a traumatized victim realizing they almost became the dinnertime plaything to demon minions. "The thing to focus on is that they're gone, and you're safe."

The person narrows their eyes. "If you're a cop, why are you dressed like that?"

Right. I'm in a hoodie and yoga pants. "I was off shift when they grabbed me too. Were you at Casse Croûte?"

"Yeah."

"Well, it seems there was a coordinated sweep for fae tonight, and we all got caught in the net. Thankfully, they didn't anticipate my powers or the fact that I'm a cop. I was able to stop them and end their plans."

"How?"

I step back and invite them to exit the car. Bakkali's team is buzzing around, and Zephyr and Briar are pulling up in the truck. "With a bit of help. Now, let's get you two home."

"Thank you," the girl says.

The other one still isn't digging me. "I'm good. Thanks anyway."

Stepping out of the car, they glance at the night sky, take a couple of steps, and burst into a large black bird. With a few powerful wing flaps, the bird lifts into the air and swoops around the side of a warehouse.

Briar's mouth drops open as we watch the bird disappear. "I'm not complaining because my powers rock, but dayam, that's fucking cool."

Zephyr nods. "I don't suppose elementals can be shifters too. Is that greedy?"

I laugh. "Maybe a little. Let's get everyone home safe so we can check on Kenzie."

CHAPTER TEN

I'm running...my bare feet slapping against the hardwood floor. I'm back in the house where I tracked Zephyr and found the dead guy. The dead guy is on the floor. When I turn him over, it's Zephyr's blank-eyed, gray face staring at me.

I scream, but no sound escapes. Instead, a rushing column of fire engulfs the body. My little brother dissolves into ashes. I keep screaming, but it only makes the fire hotter.

Someone drags me out of the building, but I can't see who. Weird runes float before my eyes. I hear clicking. I roll over, and I'm on wet, dewy grass.

Sitting up, I take in the marble tombstones. I'm in a cemetery. The grave beside me reads Laurette Gagne.

"Maman?" I grip the grass like I can dig down and find her.

Behind the gravestone, Nakey Kid is dead on the lawn of his apartment complex.

The air smells like grease and burned cookies. I hear Lamech Poreskoro laughing, but the person approaching me is Gareth. His eyes glow blood red as he reaches down to help me up.

His hand is scorching hot and burns me.

I close my eyes, and when I open them, I'm trapped in the dark box *of that trunk. We're bumping across the Champlain Bridge, and I feel the energy of the St. Lawrence River pulsing below us.*

I'm scared. Angry. Confused.

There's an explosion. This time, when I crawl out of the twisted hunk of smoldering metal, Briar is already there. He pulls me free. No... it's not me. He's pulling on a limp blue arm.

Kenzie. She's not okay.

I scream again. It doesn't sound like my voice. It sounds like a blaring alarm. It goes on and on, howling louder than anything. My ears ring with it, but I keep screaming—

"Dammit, Jules, wake up!"

A crushing wave of water hits me, and I'm pressed deep into my mattress. The fire station's alarm is going off. I sputter and sit up, choking on the water that went up my nose.

Kenzie is standing there with her arms outstretched and her palms dripping.

"What the hell? You blasted me with water."

"Because you're on *fire!*"

The scene around me comes into focus.

Briar has my bedroom window cranked open, and Zephyr has created a funnel of wind to force smoke out the window.

"You were stuck in a nightmare." Kenzie breathes heavily.

Obviously. I glance down at my soaked PJs and my poor mattress and pillows. They're burned to a crisp, waterlogged, and steaming.

"I started a fire in my sleep?"

"Got it on one," Zephyr confirms.

Jack and Jack are bobbing around their bowl, taking in the scene as if nothing out of the ordinary is happening.

Fish be crazy.

Blinking the water out of my eyes, I take it all in—Zephyr and Briar tackling the smoke, Kenzie hosing me down in her naughtiest negligee, and Tad looking damn hot in black boxers.

Looks like I interrupted something fun.

I peel myself off the bed and point at my bath towel hanging on the back of my bathroom door.

Tad does me the honor of tossing it, and I bury my face and start to dry off. Just another day in the life of me. Thankfully, these are my peeps, and they don't judge. I draw a deep breath and run the thick terry over my dripping hair.

Zephyr offers a sympathetic smile. "Finally, someone else is fucking up the sleep around here. Happy to pass that torch along to my big sister."

I groan and stare at my ruined bed. "Torch is the key word in that statement. Man, I sure lit it up."

"You've always been one to excel," he agrees.

"Achiever!" I pump my fist in mock celebration.

"Looks like you need somewhere dry to sleep," Zephyr says.

"The guest room is made up," Tad suggests. "And it's...uh, free."

Briar makes a face. "Dude. Thanks for announcing you're sexing our sister."

Kenzie busts up laughing at the flush of pink on Tad's cheeks. "He's messing with you. The four of us have lived through enough moments of oversharing that you having a sleepover in my room doesn't even blip the radar screen."

I nod. "Briar is the last person to criticize after we had to live through four months of him dating Cecilia Beauchamp."

Briar rolls his eyes. "She wasn't that bad."

"Oh, B! Yes, B. Yes!" I mimic with a breathy rasp.

"My ass!" Kenzie joins in. "Ohmygod, yes! My ass. Like that!"

Briar shrugs. "She liked butt stuff and was a bit of a screamer."

Serious understatement.

Zephyr blinks, laughing. "The neighbors called the cops thinking we were torturing someone here."

I snort. "Yeah, I still hear about that at the station too, fuck you very much."

Briar waves to stop the commentary. "I'm going to bed. Jules, try not to burn us down. Kenzie and Tad, try not to summon the cops."

"Och, no," Tad demurs. "A druid always casts a silencin' spell. Ye'll never hear a sound."

Kenzie barks a feminine laugh. "On that note of TMI, goodnight all. If the station house is rockin', don't come a-knockin'."

That clears the room quickly enough. After grabbing a dry pair of pajamas, I head into my washroom to brush my hair and get changed.

"I guess it's the guest room for me tonight," I tell Jack and Jack. "See you in the morning, boys."

I wake early, my mind having decided five hours of interrupted sleep is all I'll need today. Whatevs. Sleep is highly overrated anyway. First into the shower—especially this early in the day—means I can hog the hot water and the heater will have time to recover before my siblings get ready for work.

Winning!

First up fills the coffee maker with water, so I shuffle out to the kitchen and get things started on that front. Everyone else's bedroom doors are closed, so I have the place to myself.

I grab a couple of the Pillsbury cinnamon rolls tubes from the fridge, set the oven to preheat, unwrap the cylinders, and set the little spirals of breakfast bliss on a baking sheet.

While I wait for the *beep* of acceptance, I grab my laptop from my room and plug in the flash drive of designs for elemental sanctuaries.

Gareth wasn't kidding when he said most of the designs were for fire fae. There are some stunning fireplace images, a couple of geyser wading pools, magma pools...

Oh, cool. What I wouldn't give right now to soak in a magma pool.

The temperature notification *beeps,* and I slide the cookie sheet into the oven and set the timer. Selecting hazelnut roast for my morning coffee, I puncture the pod and slide my mug into place.

Reclaiming my seat, I scan through the waterfalls, the pools, and the misting and snow machines. Ew...snow.

The mud bogs make me laugh. I can imagine what Briar will look like when he hauls his burly butt out of a giant mud pit...hilarious.

Oooh, the wind tunnel is a fun idea. The four of us went to an IFly last year and had a blast. The idea of having something like that built in our backyard is super cool. He'd have to fight us for a turn...assuming we could ever afford any of these.

The buzzer goes off, and I jump up to take out the swirled-up bundles of cinnamon delight. Technically, you're supposed to let them cool so you can put the icing on without it melting and pooling onto the pan. Instead, I get a little bowl, pour some of the icing into it, and dip my piping hot pastry.

"Perfection." I fight not to groan as the sugary decadence melts in my mouth. As I chew the magical wonder of ready-to-bake yumminess, I pour milk into my coffee and grab two more.

After rinsing my fingers and the bottom of my coffee mug, I write a note and prop it over the top edge of my laptop. I think they're going to love the plans.

Hey, if Gareth says we need rejuvenation stations, we might all agree to use a chunk of the life insurance money we still have from *Maman* and Papa.

Grabbing my backpack and slicker, I shrug into my jacket and slide down the pole to the garage bay. I snap the silver buckles of my motorcycle boots, pull on my helmet, and walk over to open the bay door.

Because it's still early, I walk Scarlett outside, wait for the door to close behind me, and roll out to the curb before I fire her up. Once on the city streets, I open her up and leave my troubles in my wake.

I head south, down Avenue Souligny. The morning crowd is starting to fill in, but there is still plenty of space to weave in and out of pockets.

A few blocks down, I see a storefront in a well-maintained area splashed with hot pink paint across the glass front. "FREAKS."

One of the windows is smashed in, and there is nothing stopping looters or passersby from an easy snatch and grab. Gearing down to stop at the side of the road, I dig out my phone and call it in.

"Yep, it was logged in less than ten minutes ago," Reese tells me. "No one was hurt, and Rene's task force is en route to see how they can help."

"Thanks, man." I put my phone back in my pocket and get back to my bike. I take a few quick corners and hop on the highway so I can drop the hammer.

I'm not sure why I'm so unsettled today.

I got kidnapped last night, but I'm an adrenaline junkie. Yeah, Gareth walked away, but it wasn't like we were anything. He helped me out of a couple of scuffles and looks good in a muscle shirt. That's hardly a reason to get mopey.

Yes, I hated seeing Kenzie unconscious and at the mercy of monsters—again.

Yes, I'm still pissed about Nakey Kid being dead before his life really began.

What has my cells firing and sparks pushing the envelope of my control? Last night I let my flames fly, and it was a beautiful, freeing thing.

I need to do that more often.

Maybe that's it. Maybe I need to go full flame on the regular to burn off some of this energy.

It worked for Zephyr.

Z is much calmer and more focused now that he understands

the storm twisting inside him. He practices the most out of the four of us.

Maybe that's why he's doing so well.

Without meaning to, I find myself in Rougemont Park. The trees and flowers have grown lush since I came here a couple of weeks ago. It looks more like a tropical jungle than a Montréal city park.

I know the budget for the city's landscaping department, and there is no way tax dollars paid for this.

The trees are huge, their leaves stirring in shades of rich emerald green. The gardens are blanketed in bright jewel-toned flowers bordered by ebony mulch chips.

The effect is quite dramatic.

Is it a coincidence the park where Gareth held his underground rave for magical kids is teeming with prana?

I frown at the clearing where I first met him.

Despite his surly exterior, I glimpsed the guy beneath the flames. I won't deny his knowledge of fire powers draws me. I've never been one to chase men, but chasing answers—that's entirely my jam.

Unfortunately, he's a mystery that doesn't want to be solved.

A commotion in the clearing draws my attention to a group of twenty-somethings in distress. I park my bike and jog over, untucking my badge from my shirt.

It swings freely against my chest, and I lean into the group to get a better look. *"Service de Police de la Ville de Montréal. Qu'est-ce qui se passe?* What's happening?"

The crowd parts and I'm left looking at a wee pixie of a teenage girl with bright pink hair. She's doubled over on her hands and knees, vomiting onto the grass. Damn, she looks like roadkill. "What happened?"

The crowd goes silent as all eyes flicker toward the treetops, the ground, or the horizon.

"Guys, I'm not trying to bust anyone here. I need to know so I can help her."

"I think she's on Second Sight," a freckle-faced boy mumbles.

"Does anyone know where she got it?"

No one's saying.

Awesome. I hook under the girl's arms, hauling her off the ground and to her feet. "Come sit in the shade, and we'll get you some help."

I pull out my phone and call for an ambulance.

Her friends hover nearby, worried but unwilling to get close enough to be questioned by the cop.

"What's your name?" I ask.

"Sammy."

"I'm Jules. Help is on the way, and I'll stay with you until the ambulance comes. Was your friend right? Did you take Second Sight?"

She shakes her head.

I check her fingernails—they're clear.

I study her eyes—she doesn't have the glazed look of a Second Sight user.

"What did you take?"

She shrugs. "I don't know."

"You don't know? Where did you get it?"

"My stepdad."

"Your stepdad gave you drugs?"

"No. I stole his pills."

"Why?"

Her head snaps around, and she pegs me with a glassy-eyed glare. "Because he's a judgy dick. He kicked me out when I got powers and said his charity was over. He wasn't supporting a fae freak so I should fuck off."

"Where's your mom?"

"She died a couple of years ago."

"Do you have any other relatives or someone who will take you in?"

"Nope. So, yeah, I stole his stash." She leans back against the trunk of the tree we're under and takes a deep breath. "I thought maybe I could sell them. If I'm on the street, I need money. No one wanted what I had. Everyone wants Second Sight."

"So you took them yourself?"

Sammy shrugs. "I thought if I knew how they made me feel, I could use that to sell them. Nobody wants something when I can't tell them what it is. What did I have to lose?"

"Your lunch at the very least." I gesture at the puke in the grass.

As stupid as her choice seems, I've seen enough desperation on the street to understand where this kid is coming from. Newly homeless and going through an awakening at the same time is rough.

Not to mention young and unsure about who you are and where your life is going. "I don't blame you for wanting to escape, but next time, pick something that won't kill you, yeah?"

The look she flashes me says she'd rather not relive this moment. "Yeah."

"Give me your phone."

Her brows come down hard and fast. "Why?"

"Because I'm giving you the number of my Aunt Charlie. She took in my siblings and me when we were facing foster care at your age. She'll make sure you have a bed and all your meals until you figure shit out. She'll kick you out on your ass if you pull any of this drug bullshit, but if you're on the straight and narrow, she'll stand by you."

The little pink-haired pixie eyes me up and down. "For real?"

"Yeah. She already has two sixteen-year-olds she took in a few years ago. If you play nice and try your best, you'll be good. Call her after the hospital checks you out."

I hand her back her phone, and she looks at the screen, confused. "I don't know what to say."

"Don't say anything. Stay out of trouble, don't piss off Charlie, and say no to drugs."

The ambulance arrives, and the EMTs begin examining her. "What did you take?"

She tilts her head toward her purse, and I unzip the top. There's a rainbow of pills divided into smaller baggies within. "I took a couple of the orange ones."

I take one out and hand it to the paramedic. "In case you need it." Then I take the rest of them, seal the baggie, and shove them into the deep pocket of my slicker. "You're officially done on the street."

Sammy groans in embarrassment and nods. "I'm such a dumbass."

"Maybe, but everything happens for a reason, and this is where you are now. Eyes forward, yeah?"

"Yeah."

I help her get settled in the ambulance, and she squeezes my wrist. "Am I in trouble? About the pills?"

"Nah. Stealing your stepdad's stash was stupid but understandable. Plus, I'm not on the clock. I'll fix it."

Sammy's smile is relieved. I hop out of the ambulance so they can get going.

"Is she going to be okay?" the freckle-faced boy asks.

"She'll be fine."

"Her stepdad sucks."

Murmurs of assent rise from the rest of the group.

"Yeah, I got that. Give me his name and address, and I'll see what I can do about him. Don't worry. I've set Sammy up. She doesn't need to go back there."

Freckle Face's eyes narrow. "Why would you help her? He kicked her out because she's fae."

I lift my hand and push a small ball of flames through my palm. "We fae freaks gotta stick together, amirite?"

I hand the kid a bunch of my cards, wishing I had information for the task force too. He passes them out, and I realize how hard-hit the younger sector is with all this. "If you need help, call me. Between my friends on the force and me, we've got you."

Freckle Face cracks a smile as he pockets the card. "We're good. We've got a guy too."

"Gareth?"

"You know him?"

I nod. "He's a good guy to have on your side. Next time you see him, tell him I say hi."

CHAPTER ELEVEN

I make my way home, and by the sounds of chatter and the amazing smell of bacon filling the air, everyone else is finally awake. I hustle to get my boots and helmet off and get upstairs. "Did you save me some?"

"Of course." Briar gestures at the covered hot plate on the table. "You left us cinnamon treats. We could hardly repay that by eating all the bacon."

"Then my evil plan has succeeded."

He chuckles and lifts his coffee in a toast. "How are you feeling this morning?"

"Fine. Sorry about the fireworks last night."

They all good-naturedly wave that away.

"Do you work today?" Kenzie asks.

"Yeah, but not until later. I've got the morning off."

"Awesome. Maybe we can all sit with the sanctuary ideas and come up with—"

My phone vibrates on the table, and I flip it over to see Luc's name. "Sorry, guys." I answer the call and step away from the table. "Dude, tell me you just missed me and wanted to hear my voice."

"Well, duh, that goes without saying, but this is more about giving a voice to the dead. Can you come? It's important."

I meet Kenzie's disapproving gaze from across the kitchen. "How important?"

"While figuring out the timeline for the Second Sight manifestations, I came up with a few new mysteries we have to consider."

"Why am I not surprised?"

"It can wait if you really are busy, but you said you wanted to stay on top of this."

"Yeah, I do. You're putting me in the doghouse at home, but I'm on my way."

"I have a couch if you ever need it."

"Not a chance in hell. I've heard the stories of what you do on that couch."

He laughs. "Suit yourself."

By the time I disappoint my siblings and drive to the morgue, I feel the lack of sleep deep in my bones. I'd sit in the parking lot for a quick cat nap if I drove a car.

Scarlett doesn't offer the same opportunities.

"Look at this." Luc waves me over. He's sitting at his microscope and stands to give me his seat. "What do you see?"

I glance through the lens and study the wriggles and squiggles of cell stuff. "I'm too tired for scientist show and tell. Tell me what you see."

"Rawr, someone woke up on the wrong side of the bed this morning."

"Actually, I woke up in the wrong bed this morning."

His expression brightens. "Do tell…and I want details. I always give you details."

I wrinkle my nose at him. "I know. I'll never look at a subway platform the same way."

He laughs. "That was a great night."

I roll my eyes. "Sorry to disappoint you. I slept in the guest room of my house after catching my bed on fire during a nightmare."

He blinks and bursts into another round of laughter. "You started a house fire in a firehouse? That's epic."

"I'm going to start a coroner fire if you don't get to the point."

Luc points at the microscope and curbs his amusement. "Fine. When I compared the cell cultures from the evidence kit to the kid you sent me, it looks like your boy had been taking Second Sight on the regular for maybe two months."

"Seriously? Other than seeing fae, what's the attraction? Two months?"

Luc shrugs. "By its chemical makeup, it's also a feel-good drug...well, at least until it bastardizes your cells and kills you."

"Yeah, until then. You can tell all this by comparing two swabs?"

"Think of the composition of human cells like the rings of a tree. On the night you first arrested him, there was evidence of the drug but no trace of fae mutation. Now, his cells are fried."

"The mutation went that fast?"

Luc nods. "It's bad, but it's good too."

"How so?"

"Based on the chemical factors and the magical unknowns, I'm fairly confident it's not a new strain of Second Sight on the market causing the deaths. It's a cumulative effect. Doing the drug for an extended time is what makes this happen."

"What's the timeframe?"

"One to two months for light users. Two weeks to a month for those hitting it harder."

"Shit. With a deadline like that, we need to find the rest of the drug and get it off the street."

"*Dead*line being the operative word."

I roll my eyes. "That's bad."

Luc opens his mouth to say something and hesitates.

"What?"

"I, uh, I wondered…I'd like to study your cells."

I straighten, my pulse picking up speed. "My cells? Why? Do you think I'm at risk for something?"

"No, nothing like that." Luc waves away my concerns. "Your awakening was natural and organic, and it went smoothly."

I chuckle. "Depends on your definition of smoothly."

"Well, it didn't give you a horror movie manicure and kill you." Luc shrugs.

"True story."

He presses his palms together with a cheesy grin. "If you give me a sample of your cells, I promise to keep the results private to my lab, and I won't put your name on anything. I think it'll help."

"Help how?"

"The more I learn about fae cells, the better I'll be able to figure out what's going on. If people are picking you out of a crowd, maybe I can figure out a way to stop that from happening."

"People are finding me because Second Sight gives them the ability. The best way to stop that is to get that shit off the street."

"Agreed, but that's your department. I'm the science guy and I can science better with more information."

"Science better? Since when is that a verb?"

"My lab, my rules. So, can I get that sample?"

"Okay." I let him swab the inside of my cheek, pluck a few strands of my hair, and prick my finger to squeeze out a couple of drops of blood.

"Ouch. Careful."

He snorts. "Don't be a baby. It's completely painless."

I stick my recently pricked finger in my mouth, sucking to

stop the bleeding. "You have a strange concept of painlessness. You jabbed a needle into my hand."

"A lancet. A very tiny lancet." He seals all the samples into a sterile collection bag. "Aren't cops supposed to be badasses?"

I make a pathetic pouty face. "I won't tell if you don't."

"Hey…uh, do you think your siblings would be willing to give me samples too?"

"I'll ask, but I won't make any promises. After all, the last time someone took our samples, we ended up on the radar of the evil fae demon elites, who opened a portal to Hell and intended to eat us."

"That was a bummer."

I snort. "It was."

Luc hands me a white envelope with three more sample collection kits. "I swear, no one will know about any of this except me."

"And Teresa." I pat his microscope.

Luc laughs. "Of course, but my bitch ain't no snitch."

"You're so weird."

"You love me for it."

True. I tuck the envelope under my arm. "Anything else I can do for you?"

"Next time you kill one of those things that keep coming after you, could you bring me a body?"

I groan. "You're so needy this morning!"

When I get to the station, Rene is already there, which isn't surprising considering I'm nearly forty-five minutes late, and he's incredibly punctual. At least he's not at my desk, messing up my files or putting up his feet.

Instead, he's in one of the meeting rooms with a visitor. As I walk by, I glance through the window and read the badge on the visitor's uniform.

"What's a Kahnawake Peacekeeper doing here?" I ask Morin as I get to my desk.

Peacekeepers are a First Nations police service located in the Mohawk Territory of Kahnawake, very close to Montréal.

"*Je ne sais pas*, they were talking before I got here."

Rene sees me dropping off my stuff and waves me in.

I hold up one finger and pull the baggie of Sammy's stepdad's pills out of my pocket. "I snagged these off a kid puking in the park this morning. Can you take them to Disposal for me? Looks like I'm needed in there."

"Can do."

"Thanks." I give him the bag of pills and head into the meeting room.

"Officer Jules Gagne," Rene says, as I enter, "allow me to introduce Officer Chase Goodleaf of the Kahnawake Peacekeepers."

"*Shé kon.*" I extend my hand.

"You speak my tongue?" he asks.

"Only a few words of welcome and thanks."

"Still, I'm honored you made an effort. It's a pleasure to meet you."

I take an empty seat and join them at the meeting table. "Has something happened? What brings you to our door, Officer?"

Officer Goodleaf's expression becomes sad and serious. "We had an incident two nights ago on the reservation. Two youths collapsed and died during a garage party at a friend's house."

"The Peacekeepers confiscated packages of Second Sight at the scene," Rene adds. "When the ME logged in that the bodies had hot pink spider veining under their fingernails, the system flagged us."

"Thank you for bringing this to us." I nod at Peacekeeper Goodleaf respectfully. It's not every day the First Nations police force trusts us enough to collaborate on an investigation.

I can't blame them. There are many ways our criminal justice system could improve how we interact and communicate with other branches of law enforcement.

"Do you know where the kids got the drugs?"

Chase Goodleaf's ebony braids sway as he shakes his head. "The two made weekly trips into the city for a university night course they were taking."

Rene squints. "Any chance they weren't going to school and doing other things in the city?"

"Not likely. The car they used belongs to one of the kids' moms. She outfitted it with GPS tracking because the older sister has a sketchy boyfriend and she keeps tabs on her."

"What did the GPS tell you?" I ask.

"According to the data we pulled, they went straight to the campus every week, then straight back."

"So they either got the drugs at the university campus or via a quick stop on the way."

"Unless someone is distributing it somewhere close to the Kahnawake territory," Rene adds.

Goodleaf shakes his head. "We keep a close eye on anyone coming in or out of our territory. If someone is dealing on our land, we'd know."

"Which school were they attending?" I ask.

"McGill."

Rene and I exchange a look. That's where one of our original three victims was a student.

"Peacekeeper Goodleaf, are you familiar with a youth named Deganawida Brant?" I ask.

"I don't think so. Is he somehow involved?"

"We're not sure. He's another First Nations student at McGill who was found dead in connection with Second Sight."

Goodleaf's lips press together into a thin line. "If you send me his information, I'll ask around."

Good. That will help. "In the meantime, can you have your

pathologist forward his report to Luc Leclerc so we can compare notes?"

He accepts Luc's card when I offer it. "This guy is with your coroner's office?"

"Yes. He has a working theory on what the drug is doing to users on a cellular level, but having more data can help him figure it out fully."

Rene assures Goodleaf we'll follow up on everything he gave us and he gives us the same assurance.

Cooperation is a good thing. The Peacekeepers don't have any jurisdiction beyond the Mohawk Territory, and we don't have any jurisdiction over there.

With this Second Sight problem spreading, we need to work together.

After Peacekeeper Goodleaf leaves, I hang back in the meeting room to talk to Rene about last night and ask if the blue-haired sprite contacted him.

"She did. I sent Caitlin to meet her at a coffee shop this morning."

"Good. I'm glad she reached out."

"What about the skoro who grabbed you? Do you think they were targeting you specifically or did they think they were grabbing random fae girls at a bar?

"The latter. From what I gathered, they picked up some fae takeout and headed to a warehouse to get their party on."

Rene frowns. "I shudder to think what would've happened if you weren't there."

Yeah, me too. "Because I'm a fire elemental, I burned off the sedation faster than expected and woke up early. We got my sister clear of it, then checked in with the other empowered folks they'd taken. They were shaken but unharmed."

Rene taps his pen against his notepad. "Do we have any of the involved men to question?"

"Sorry, no. They were the fight to the death type."

Rene sighs. "That's unfortunate."

"Doesn't mean we're without leads. We impounded the vehicles they were driving. I have photos of the license plates and their ugly mugs."

Rene scowls. "That's something. Next time, I want to be the first person you call."

I smile. "You're assuming there will be a next time. Do I look like the kind of girl that gets herself tranked and tossed in a trunk on the regular?"

Rene looks at me. "Do you really want me to answer that?"

"Yeah, you're probably right. Hopefully it's not another car trunk incident. Fuckers didn't even have a glow-in-the-dark emergency release pull!"

Rene chuckles. "So, cite them."

"Oh, they felt the full wrath of Montréal's law enforcement, don't worry about that."

Rene laughs and gets out of his seat. "Enough chit-chatting. Let's get back to work. Tell me. What had you so late this morning that I got stuck listening to Tremblay talk about his dog's girlfriend for twenty minutes?"

"Tremblay's dog has a girlfriend?"

"They met at the dog park. Little Oscar can't get enough of Miss Junebug."

I roll my eyes. "At least someone in that house is getting some."

Rene chuckles, and the two of us head out.

At my desk, I pull Marx's chair over for him to sit and I boot up my computer. "I was late because I was down at the morgue talking to Luc."

"And?"

"He thinks the mutations we're seeing are a side effect of prolonged use, not an aggressive strain. Anyone who takes the drug for up to two months is at risk."

"Yikes." Rene grimaces. "Then every day it's out there, more people will die."

"I think we should go public with at least some of it. Maybe we can convince people to stop taking it."

Rene shakes his head sadly. "No public service announcement is going to derail this train."

"We could try."

He considers that. "Go put your shit in your locker and meet me in the coffee room. You look like you could use a jolt."

"Is it that obvious?"

Rene looks me up and down. "You doing all right?"

"It was a long, shitty night. I'm fine. Just a few growing pains to being a fire girl."

"You swear you're one hundred percent?"

I'm not. Fire is coursing through my blood and threatening to spark. I feel volatile and aggressive. "I need to train more and release some of this excess energy. It's a lot…but I'm good."

I'm not sure he believes me.

I flash Rene the most confident thumbs-up I can muster. "I'm good. Top form."

CHAPTER TWELVE

When I meet Rene in the break room, he has two coffees and a couple of chocolate croissants for us to take downstairs. We take over one of the smaller meeting rooms to lay out everything we know about the Second Sight case, the deaths, and how that ties back to the Poreskoro family.

Point by point we tape photos on the large whiteboard, filling in notes beside them and drawing lines to connect things that are tied.

"The file from Goodleaf highlights the same things we're seeing here." I pull out a photo of each of the two First Nations boys that died on the rez.

Each of the six overdose victims with known cellular mutations runs near the top. Below we stick Post-it notes with the information we have on them.

Rene prints a few images from Luc's microscope samples, although what we're going to glean from them, I don't know. "Put the kid from the dorm next to the two from the rez. Those three have the closest tie to where they might be sourcing this shit."

I cluster those three photos and write "McGill" with a line joining them to the connection.

The rectangular table skids on the linoleum floor when I lean toward the center and check out the map Rene is unfolding.

It depicts Montréal and the surrounding areas.

"Read me the locations of where the bodies showed up and where they lived." Rene grabs two markers. "Black is dead. Green is home."

Together, we comb through the files, mapping out where the victims lived and died and where they worked and frequented.

"These GPS routes Goodleaf gave us are handy." I draw the path the two night-school students took each week to get to the university.

"There's nothing unusual about this drive." Rene sighs and rubs his forehead.

"He said they only left the reserve to go to school so if they didn't score the drugs at home, it's gotta be somewhere on campus."

Rene pulls out his phone. "I worked with the head of university security a few years ago on a sexual assault case. I'll call him. Meanwhile, you start adding what we've got on the skoro you took down last night."

Rene leaves to call his guy, and I text Tad.

Any way you could bring the bag of personal effects we took off the guys last night to the station?

Sure. Is it okay to portal there?

Probably best to *poof* to the parking lot out back and come through the front door. I'll meet you at the front desk.

Everyone here has been chill about me having powers, but I'm not sure how a bunch of cops would react to a random Irish dude materializing in the middle of the precinct.

I meet Tad at the front desk, hug him, and grab the bag. "Thanks, man. Want to stick around and see how Montréal's Twenty-Third gets things done?"

Tad shakes his head. "We've got a rousin' game of El Dorado goin', but if ye need me, I'm there in a flash."

"I'll keep that in mind."

Part of me is sad to miss out on a family board game day. The other part of me knows that time matters and we need to stop Second Sight before more people die.

Tad wanders out through the front door, presumably to disappear without raising the alarm.

Back in our meeting room, I dump the bag's contents onto the table so Rene and I can sift through it.

There are three black leather wallets, all stuffed with high denominations in cash and a fake ID. They're good forgeries, but not that good.

Rene photocopies them for our wall and bags the originals to send down to Counterfeiting.

"Only cash and fake ID, eh?" I toss the third wallet into the discard pile.

"They aren't as dumb as they look."

I chuckle. "They don't look dumb. They look creepy. It's those beady demon eyes."

"Hater. Demons need love too."

"Not when they're trying to suck out my soul."

"True. Resume your hatred with my blessing."

We catalog some fine leather shoes, a pair of Ray Bans, a pack of menthol cigarettes, a gold chain with a weird pendant, and a white paper bag with packets of butter and syrup.

"Looks like they stopped for a snack." Rene slides the white paper bag to the side of the table.

"Better they consume takeout pancakes than local citizens."

"True enough." Rene scrutinizes it all and sighs. "We'd get further with the investigation if you didn't kill every person who comes at you."

"My bad. The next time I'm trapped in a trunk and shaking off the brain fog of being drugged, I'll be sure to consider how to make your life easier."

"That's all I'm saying." Rene grins. "A little courtesy would go a long way."

The two of us laugh that off and spend the next half-hour flipping through the files, searching for anything that could help this case.

Marx eventually pokes his head into the room, holding a slip of yellow paper. "Registration information on those black sedans you had impounded, Gagne."

"Awesome. *Merci.*"

"*De rien.*"

Marx departs, and I sit at the table with Rene. The scrawled notes in Marx's horrible handwriting are exactly the change in direction we need to get new ideas sparking again.

"Both cars were rentals secured to a fleet by Harvey Funk, a sleazy lawyer here in the city."

"Whose fleet? One of his clients?"

"Seems so." I scan the list of his clients to see if anything jumps out at me.

"That's not helpful."

I pause on a name and shrug. "It is if one of those clients is the Poreskoro Corporation."

Rene steps in and takes a look. "Not surprising. It's pretty likely that if skoro are involved, so too are the Poreskoro Six."

"The Four," I correct.

"Right. What do we know about them?"

"They are the deadly offspring of a fae queen and a demon king. There used to be six but two have ceased to be a threat to my family. When they feed on elemental energy, they gain the ability to create an army of minions."

He makes a face. "How do they do that, exactly?"

"I like to imagine it like Mogwai fed after dark and popping off an army of gremlins."

He chuckles. "Who are The Four we have left?"

I pull out my phone and open my notes from when Azland taught us about our enemy. "The oldest and youngest are the men, Rance and Razgarath, and the two middle siblings still alive are girls, Zissa and Sasobek."

"Are they all ten-foot green monsters with horns and poison halitosis?"

I scroll through the descriptions. "Azland says Zissa has long red hair, graceful antlers, and natural body armor plating her shoulders like an armadillo."

"She sounds terrifying."

"According to him, she's quite sexy and striking."

"We definitely have different tastes in women."

I chuckle and go back to my notes. "Sasobek is arguably the most dangerous of all of them. She takes after their demon father the most. Azland says she revels in nothing so much as the suffering of her prey."

"Charming."

"He also says she could almost wholly pass as human in her natural form…other than the glowing yellow eyes that give away her demon nature."

"Awesome, give the psychotic one a pair of sunglasses, and she's the least identifiable. Lucky us."

I chuckle and continue to read. "Rance is the oldest of The Six. He's a businessman and manages the family fortune. His true form is humanoid, and he conducts electricity—natural and processed."

"And the youngest?"

"Known as Raz, he's the one who most took after their

mother. Azland says he's more fae than hell beast and while he has demonic hell powers like the rest, he tends to be a pacifist."

"A passive demonic hybrid. I like it." Chuckling, Rene addresses the whiteboard and uncaps a marker. "So, we've got four living Poreskoro, plus the thugs they spawned."

"The skoro."

"They are more dangerous because of numbers rather than lethality, right?"

"Right. They also smell like burned cookies and have soulless black eyes so they're fairly easy to identify."

"Nice. I'd rather the assholes of the world smelled like confectionary delights than death."

"Agreed."

Rene closes his eyes and stretches his neck. "If the minions die when their sire dies, that means we still have active hybrid siblings in the area."

"I'd say so, yes."

"You'd be right," a deep voice says in the doorway. "Trent mentioned you two are going after the Poreskoro family. I thought you might need intel."

Peter Trent is our acting staff sergeant, but he's also a damned good cop and cares about the success and survival of our department.

He's been good to me since the whole awakening drama, and I'll be forever grateful for how he handled things.

I extend a hand to Max Deacon from Guns and Gangs. Stocky and strong, with long shaggy hair that works well for undercover, he's making a name for himself downstairs. "Welcome to where the magic happens, Deacon."

He laughs. "Yeah, thanks."

"What can you tell us?" Rene asks. "Are you boys edging in on my department now?"

He shakes his head. "No. It happened that a bunch of the city's criminals—assholes we've been watching for years—turned out to be empowered."

"The veil dropping exposed a lot of truths," I agree.

"It did at that."

Rene offers Deacon a space at the table to spread out the file he brought. "Let's see what you've brought for show and tell."

Deacon accepts the invitation and opens the folder. "Keep in mind these players earned a name for themselves long before the Poreskoro Corporation came to town. It just so happens assholes gravitate toward one another, and they seem to have formed alliances."

Lucky us. "It hasn't even been seven months since the veil dropped and the prana started to flow in our city. They work fast."

Rene grunts. "Evil is opportunistic."

Yeah, it is. "Okay, Deacon, walk us through this."

Deacon pulls out a picture of an attractive, well-groomed businessman standing at a podium and smiling at the audience. He has deeply tanned olive skin and strikingly chiseled dark features.

"Rance Poreskoro is the big boss of his family corporation. He's the face of the business, and from what we hear, he has the veto vote on anything to do with Poreskoro money."

"I've seen his picture a dozen times since starting our investigation, but I can't find any of his siblings."

"I'd be surprised if you did," Deacon says. "The others don't seem to want to be identifiable."

"Not surprising, considering they're tying themselves to organized crime, arms dealers, and assassins." Rene scans the information Deacon's laying out.

"Rance is the only one we know anything about?"

"The only one of his family, yes. But we know a lot about his go-to players in the city."

"Excellent. Enlighten us."

"Andre 'Blackout' Bergott." He pulls the first photo from the pile. "He gets his nickname from his ability to plunge an entire area into darkness and blind his opponents with a cloud of inky magical smoke."

"I'll make sure to keep a flashlight on hand," I quip.

The next photo is of a guy wearing a blocky cut blazer, aviator sunglasses, and a cigar dangling between his teeth.

"This is Matthias—no last name. He rolled into town about five years ago and leads a crew of assassins and brutes. If a point needs to be made or a witness dispatched, Matthias is the one who takes care of it."

Rene slides the photo of Matthias next to Blackout Bergott and Rance. "He's built like a brick shithouse. Is he all muscle or does he also have magic?"

"The closest we can figure is that his power is sadism. He hurts people, and their pain recharges his powers. He becomes stronger the more his victims suffer."

Rene groans. "I miss the days when bad guys were only greedy, self-serving assholes."

Yeah. Me too.

"The good news is that the last we heard, he left for London," Deacon adds.

"London, Ontario or London, England?" Rene asks.

"The second one."

I shrug. "Honestly, what does it matter? With portals and people who can teleport, distance means nothing."

Rene pegs me with a look. "You're a regular ray of sunshine these days, Gagne."

I chuckle and point at the last mug shot. "Last but not least?"

Deacon pulls out the photo. "The last two are called The Twins. Their power is entrancement and seduction. Whether they work together or solo, they're scary powerful."

My jaw drops. They're two of the most gorgeous people I've

ever seen. "There's no way they're human. They have to be full-on fae."

"We think they come from either siren or maybe succubus lineage, but that's more your department than ours. All I know is that the guys in our unit say they can get your heart pumping, make your mind go fuzzy and blank, or convince you that you're obsessed with doing whatever they want."

"Where do they work out of?" Rene asks.

"They have a suite at the Ritz-Carlton."

"Swanky. What kind of business do they handle for the Poreskoro Corporation?" I ask.

"In public, they're rich philanthropists. Behind the scenes, they're into prostitution and sex trafficking."

I shake my head. "Just what we need. More rich assholes with evil intent."

"Rance is into the sex trade?" Rene asks.

"We don't think so. It looks like he uses them to wash and launder large amounts of money through various charities. We can't prove it yet."

"Maybe we need to send someone undercover at one of their fancy parties," Rene suggests.

I raise my hand. "Not it."

Rene laughs. "I don't believe in sabotaging missions. There's no way I'd send you to an upscale gala."

"I appreciate the insult."

While Deacon checks out our case board, I mull over the information. "As far as we know, Rance is the only Poreskoro currently operating in Montréal, so he probably sired the guys I took down last night."

"Probably," Rene agrees. "The only way to know for sure is to track the cars through Harvey Funk and see where that leads us."

"Funk is slime." Deacon readies to leave. "Not a bad attorney but sucks on the human front."

I hold up a fist to bump knuckles. "Thanks for the briefing. We owe you one."

He winks. "Careful, Gagne, I might call in the favor. I've seen you drive in on that Multistrada. You're my kind of female."

I chuckle. "Thanks, Deacon, but I don't date cops."

He nods. "Let me know if you ever change your policy."

"Will do."

Deacon closes the door behind him. Rene and I regroup and get back to it.

"The best lead we have to the drugs is the connection of the three kids at McGill. Why don't you and Tad take a car and follow the route from the Mohawk Territory to the university? See what you find."

"And you?"

"I'll take one of my guys and arrange a meet with Rance Poreskoro."

Oh, hells no. "Dude. If you're facing the spawn of the devil, I'm going with you. These assholes have tried to kill me and mine what...three times now? Four? You're not benching me to deal with them on your own."

Rene looks exasperated and concerned. "I'm not benching you. I'm sending you to follow another lead. We're dividing the work."

"In that case, I'll confront the Poreskoro. You can drive the route to the university."

"And put you—a fire elemental—right in his lap? Not a chance. As you said, they've tried to kill you three or four times already."

I put my hands on my hips. "You know I can handle myself. I deserve a chance to take these fuckers down."

Rene sighs. "You're a good cop, and you'll be a huge part of closing this case, but why on Earth would a rabbit go into a wolf's den? His kind eats yours."

"I'm not a rabbit, and the Poreskoros aren't big bad wolves.

I've held my own against them and their minions. I can take care of myself."

"You think that, but your powers are still new. You haven't gained enough proficiency to take on a big boss and his army horde on your own."

"In your opinion," I snap.

"Okay, fine. Say I'm wrong, and you're totally up to the task. What if Lamech didn't tell Rance about you? What if he planned to feast on you and your siblings himself? If you walk in there, you'll expose Briar, Zephyr, and Kenzie as elementals. Are *they* ready to defend against that kind of organized force?"

I open my mouth to argue, then let it fall shut.

Dammit, he's right. I can be cavalier about my safety when it suits me, but ego and stubbornness aside, I won't put Kenzie, Zephyr, or Briar into the line of fire.

"So we're agreed," Rene says with finality. "We keep you and yours out of the crosshairs as long as possible."

"Fine."

He flashes me a smug smile, and I fight the urge to punch his face. "You track the route and work on the drug. I'll handle the first contact with the hybrid from Hell. Then we'll catch up with each other when we finish."

I'm still cranky about being sidelined, but he won the moment he invoked the well-being of my family.

Reality sucks.

I sign out the keys to an unmarked car and go see what I'll be driving today. I figure it'll be a treat because the guy on the motor pool desk is chuckling as I walk away. "Oh, you're not as bad as I feared," I say to the little powder blue hatchback.

I'm scarred for life from the week I spent with Morin in the surveillance van last year. The interior smelled like rotten fish and stale cigarettes, and there were mystery stains on the seats I was afraid to think about.

"You'll do fine," I say. "You're almost the same color as my sister." I slide into the driver's seat and adjust the mirrors and the seat. Nothing beats my bike, but if Tad is coming with me, we can't exactly chat if he's clinging to me on the back of a roaring motorcycle.

Plus, now that he's Kenzie's guy, I doubt it would be very sisterly to make him ride bitch.

Pulling my phone out, I call him. "Hey, do you want to play Montréal cop for the afternoon? I'm going to be touring around in a car and thought you might like to expand your portaling range."

"Aye, sure. Do ye want me to come yer way?"

"Yep. I'm in a blue car in the parking lot."

"Give me two to tell yer sister I'm off."

I hang up and tuck the phone into the thigh pocket of my tactical pants. Scarlett sits pretty under a tree at the side of the lot by the fence. "Don't be jealous, girl. I'll be back for you in a bit."

Damn, I love that bike.

The door creaks open, and Tad slides into the passenger seat beside me. He grunts, reaches under the seat, and moves it back to make room for his long legs. "Do ye have a thing fer wee clown cars? First yer Beetle and now this thing."

I chuckle. "It's the luck of the motor pool. I usually pair up with a partner in a cop car or check one out but today, taking an undercover car was my only choice."

"All right, so what's our mission?"

I tell him about the Second Sight mutations and deaths that resulted. Then, I let him know we've got a potential lead related to three students of McGill University. "We're going to trace their route and see what we can find."

"Ye don't seem all that pleased about it."

I wave away his concern. "It's not you. I didn't want the road trip assignment. I wanted to shake down Rance Poreskoro."

"Did ye lose the coin toss?"

"Something like that."

"All right, then. It's lemons to lemonade time." Tad reaches to turn on the radio. He tunes it until a classic rock station comes on. "Does this work? I noticed ye had a decent collection of vinyl in yer part of the living room cabinet."

I put the car in gear and get us moving. "Yeah, this is good. What kind of music do you like?"

"Och, all sorts. Growin' up, I had to listen to classical and have a fondness fer a great many pieces. I also like Celtic rhythms, classic British bands, and classic American rock. If ye get me drunk enough, I've been known to croon Bublé at karaoke."

I laugh, imagining that. Tad has a voice like warm honeyed whiskey and the swagger of a sex god. I imagine he could put on quite a show. "Are you any good?"

"Aye, I think so. There've been more than a few catfights in the parkin' lot over who got to take me home."

"Seriously?"

"Oh, aye. I admit I haven't always been as restrained and discernin' as I am these days. I was a bit of a scoundrel and a rake growin' up."

"But you're reformed?"

"Aye. I think my ego took enough hits that it'll never inflate so big again. Livin' a quieter life suits me just fine and bein' part of Fi's and Sloan's extended family has taught me a great many things about what I want in my life goin' forward."

I take the eastbound ramp onto the highway and head out of town toward the Kahnawake reserve. It's not that far. Twenty-five minutes and over the Honoré Mercier Bridge and we're there.

Since I have no jurisdiction here, I don't stop. We start at the first GPS address and put ourselves into the minds of two university kids.

"All right, we know the boys were taking night classes. I called the school, and the class began at six-thirty. It takes twenty to twenty-five minutes to get to the university from here. Since they'd be in traffic, they likely left around five-thirty to give them time."

"Did the GPS route show them stopping anywhere?" Tad asks. "If it were me and I didn't get off the reservation often, I'd stop for food."

"All right. We'll keep our eyes open for any promising places along our route. Pretend it's early evening, and we're a couple of college students on our way to Modern Anthropology."

"Sounds thrilling."

"You're the navigator. Most of the trip is a highway drive, but you can guide me through the streets when we get closer."

Tad takes the printout description of the driving route and nods. "Seems straightforward. Let's do this."

For a while, there's nothing much to see. We retrace our path on the highway, then exit and make our way to campus. It's a school day, so teenagers are all over the place, wearing heavy backpacks and zipping around on skateboards and scooters.

"Did you go to college or university?" I ask Tad as we pull into a visitor parking spot.

"I was a business major at Trinity College Dublin."

"Did you enjoy it?"

He shrugs, then pulls the door handle and gets out. "Aye, sure. Great craic. I wasn't much interested in the school part, but I was the life of the party when it came to extracurriculars."

"Sounds like more fun than the police academy."

Tad chuckles. "Doesn't surprise me."

The two of us make our way toward the main building, following the signs directing us to the registrar's office. A student with a blonde bob and a nametag that reads Christie Kellwether, Student Ambassador, greets us. "Can I help you?"

"Can you direct us to the Modern Anthropology classroom?"

She hustles around the registration desk and returns with a tear-off map the size of a placemat. Reaching across the desk, she sets it on the raised counter. "You're right here, at the front." She circles the registrar's office on the map. "You want the seventh floor of the Leacock Building, right here, off the quad."

She circles another building, then draws a line between them, following the footpaths marked on the map. Christie Kellwether is good.

I wish everyone were this skilled at telling me exactly what I want to know.

She gives us the map and checks something on the computer. "There are no classes in session now, but you might find a prof or a TA in the classrooms. Are you parents of a prospective student?"

I'm about to pull my badge out from where it's hanging beneath my shirt when Tad slides a hand across my lower back and pulls me against his side. "Aye, our wee Gemma is bustin' her buttons to get here. Lives and breathes anthropology, that one. We wanted to check where her classes will be before she starts in the fall."

"Well, welcome to McGill." Christie hands us the map. "I have no doubt she'll love her time here."

Once we're outside, I burst into laughter. "Does that poor girl honestly think we're married with a teenage kid? Wait until Kenzie finds out about this."

He grins. "Trust me. It's better than letting anyone know cops are snoopin' around. At least it was in my days of college."

We cross the quad and pass a group of girls in ponytails slicing the air with a Frisbee and a couple of guys making out on a blanket under the shade of a maple tree.

The smell of weed wafts through an open dorm window, and I hear raucous laughter from somewhere inside.

"Cannabis is legal now, but that doesn't mean it smells any better," I say. "Gah…how can people stand it?"

"The good stuff doesn't smell bad," Tad points out. "The really good stuff even smells good."

I arch a brow with a sideways look.

"Or so I hear." Tad grins.

I shake my head. "Edible brownies are as far as I'll go. They're a good time and are chocolatey goodness."

"There it is." Tad glances up from the map and then points at a ten-story concrete building with a pale green roof.

"All right, let's see what we can find."

Tad grins beside me. "Maybe there will be a table set up with a sign, Sellin' Magical Drugs That Will Mutate Yer Cells."

"That would be so helpful."

We wander the seventh floor, glancing in several empty classrooms and passing the full lecture halls so we don't interrupt.

"What was the field of study fer the other student who died in the dorms?"

"Principles of Statistics."

"Math department then. I assume that's a different buildin'?"

I pull out my phone and Google that. "Yeah, math is in Burnside Hall."

We exit through a side door, squinting in the sunlight as our eyes adjust. The footpath that runs along the side of the building takes us between two other buildings facing Rue University, one of the main roads bordering the McGill campus.

We wander the campus for half an hour but don't see anything beyond normal university activity.

Something sweet lingers in the air, and my stomach is growling by the time we're on Rue University.

A food truck is parked and serving a line of kids. "Poor Boscoe's Beaver Tails. Yummy. Want one?"

"What on Earth is a beaver tail? Is it somethin' a druid would eat?"

I laugh. "Oh, my druid friend. You are in for such a treat. A beaver tail is a sweet, yeast-risen pastry. Sort of like a Danish or a fritter."

"Ye have my attention."

"They have different flavors, like almond or maple or fruits, and they're covered in sugar and icing. So much sweet sugary goodness."

"All right, I'm convinced."

After a short wait, it's our turn to speak into the little window of the truck and order. I get an apple and cinnamon beaver tail, while Tad goes for the standard.

Warm and melt-in-your-mouth fresh, we're lost in our sugary treat as we walk back toward the main parking lot. Despite the white paper wrapping, we both end up with crumbs and cinnamon sugar all over our hands.

"Hope yer colleagues don't mind us gettin' the loaner car a bit messy."

I lick my fingers and wipe my hands on my pants. "It'll have to do."

We get back to the station before Rene, so I text him before sitting down to type up my notes. Tad *poofs* back home to check on Kenzie, which gives me plenty of time to write up my report.

Not that I have much to report.

Marx and Tremblay come in, both looking exhausted. Tremblay flops into his seat. "What a day."

I look up from my computer. "What did you boys get up to that tuckered you out?"

Marx sighs and pulls a meal replacement shake out of his desk drawer. "We caught a lead on de baby food burglaries and raided a warehouse down by de docks."

"Yeah? Did you wrap it up?"

Tremblay flashes me a cocky grin and pats his barrel belly. *"Mais, bien sur."*

"Nice. Congrats. Does that mean I can stop inventorying Enfamil now?"

Marx nods. "You're off de hook. ASS Trent says all we need to do is get things together for the prosecutor's office. All de lawyers want are photos of what's going on in de warehouse."

Lawyers. Warehouse.

Right.

Since searching the campus didn't get us anywhere, I switch gears to try another tactic. Last night, the skoro were taking us to a warehouse. Wondering about their intended destination, I go into the department files and pull up a list of company assets handled by Harvey Funk, the Poreskoro lawyer.

Bingo.

Three of the properties listed are warehouses near the area where I blew out their gas tank.

Grabbing my phone, I pull up his contact info and call Tad. "Road trip—take two."

CHAPTER THIRTEEN

I leave a note for Rene, listing the warehouse addresses, and tell him we're going to check them out. I finish with a polite request that he text me as soon as he gets back.

I am desperately curious to find out how his first contact went. I'm also worried that he's not back yet. The conflict has my emotions vacillating between anger at him for not letting me come and concern about his safety.

I leave the note on my desk, figuring he'll find it for sure.

When Tad *poofs* in, I update him on the three warehouse properties. "Can you *poof* me back there?"

"Not a problem." He brings us to where I blew up the car, although you would never know it.

"Damn, Bakkali's people are good."

"Aye, they are. Garnet's people are the same in Toronto. Magic is a crazy thing."

It is. Briar did a great job on the asphalt. The street doesn't look any more busted than your average Montréal pavement.

"How's Kenzie doing?" I ask.

His soft smile makes my heart melt a little for them both. "Och, she might look like silk and honey, but she's a tough one. I think she's finished with bein' shaken and has moved into indignation and anger."

I chuckle. "That sounds about right. Although, between you and me, I was worried. She's had a lot to deal with over the past month. The change in her appearance was a shift of her foundation."

"Aye, I know it was. I also know the more time she spends with members of other fae sects, the faster she'll realize that not lookin' completely human isn't a bad thing. She's an exotic beauty representin' a proud and magical race of fae." He glances at me and smiles. "Ye all are."

"Are you hitting on me, druid?"

He laughs. "Ye know I'm not."

"Yeah, I know. The way you and Kenzie look at one another, there's no mistaking that you two are heading for something epic."

He shoves his hands deep into his pockets as we walk. "It feels like that on my side too, but let's not jinx it. My life has been a heapin' pile of shit lately. I don't want to get ahead of myself."

I can respect that. "Your secret is safe with me."

The closest of the three addresses is only a few blocks over, and the weather and the company make the walk pleasant.

"There." I point at a squat, whitewashed building. "That's the one."

The sign on the front reads Monster Hot Tubs. We push through the double glass doors and meet a blast of air conditioning and the glare of fluorescent lights.

"What is this place?" I mumble, blinking and glancing around to get my bearings.

"It's a hot tub showroom."

It is. A tanned woman in an extremely short sundress weaves through the floor displays to greet us.

"Welcome, you two!" Her accent is strongly Deep South, USA,

and her teeth are extremely white. "Are y'all in the market for a new hot tub?"

"Maybe," I tell her.

"Well, come on in, and let me show you some of our top models. I'm Brandi-Rae, and you are?"

I take a page from Tad's book and hook my arm around his elbow. "Andy and Andie. I know, it's crazy that we have the same name, but we can't help it."

Tad almost laughs but manages to get into character. "Our friends think it's weird, but we don't care. We think it's cute."

"Cute as a speckled pup," Brandi-Rae agrees. "Let's show you some hot tubs."

Brandi-Rae shows us a hot tub they call the Brick House. The tub's raised sides are deep red terra cotta bricks. "Landscapers love this one because it fits with any garden style, and you can customize the bricks to include little pots for your plants."

The thought of having a big tub full of hot water in my backyard sounds enticing. Could an enrichment station be that easy?

"How hot can the water get?" I ask.

"There are safety mechanisms in all our tubs to regulate the temperatures," she assures me. "No need to worry. The water will never get too hot, or you'd blow out your heater. Then where would you be?"

Not exactly the answer I was looking for.

We wander over to another tub, this one called Neptune's Serenity. It's made of turquoise and white tiles, inlaid with shimmering glass.

"Now, this one is beautiful," Brandi-Rae gushes. "A common favorite for those installing an indoor hot tub because it really elevates the décor, don't you think?"

I don't give a damn about elevating my décor, but I pick up the little booklet attached to the hot tub by a long silver chain. The price listed for the base model makes my eyes nearly pop out of my skull—and that's without any of the luxury jet attachments or aromatherapy add-ons.

Tad speaks up. "My lovely wife's brother is in construction. Who can we speak to about wholesale?"

Brandi-Rae looks disappointed that she might miss a commission, but she dutifully walks us to the back of the warehouse. We make our way into an area cordoned off from the showroom floor by hanging plastic sheets.

This storage and work area is quite different from the showroom floor. It's dusty, loud, and much hotter.

A handful of people rush around hauling boxes of tiles and huge empty hot tub shells, loading them onto flatbed trucks, and checking off carbon copy sheets held on clear plastic clipboards.

"Ernest is our wholesale guy." Brandi-Rae cranes her neck to look for him. "I don't see him. He's probably out on a delivery run. We have a lot going on to get ready for the home show."

"Maybe we could wait somewhere?" I ask.

The warmth of her Southern hospitality waned when it became clear there would be no showroom sale. Now that we're Ernest's problem, she seems more than ready to return to the pristine showroom. "The lunch room is off the hallway back here. Y'all are welcome to fix yourselves a coffee and wait."

"That sounds fine," Tad agrees.

She escorts us to a room with a kitchen counter, a round table with four chairs, and an old couch against the far wall. "Give me a holler if any questions pop up. Otherwise, have yourselves a monster of a day."

She giggles as she exits, delivering her hot tub tagline with true salesperson flair.

I fake a laugh. "Monster of a day, because of Monster Hot Tubs. Good one."

Tad and I give it a moment and slip across the hall into the office. The desk is a mess, covered in scribbled notes and half-completed receipts. We look through everything left out and come up empty.

"I don't think there's anythin' criminal here." Tad flips through a clipboard crammed with delivery notices. "Other than their prices."

"Seriously. I bet Briar could build us a nicer one for a fraction of the cost."

"Well, Andie, shall we take our leave?" Tad asks.

I hold out my hand. "Why yes, Andy, we really should be getting back to the kids."

Tad snorts. "We have kids now?"

"What about wee Gemma? Shouldn't we get home to help her with her anthropology homework?"

"Och, right. She's such a good girl I almost forgot all about her."

I help myself to a pink lollipop from the bowl sitting on the office desk, and Tad grabs one too. We *poof* outside, unnoticed among the chaos and noise, and check the addresses on my phone. "The next place is a few blocks north."

We walk in companionable silence, and I think about what Tad said about Kenzie and me being exotic members of a rare fae race. "Should we be getting together with other elementals in the area? Is repopulating a fae race a thing?"

Tad blinks at me. "Ye mean like arranged marriages with others from yer kingdom to revive yer sect?"

"Yeah. I'm not saying I *want* to, but is that a concern? As you mentioned, I'm one of the last members of the fire kingdom, Lasair. Is it my duty to ensure people like me don't die out?"

"Do ye intend to have children?"

I blink. "Yeah, I…uh, eventually."

"Then the people of Lasair will live on. There's not the same focus on lineal purity in the fae kingdoms as in the witch and wizardin' worlds."

"Yeah? You're sure?"

He lifts a shoulder. "When yer kids are born, they'll be fire elementals. They might be solely fire or take on their father's traits, but fire will be represented. When the others have kids, their children will be elementals as well. Whether ye return to Lasair to revive yer sect is another story altogether, but it's not yer duty, no."

"Still, I think we should find them and make sure they're safe and know what's happening."

Tad nods. "Of course. That's a fine idea."

"Maybe we could offer training and advice to keep them safe."

"I'm not sure how Azland would feel about ye signin' him up to start trainin', but I'm happy to help. Between Fi and us and her family, we could do a lot."

"Plus, Rene and I could connect them to Bakkali at the Guild of the Laurentians if they wanted."

"Aye. I think it's a good idea that the others learn they aren't alone. Did Rene give ye any idea of how many others there might be?"

"No. I haven't had a chance to look into the files he gave me access to."

The more I think about it, the more committed to this idea I become. It's something I can do to start being more proactive rather than reacting to all the craziness that explodes in my path.

"I think we should take a page out of Fi's book and have a meeting where the other elementals can get to know one another. We can learn more about our powers, hang out with other people who get what it's like, and maybe figure out what we'll do about the psycho hybrid assholes who want to eat us."

Tad shakes his head. "A meetin' is a very bad idea. It would put all the most delectable psycho-treats in one location. Easy pickin's."

Man, it seems like all anyone tells me lately is that it's too dangerous for me to do what I want.

"A virtual meeting, then. We'll build a website with a private chat room. Fi mentioned you're good with computers. Is that right?"

"Aye, I went through a hacker phase in my destructive youth."

"Zephyr's good too. Maybe between the two of you, we can create a landing page to post the plans for the elemental recharging stations Gareth shared with us. We can also discuss what we're up against with the skoro. Does that sound safe?"

Tad smiles. "I think that's a grand idea. I know of a few access points on the dark web where we can hide the site."

I frown at him. "You have experience on the dark web? You know I'm a cop, right?"

He holds up his hands and laughs. "Just some herbs and mushrooms for my druidic work that ye can't get anywhere else. I'm happy to take a polygraph if ye need me to, Inspector Gagne."

I laugh. "Nah, I believe you. But just so there are no secrets, the moment you and Kenzie started making fuck eyes, I might have had one of the cyber guys at my precinct run a background check on you."

"Can't blame ye. Kenzie is worth protectin'."

"Anyway, the website then—it's a plan?"

"Aye, it is."

We arrive at the second warehouse. This one doesn't have a sign or doors that open for the public. Whatever they do in there, it doesn't include a shiny sales floor with a Southern salesgirl named Brandi-Rae.

Whether that's good or bad, I don't know.

"It says here this is a holding warehouse for a chain of art—"

A woman's blood-curdling scream rents the air.

The two of us race toward the entrance. I draw my gun and approach.

There is one door into the warehouse. It's a blind entrance. There's no way to know who or what is inside.

Pulling out my phone, I call it in.

"911, what's your emergency?"

"Dispatch, this is Inspector Jules Gagne, badge number 361. I've got a female crying for help in a warehouse at 6114 Dollard Avenue near Rue Marie Claire. One officer and one friendly on scene."

I finish the call and slide my phone back into my pocket. "ETA four minutes."

Another harrowing scream raises the hair on the nape of my neck.

"The lass might not have four minutes."

My gut says to go in, but my head says we don't know who or what's inside and I hate risking Tad's safety—especially because Kenzie will kick my ass if I get her sexy new boyfriend killed.

Then again, he's a trained warrior with more experience than me with fae dangers.

"Do we play it smart and wait or play it stupid and go in blind and unprepared?"

Tad gives me a look that's part grimace and part smile. "I've been called an eejit more times than I can count. Why change my nature now?"

I love how we're always on the same page.

We get to the door as quickly and quietly as possible. I try the handle.

It's unlocked.

Turning it slowly, I ease it open, doing my best to keep it from making noise.

Tad peers in over my shoulder and *poofs* inside.

With my gun raised, I enter the building. It's largely open with some offices up and on the left with a metal staircase down to a fleet of box trucks.

Inside, it smells like dust, old concrete, and—yep—burned cookies.

Gotcha.

The woman is crying, and I make my way toward the sound

of her struggling as quickly as possible without calling attention to myself.

Weaving through the trucks, I check the sightlines and make sure I'm not exposed from above.

Where the fuck is Tad?

Rounding the back fender of a truck with a swirl of vanilla ice cream on it, I spot the woman fifty yards across the warehouse.

The scene is bizarre and grotesque.

There is a living room setup with leather couches, tables, lamps, and an expensive-looking carpet. Gathered at the leather couches, half a dozen skoro are lounging around, some passed out, some enjoying their pastime—torturing two naked faeries, their shimmery skin and delicate wings exposed.

The mauve one is trapped in a massive hookah bottle, tumbling in slow motion within the belly of the strange vessel. Her body is suspended in a pale pink cloud of smoke and is withered...desiccated.

The moment one of the skoro drags a long pull on the hose's mouthpiece, a horrifying understanding of why strikes me.

He's toking her essence.

The beady-eyed fucker inhales deeply, and the pull causes suction within the bottle. The female screams, twisting in agony as he consumes more of her life force.

In all my years on the force, I've never seen anything so vile and sadistic as this.

The whimpering of the other female draws my attention to the sage green faery face down on the ottoman. Two skoro are plucking at her wings. Each time they yank off a piece of iridescent flesh, she shrieks.

My stomach revolts and I fight not to gag on the acid pushing up the back of my throat.

A hulk of a man in a suit jogs down the metal steps. I recognize him from the photos Max Deacon showed me earlier. Figures. He's the one Deacon said levels up on the pain of others.

Matthias.

He smiles at the skoro torturing the faery and tugs the cuffs of his suit jacket. "As much fun as it is to watch you fuckers play with food, finish up. There's trouble at the house. Don't spill on the Persian rug. Your master won't appreciate you sullying his possessions."

The one ripping the faery's wings leans over the ottoman and grips the faery by the sides of her face. "Fast food never tastes as good."

With one quick breath, the faery goes limp, and a wisp of pink energy is sucked from the faery's mouth into the skoro's.

He's consuming her power.

I point my gun at the skoro feeding, but he's got his arms around her, and there's no way I can fire on him without endangering her further.

Aiming high, I send a warning shot over his head. He straightens and my second shot takes him down.

"Police. On your knees!"

Unfortunately, I've woken the crowd, and now it's seven against one. Sadly, they don't seem like the type to surrender.

Oh shit.

CHAPTER FOURTEEN

The battle is on, and I've declared war against the sadist assassin. *Yay me.* The skoro I shot gets back up despite the center mass hole in his chest. I shift to gain cover behind a metal column and squeeze off a couple more rounds. Where the hell is my backup?

It has to be four minutes, right?

The skoro with the hole in his torso runs at me like a juggernaut. Matthias is tucked in behind him, using the wall of his body as a living shield.

Fuckety-fuck.

Tad *poofs* in behind them and cuts off half the pack, laying into them with a length of pipe.

It's me against three and Tad against four.

Better, but still not good.

Skoro aren't overly dangerous as opponents. Their threat comes in numbers. Matthias, on the other hand, scares the bejeebers out of me.

Round after round, I fire into the skoro running the gauntlet toward me until chunks of him fall to the floor. How is he still on his feet? It's like he's on PCP.

No time to figure that out now.

I'm about to get overrun.

As the last space between us vanishes, I grab the truck's passenger door and swing it hard. The crack of steel to body is satisfying but not nearly as gratifying as seeing the skoro finally end his advance.

He falls to a lifeless heap, and the next moment, the momentum of Matthias' attack sweeps me up. He grapples me hard, lifting my feet from the floor as he slams me against the truck.

Oxygen exits my lungs in a gasp, and my world goes black for an instant. Fire roars inside me as my cells ignite. There's no way I'm blacking out and falling to the mercy of this psychopath.

Embracing the fiery beast within, I call flames to my hands and get a solid punch to his face. The strike is hard, but it's the heat and fire that land it.

He staggers back with a roar, clutching his cheek, but when he straightens, sadistic pleasure lights his gaze. "Oh, we're going to have some fun, beautiful."

"Hard pass." I flex my muscles and call my flame to engulf me, but nothing happens. Why? I glance down at my fists as my fire fizzles out completely.

Where the fuck are my powers?

I try again, but I've got nothing.

Matthias's tackle slams into me, and I fly. I brace for the impact a moment before the concrete floor rises to meet my face.

To avoid coming out of this looking like one of those smushed-face cats, I tuck and try to roll to absorb the impact.

I manage to save my head from cracking open, but a sharp pain in my side and the *snap* of bone tell us that my ribs didn't fare as well.

I gasp for breath and curl into myself a moment before Matthias is on top of me. The searing heat of a blade puncturing my side envelops me.

"Hmm," the bastard hums, the green irises of his eyes glowing as his smile grows wide. "The power of your pain is incredible."

"You're a twisted fuckwad."

Male voices shout at the entrance, and I sag a little.

Thank the stars.

Only, when the men flood into view, they're skoro, not SPVM officers. Matthias yanks the blade free from my body, his hand and the weapon slick with the dark red stain of my blood.

Tad is there the next second, fighting to get through the skoro reinforcements.

Matthias is practically vibrating on the high from my pain. "You four, take the blond. You come here."

As he directs the skoro men, I stagger toward the living room setup. My footing is sloppy, and my hand is warm and wet where it's pressed against my side.

I flop onto the ottoman.

The leather is cool and soft, and for an instant, I toy with the lure to close my eyes and rest.

Then meet the gaze of the mauve faery in the hookah bottle. She's dead, but the sage green one who was having her wings plucked off isn't.

Still...her end is not far off. Her eyelids are fluttering, and her breath is shallow and rapid.

"It's going to be okay." It's a total lie, but it makes me feel better to say it. I haul myself off the ottoman and lift the faery. She's smaller than me, with iridescent skin and big wings. I gently lay her limp body on the sofa, grunting with the effort and agony of moving.

I check to see where Matthias is, and he's pointing at me, sending the two skoro over. He's in no hurry and having him stalk me like wounded prey is unnerving.

Tad is cursing up a Celtic storm. He's holding his own against the skoro, but he's not portaling or using his druid abilities, so I assume whatever cut off my powers cut off his as well.

A hand clutches my side, and I cry out. A rush of dizziness hits but I fight to stay conscious. The two skoro he sent over have me, and I don't have much fight left.

Sirens wail in the distance, but they're too far off.

With a yell, Tad swings a massive burlap bag. The open end spews out a sandstorm of cinnamon. It smells amazing, and it chokes and scatters his attackers.

I cry out as rough fingers tighten at the back of my skull and two brutes secure my arms behind my back. The position tweaks my ribs and my world spins, my consciousness threatening to abandon me.

My boots dangle as the skoro presses his face close to mine. I'm not sure if it's faery breath or demon halitosis that hits me, but it's bad. My eyes tear up, my sinuses tingling from the pain and the stench.

He grips my jaw, digging his fingers into my flesh. "You smell good, bitch."

I gasp as he forces my mouth open.

Understanding what he plans to do, I fight harder. The skoro pinning my arms behind my back tighten their hold. They keep their legs out of range from my flailing kicks, rendering my struggle useless.

I glare at the asshole in front of me, taking in every inch of his face, the sharp features, the cruel smile.

Sirens continue to blare. They should be closer, but their wails sound distorted...far away, or maybe...underwater. Everything seems muffled.

Shit. I can't pass out. Not now.

Then the asshole starts breathing in.

My breath catches as my heart slams to a halt in my chest. An itch tingles in my lungs and builds to a pull, then to an excruciating tearing.

He's tearing the fire inside me from my soul.

I squirm and scream, but no matter what I do, the fucker's hand remains clamped on my jaw, and he keeps feeding.

Bone-deep, mind-numbing cold crystallizes through my body, extinguishing my fiery side and encasing my organs with ice.

I can't fight it.

I'm powerless to stop him from consuming everything that makes me…me.

Shots ring out, and I drop. My boots hit and my legs fold, crumpling me onto the Persian rug. My head *cracks* to the floor, and I'm thankful for the cushioned fall.

I want to get up…to fight…to get the faeries to safety.

I can't.

"*Arragh.* Feckin' hell, Jules." Tad scoops me up and runs. He says something, but I can't hear him. I can't see him, either…

My eyes flutter open, and I'm on the sofa in the living room of the firehouse. Kenzie and Azland are hovering, both of them looking despondent.

Shit. Things must be bad.

I try to sit up…

A wave of weakness and nausea hits and I collapse against the cushion as the room spins.

"Lie still." Kenzie sets a hand on my side, where the sadist stabbed me. Her healing waters trickle down over the wound, sealing the puncture and knitting my ribs back together. Her eyes are red-rimmed and puffy.

"I feel awful."

"A skoro consumed your fire," Azland says.

No shit. I was there.

"How long until it replenishes?" Kenzie asks.

"It won't." Azland's tone is sharp, his words laced with anger.

Briar rushes in to join us. "What the fuck does that mean?" He chucks his jacket and kisses my forehead. "Why won't it replenish?"

"Her fire was consumed. She'll die."

Kenzie turns a defiant glare at our mentor. "You don't know that. Jules has an inextinguishable spark. It's still in there. I know it."

I'd like to agree with her, but I feel like I'm lying naked on a sheet of ice…and I'm wet…and there's an Arctic wind…and I'm eating ice cream…

"A fire elemental with no fire cannot survive."

"Then what the fuck do we do?" Zephyr joins the party. I appreciate my siblings freaking out about my impending death because frankly, I don't have the energy to do so.

"Unless you have a way to reignite her soul's elemental fire, there's nothing," Azland says. "You don't have a volcano handy, do you?"

Not many volcanos in Montréal, no.

"What about that Laurentian guy in the tower?" Kenzie swings her gaze to Tad. "He has magic. Can't he help? Or maybe Fiona?"

"A Viking and a druid have their powers, but they aren't rooted in fire."

Rooted in fire…

My consciousness fades, and I drift into a long, dark, icy sleep.

I dream of that scene in *Titanic* where Leonardo is bobbing in the glacial waters clinging to the door, and Kate won't scootch her aristocratic ass over a foot to give him space to climb out of the cold.

Seriously, woman. Learn to share.

I'm freezing from the inside and know that stupid Azland is right. My spark is extinguished.

"Don't you fucking give up, Juliette. Not yet." The voice is throaty and gruff and echoes inside my mind. Warm lips press against my mouth and my heart hiccups in my chest.

I try to open my eyes, but I'm dreaming and mostly dead, so that's a no-go. Still, this kissing part of my dying dream is quite nice.

I groan when the contact is lost, missing the heat of the connection. Kissing guy…come back.

A long, soft *hiss*…a powerful *whoosh*…and warmth envelopes me.

When I wake next, bright blue light surrounds me. It wraps around me, cradling me in a blanket of bliss, filling my lungs with each breath I take. I'm naked with nothing between me and the light…which now that I think about it, is more than bright—it's warm.

I'm warm.

I blink and lift my head. I'm lying on a porous pad of ivory-colored stone. It glows like magma heaving with heat and fire after an eruption.

Only, the flames aren't orange and red—they're blue. I'm living within blue lava…and it feels amazing.

I stretch and roll over on my side. The warm stone beneath me is a perfectly flat slab, yet it contours to my curves like a memory foam mattress.

The room beyond the flames is dark, lit only by the fireplace's blue glow. In the middle of the room, facing me, a man sleeps on a leather sofa.

My heart skips a beat.

It's Gareth. Judging by the slow motion of his chest, he's dead asleep.

Which is fine by me. I could use a few more moments of privacy in his elemental sanctuary. He said it was like ten trips to the spa, and he's right.

It feels spectacular.

With him sleeping, there doesn't seem to be a pressing need for me to give it up.

I draw a few deep breaths of fiery air and revel in the elemental power infusing my cells. Then I close my eyes and settle back down to sleep.

The next time I wake, the room is light, and the couch is empty. The fireplace is still on, and I wonder what kind of draw that takes from the world. Does he pay for this? If so, I might owe him a year's salary for the fire I used up.

Not that I feel guilty.

Nope.

I needed that more than I could say.

Still, all good things must end, so I swing my feet over the edge of the stone hearth and take inventory of my injuries. My ribs feel good. The hole in my side is sealed and other than a faint pink mark, there's no trace of being stabbed.

Rolling my neck and shoulders, I pop a few vertebrae and rise to my feet. "Gareth? Are you here?"

There's no answer, and I'm relieved.

As thankful as I am to him for whatever series of favors led me to recuperate in his sanctuary, I can't help but remember how annoyed and determined to get away from me he was when we last spoke.

"Jules...as much as I like you...this was a mistake. I can't get involved."

Right. He helped me because he's a good guy and Kenzie probably soaked his black muscle shirt with huge, sobbing tears.

Forget the fact that I'm freaking naked.

Even if a guy hadn't totally rejected me, I'd prefer not to have my lady bits on display.

Not that he didn't see me when he was watching over me while I slept.

I push that thought out of my mind. *Awkward.*

A decadent black, fluffy robe with an embroidered G on the lapel sits next to a neatly folded stack of my clothes. On top of it is a note with my name on it.

The handwriting is masculine and neat.

> *Gone to work. The fireplace will shut off automatically once it's no longer in use. Give your skin time to cool before getting dressed, or your clothes will burn. Help yourself to anything in the kitchen. Your siblings are eager to hear from you. Call Tad for a pickup when you're ready. He dropped you off so he could pick you up without issue.*

Clipped and to the point, much like the man.

Nice penmanship though.

I slip on Gareth's robe, chuckling at how long and floppy it is on me. The fact that he doesn't have a spare one around in a women's size wins him bonus points. Yet another tidbit about the enigmatic fire guy to tuck away in my detective's file folder.

Considering I can't go anywhere until my skin cools enough to get dressed, I accept his invitation and head into the kitchen.

Holy crapamoly. The cabinets are slate gray lacquer with black marble countertops, black appliances, and brushed pewter fixtures. Damn, his kitchen is as dark and sexy as he is.

My stomach growls. I check the refrigerator and snort. Even with a kitchen that probably cost him sixty grand easy, he's still in touch with what's important.

I grab the bucket of day-old fried chicken and set it on the counter. Ripping off a couple of paper towels, I make myself a picnic area. I pick out a breast and a drumstick. Man, I'm starving. *Annnd* another breast.

Don't judge. Almost dying does that to a girl.

I bite into the seasoned skin of cold fried chicken and lean into my elbows on the counter. The time in Gareth's fire spa has left me chipper and relaxed.

Life is good. I'm alive, I have cold chicken, and my fire is burning hotly inside me. While I get ready to return to the world, I get to unravel a little of the mystery of Gareth.

Score.

CHAPTER FIFTEEN

After finishing my chicken feast, I tie the silk sash tight around my waist and decide to have myself a little wander around Gareth's home.

The kitchen is off the main living room, and I pad barefooted back to the huge fireplace where I began. The thing is a stone masterpiece and is the centerpiece of a sleek but comfortable home.

It's two-sided. I bend to look through the empty fire pit to the master bedroom beyond.

Handy.

It's easy to tell he designed the space for himself and not to impress anyone else. Everything about the fixtures, the furniture, and the finishes screams Gareth.

I brush my fingers over the plush leather of the couch and admire the marble top of the coffee table. The coasters look like brushed platinum, but that's crazy. Who would spend that kind of money on coasters?

Everything is masculine and tidy. There's not much here, but what is here is high quality, built for his comfort, and has an air of style.

I go into the den next. It's a rather small room, a bit dwarfed by a large, sleek desk with two massive curved monitors stacked one above the other. I swivel the contoured leather chair and smile at the gamer setup.

"I didn't peg you for a VALORANT guy. Nice."

I keep the tour going, the silk of his robe swishing around my legs and behind my feet as I step. What is this made of?

Gareth has a lead on fireproof fabric. I rub the material between my fingers, trying to pinpoint what's so exotic about it.

Oooh, nice. There is a bag of Oreos on his bedside table with my name on it. They're already open, so I figure it won't be a huge deal if I grab a few.

I ease them free and look around.

There's no TV in here, but there is a floor-to-ceiling bookshelf.

Munching on the sugary goodness, I wander around some more. My detective's mind is loving all this input. It's amazing what you can figure out about a man simply by examining the stuff in his home.

Like the fact that his formal dining room is set up with a treadmill and a weight machine.

"No formal dinner parties then."

I laugh and take another bite of my cookie.

Gareth is broody and quiet. I can't imagine him pulling a Martha Stewart.

The other two bedrooms are on this end of his home. The first is off the kitchen and is set up like a miniature recording studio. It has a DJ deck, another desk and a computer, and a handful of microphones on stands.

It also has a stack of cardboard boxes sitting on a chair. I bend back one of the open flaps and look inside. It's a printing box filled with flyers with motivational quotes on them.

Weird. Gareth is a good guy, but I don't get any glass half-full, Eat, Pray, Love vibes from him.

I take a closer look. They appear to be like any other brightly colored advertisement plastered to the telephone poles all around Montréal. But then...

I lean closer, studying the rune markings hidden in the border design. What looks like graffiti art at first glance is a language I've seen in different parts of the empowered world since my awakening.

There's a secret message written in a code of some kind. I bet it lets fae and empowered kids know about the private events he holds for them.

He spreads the word privately so they'll be safe.

I take one off the top.

On the computer desk is a little box filled with flame-style thumb drives like the one he gave me with sanctuary plans.

I wonder how many other strangers he's helped in his time.

My detective instincts remind me I barely know anything about this guy. He has secrets he isn't interested in sharing, and he has connections in the magical world that I don't have the full story on.

I like Gareth and want to trust him, but it's not only my safety on the line. If I let this guy get close to me, my whole family could be at risk.

There isn't much else on the desk, only a photograph in a fancy frame. It's of a woman, dark-haired and beautiful. She's smiling over her shoulder at the camera, the ends of her hair a little blurry like she's just turned.

It's the only photo in the entire house. Actually, it's the only personal item I've seen. I pick up the frame, examining the photo.

The woman in it looks a lot like Gareth.

A sister maybe? Or maybe a picture of his mom from years ago? There's no way to tell because it's a head shot and she's on a beach walking toward the water.

Maybe he has a woman in his life and hasn't shared that information with me. Then again, if there is a girlfriend in the picture, what's he doing leaving a naked girl lying in his fireplace overnight?

Off the main hallway, there's a closed door with a note taped to it.

Nope, not in here. Jinx has puppies and is protective. Think rabid wolfhound on bath salts.

Yikes. I lean toward the crack of the door frame. "It's okay, Jinx. I'm not coming in. You're good."

A deep-throated growl behind the door tells me I've made a wise decision.

I read the note again and chuckle. Gareth expected me to snoop. *Smart man.*

Of course, he left a detective alone in his house for an indefinite period—snooping was bound to happen.

Which means there's nothing in here he doesn't want me to see. Either it doesn't exist, or he hid it in the room with Jinx.

Back in the kitchen, I eat my last Oreo and wash it down with half a glass of almond milk. Is he lactose intolerant or does he prefer his milk to be nutty?

With my tummy full and my tour complete, I write him a quick thank you note, get dressed, hang the robe on the hook on the back of his bedroom door, and grab my phone.

I call up Tad's number and dial.

"Welcome back to the land of the livin', lass. Howeyah?"

"Honestly, I'm alive and well and feel the pilot light of my inner flame burning strong inside me."

"I'm incredibly relieved to hear it. Yer sister won't be satisfied until she sees fer herself that yer well. Can I come and get ye then?"

"If you don't mind, please."

In an instant, Tad is standing in Gareth's living room. He looks relieved as well. He strides forward and pulls me against his chest in a hug. "Ye gave us a mighty big scare yesterday, Jules. I'm glad ye made it."

I ease back with a reassuring grin. "Thanks for getting me out of there. Did either of the faeries make it?"

"The one they were torturing will live. The one suspended in the glass bottle was in a bad way. I took them both to Bakkali but can't say what happened since then. Bakkali's healers said they'd do what they can."

I grimace. I've been a cop long enough to know what *in a bad way* and *do what they can* mean. "I wasn't quick enough to save her. I should've taken the shot sooner…before that asshole took those last few drags."

"Ye did what ye could and then some," Tad assures me. "And almost lost yer life in the process."

"Well, I'm fine now. Take me home so I can show everyone I'm alive. Then I need to check in with Rene and find out how he did yesterday."

"Do ye ever give it a rest? Ye almost died, Jules."

"Yeah, I know. The minute the bad guys start taking days off, I will too."

He chuckles. "Yer as bad as Fi."

"I'll take that as a compliment."

"Aye, I suppose ye would."

Back at the firehouse, Zephyr welcomes me with a massive hug, longer and tighter than usual. He looks like he didn't sleep a wink. Kenzie rushes out of her suite and crashes into us, wrapping her arms around us. Briar is right behind her, and it's a four-way Gagne cluster hug.

"Guys, you're crushing me," I gasp.

"Suck it up," Zephyr retorts.

"Yeah, you deserve this and more for almost dying on us," Kenzie snaps. "Not to mention almost getting my very new and sexy man toy killed."

"I knew that would come back to bite me in the ass."

As much as I get annoyed by my family fussing over me, I realize they spent the last who-knows-how-many hours not knowing if I would survive.

Briar eventually releases us, and we peel apart. "It's good to see you upright, Jules."

I kiss his cheek. "Thanks, big guy. Honestly, though, me being here has nothing to do with me and everything to do with you guys reaching out to Gareth—and him giving enough of a shit to save me even though he doesn't want to be tied to me."

Kenzie rolls her eyes. "I don't believe that for a second. Tad said he was throwing sparks the moment he saw you collapsed in his arms."

Tad nods. "I'm not sure why he said the two of ye were a bad idea, but it isn't because he doesn't have feelings fer ye. That much is plain."

"Are you hungry?" Zephyr asks.

Briar takes that as his cue to hustle behind the counter and turn on the griddle. "Chocolate chip pancakes with a side of bacon?"

When I think about it, I'm starving.

"As crazy as it is, I had three pieces of chicken and a handful of Oreos less than an hour ago. How can I be hungry?"

"It's your elemental side powering up." Azland frowns at me. "You almost died." He practically growls it at me.

I take it as his way of expressing he cares and doesn't like the idea that I was hurt.

Yes, that's my dime-store psychology kicking in.

Briar is whipping batter and spreading out dollops of delight a few minutes later. Kenzie grabs the bacon out of the fridge as Zephyr sorts through the coffee pods, looking for one I'd like.

"Guys, I'm fine. Really." I perch on one of the stools at the breakfast bar, facing them. "I love you all, and I'm grateful you want to take care of me, but I'm good. One hundred percent."

Zephyr slides me a mug of coffee. "You scared us, Jules. Shut up and eat your pancakes."

I laugh and do my part to appease their anxieties, accepting the fussing. Tad snags a couple of pieces of bacon as Kenzie makes it, but otherwise, it's a feast for me.

Zephyr remarks, "Tad told us about the skeevy lawyer and how you tracked down the addresses. We know you got there while the skoro were torturing faeries, and we understand you couldn't stand by while they killed her."

"No. I couldn't."

"The big question is, are honest-to-goodness faeries, like, Tinkerbell size?"

I laugh. "That's the big question?"

"Yeah."

I grin at my little brother. "Nope. They were regular people sized but on the petite side."

"But their skin shimmers," Tad adds.

"They have filmy gossamer wings, sort of like dragonfly wings."

"Wild," Zephyr says. "I can't wait to see faeries."

"Ye might be waitin' a good long while," Tad interjects. "Most faeries are incredibly private and don't often frequent the human world. The ones who do, use strong glamors to conceal their appearance."

Zephyr seems genuinely disappointed. I could so see him with a winged faery girlfriend.

"If they're so rare in the human realm, how did the skoro find them?" Kenzie asks.

Tad shrugs. "No idea."

Briar plates me three fluffy, golden pancakes and adds a stack of bacon on the side. "Enough about the faeries. Tell us about what happened to you."

It turns my stomach to think about it, but I slather butter and syrup over my breakfast and focus on the here and now. "They had dampening magic working to block our powers. At first, I could call fire to my palms and Tad *poofed* inside, but once we were inside, my powers fizzled out."

"Mine too," Tad says. "I portaled onto a catwalk along the ceiling at the back of the warehouse to get a good view. After I was there, I couldn't get back. I had to find a way to climb down and get back to Jules. It was stupid. I'm so sorry, lass."

I wave away his concern. "Don't be. Neither of us knew that would happen."

"Although it's reminiscent of the golf club incident," Briar observes. "Maybe we need to expect power blockers when dealing with the Poreskoro."

"Yeah, I think so," I agree.

"Did it hurt?" Kenzie's eyes glass up.

"Not really. It was cold and terrifying. It spread through me like a glacier consuming the land, and I felt the heat within me getting consumed. Beyond the panic, I was numb. Like it was stripping away my soul, the essence of who I am as a person."

Zephyr curses. "Well, you cut it too fucking close."

Agreed. "I'm thankful Tad was there during the worst of it and for the quick thinking with calling Gareth. His fireplace was awesome. Literally a lifesaver."

Azland grunts. "You got lucky this time. Let this be the lesson for all of you. Anyone from the Poreskoro family or their siring lines can corner you and consume your elemental power."

The four of us share a look and nod.

"We get it." I speak for all of us. "It was terrifying and certainly nothing I want to repeat—ever."

Briar leans back against the countertop and crosses his muscled arms. "If they ever find out we're behind Lamech's death and indirectly Draven's, they'll be after us for revenge on top of wanting a tasty meal."

"Well then, we need to ensure they never find out," Tad reminds us.

I agree with him, but easier said than done. "We'll keep it a secret for as long as we can, but given how much power and money their family has, I wouldn't be surprised if they figure it out eventually. There were too many responders to the skoro warehouse that saw us there bloody and gross: police, fire, factory workers."

"We'll cross that bridge when we come to it," Azland darkly advises.

Zephyr pipes up. "In the meantime, it's good you're back and feeling better because Charlie is bringing the twins for dinner. If she found out you were hurt, none of us would ever hear the end of it."

I chuckle. "Then we keep things on the down low."

"Hey, if I can't protect my big sister from the demon cabal trying to eat her soul, at least I can shield her from our overprotective aunt."

I finish eating and get up to clear my dishes. As I set a plate smeared with bacon grease on the counter, I spot a note in Kenzie's flowery script. "What's this?"

"Oh, yeah." Kenzie holds a spoon under the faucet to wash it. "Someone called looking for you."

"What? Who? When? How?"

"Oh my God, you sound like such a detective," Zephyr jokes. He turns the spoon in the sink, and it sends a jet of water splashing onto his shirt.

He grumbles and waves, using his air and wind powers to dry it quickly.

"Is that how you're supposed to use your powers?"

He grins. "Azland said we're supposed to practice in every free moment."

"Absolutely," Azland agrees. "If you have no free moments, you'll have to make some."

He's staring at me when he says that and I roll my eyes. "Yeah, I know. I'm trailing in the elemental training hours."

"Yes, you are."

I read the note.

Call Luc as ASAP as possible.

I chuckle at his goofy phrase. "When did he call?"

"About three hours ago?" Kenzie checks her watch. "Yeah, about that. It was before Tad met Gareth and dropped off your clothes and phone but after I had begun the weekly conference call with my office."

"All right, I'll feed the Jacks, take a shower, and get to work. My shift starts in less than an hour."

"I can *poof* ye there if ye like," Tad offers.

"Thanks, but I'll drive myself. A ride on my motorcycle will give me time to think."

Jack and Jack don't seem to have been impacted by my absence. They're lazily swimming in circles. I sprinkle some fish flakes into their bowl, watching their orange scales flash in the light.

I shower, relishing the hot water, then grab some work clothes and get dressed. After a quick towel dry, I run my fingers through my wet hair, head down to the garage bay, and cram on my helmet.

Yes, I know it'll look ridiculous once it dries.

Zero fucks given.

"Headin' out?" Tad asks when the bay door hums open. He's sitting on the brick retaining wall of the fire station's flower bed. Aurora is standing on our side lawn pulling a dove apart with her talons.

With each tug of her beak, long, stringy strands of bird innards pull free, and she throws her head back to eat them. It's gross, but Tad is watching the horror show with rapt pride in his spring green Irish eyes.

"Be sure to be home for dinner," Zephyr reminds me. "Charlie will pitch a fit if you're late again."

"I make no promises. Try to keep her sane while I serve our city."

"I make no promises."

Fair enough. Keeping Charlie calm when there is something to fuss about is as likely and as easy as me being home from work on time.

"Safe home, lass," Tad says. "Text me if ye need a partner in crime."

I flip down the visor of my helmet. "You'll be the first person I call."

CHAPTER SIXTEEN

"All right, my formaldehyde-pickled friend," I shout into the morgue as I set my helmet on the counter by the door and saunter into Luc's lab. "What have you got for me today?"

"Jules!" Luc rushes over to give me the most awkward knuckle bump and hug combination ever. "You're alive."

I step out of his weird embrace and make a face. "What's this and why is it happening?"

"The police reports said you'd been magically hurt in a warehouse raid and your condition was considered dire. Then I called your cell, and Kenzie picked up and started crying when I asked how you were. She said they didn't know if you were going to live."

"Yet here I am. Yes, it was dire, but through magical intervention, I'm back on the top of my game, no harm done."

He glances at me as if trying to decide whether or not to believe me. Hell, he looks as rough as Briar did.

I smile and give him another short hug. "Thank you for worrying. I'm good."

"I'm glad to hear it. Teresa was getting jealous."

I chuckle and pat the beige housing for his microscope. "I'm sorry. I never meant to come between you and Theresa."

Luc exhales, and grateful warmth washes me.

I have people who care enough to lose their minds when things go bad but are weird enough to jump back into cracking jokes and solving crimes once they find out I'm okay.

Just the way I like it.

"What were you trying to get hold of me for? Did you find anything new on the Second Sight front?"

"Yes, I did, and it's super weird."

"That doesn't surprise me. This whole situation is super weird. I'd be more surprised if you found something normal."

Luc's grin is mischievous. "In that case, prepare to be shocked."

He grabs a printed sheet from one of his machines and hands it to me. It's full of scientific gibberish I don't understand. I scan it, finding words like *cinnamomum cassia*, *monosaccharide*, and $C_{12}H_{22}O_{11}$.

"Luc, you'll never entice me into taking science classes. Tell me what you found."

"Well, I put the most recent samples of Second Sight you collected through a gamut of tests—everything from radioscopy to mass spectrometry to dye solutions—and found a strange trace ingredient in them that I didn't find in the earlier samples."

"A trace ingredient? Do you think it's what's causing the fae mutations and the deaths?"

"No. It's not dangerous. It's just weird to find in a street drug."

"I'm on the edge of my seat here, dude. Tell me."

"Cinnamon sugar."

I give that a moment to sink in. "Like the stuff we sprinkle on French toast?"

"The very same. You can buy it at any grocery store in the city, and it's present in every sample of Second Sight you've brought me since you blew up Lamech's warehouse."

"Allegedly," I correct him holding up my finger. "Officially, that was a magical surge of poorly contained prana energy causing a catastrophic explosion."

"Right, my bad."

I look at the printed sheet again. I don't know that cinnamon has ever turned up in drug and organized crime investigations. "What's it doing there? Second Sight pills are made from compressed powder. Were they improving the taste? Maybe people take so much of it because it's sweet and they munch it like candy?"

"I doubt it. These trace amounts of cinnamon sugar wouldn't change the taste. The tablets are supposed to be swallowed whole, and I haven't seen any indication they're trying to swap to a chewable."

"That's good, at least. Pills make it slightly less enticing to kids. How did it get there?"

"No idea. At first, I thought it was from the baggies people stored it in or maybe transferred from the fingers of a user picking up the pills, but I don't think so."

Weird. "Okay, thanks for letting me know."

"Thanks for getting your ass down here, finally. And for not dying. I'd be bummed if you were dead."

"I'll try not to bum you out. Thanks, man, you rock."

When I get to the station, Rene is sitting in the small meeting room we commandeered as our strategic headquarters. He's poring over paperwork and doesn't register my arrival until I sit opposite him and lean in to see what he's studying.

"What sucked you in? Anything good?"

He starts and scans me with an assessing gaze. "How are you? I heard from some of the guys that you went down hard at that warehouse."

"The beauty of being magically attacked is that you can be magically fixed and come out unscathed."

"I heard you almost died," Rene matter-of-factly counters. "Dead is dead, magical or not."

"True story, but I'm not, and I'd rather not dwell on it. Eyes front and all that."

Rene gauges my sincerity and gives in. "All right. You're good to go unless you tell me otherwise, but *only* if you promise to tell me otherwise."

I lift my three center fingers. "Scouts' honor."

He sits back in his chair and crosses his arms. "Okay, so tell me what you learned yesterday."

I get him caught up on driving the route from the Kahnawake territory to McGill University, the walk of the campus, and our plan to search the three properties that Harvey Funk manages for his clients in the warehouse district where the skoro had taken me after kidnapping me.

That led me to the faery screaming, the warehouse raid, and me almost dying from the world's worst skoro make-out session.

He pulls a sheet of paper out of the pile and turns it for me to study. "The boys found these in the warehouse office while clearing the scene."

It's a street map of Montréal, with several roads marked off.

I scan the map, trying to make sense of it.

Nothing jumps out at me. There are no obvious connections between the roads marked. There are notes on the side of the map, some kind of legend, but it's not in any language I can read.

"What does it mean?"

Rene shrugs. "We're not sure. The top two theories are that it's their drug selling routes or spots where they're grabbing fae off the street."

I scan the map a little longer. "I'll run the locations against existing crime reports. What about this writing here? Are those fae runes? They don't look like the ones I've seen before."

Rene shrugs. "No clue. It might be a skoro language or a cipher unique to the Poreskoro Corporation. We have the cryptology department working on it."

"Speaking of the Poreskoro Corporation, how did your interview with the oldest sibling go?"

"Rance Poreskoro is an interesting guy. If I didn't know what we know about his origins and his family's criminal pursuits, I would've found him to be a damned impressive corporate mogul."

"Knowing he's a demon hybrid intent on killing my family and my kind?"

He shakes his head. "Honestly, I didn't get any homicidal Soprano vibes from him."

"Azland did say they could be very charismatic."

"He's right. I've spoken with slick assholes, and that's not how he came off. Either he's good at deception, or there are layers to this family we haven't peeled back yet."

"Did he give you *anything* interesting? Before everything went to hell in the warehouse, Matthias said they needed to leave because there was trouble at the house. What happened?"

Rene shakes his head. "That wasn't about us. We met Rance at a swanky office building near the Quartier des Spectacles."

I sit up, my curiosity piqued. "What was the trouble at the house? Where is their house, anyway?"

"No idea."

"Ugh." I rub my forehead. That sensation of well-being I had after spending the night in Gareth's elemental sanctuary is gone.

Now I'm a ball of annoyance and frustration.

Maybe he'll invite me over again soon.

Before my mind takes me on a jaunty, X-rated daydream of how that would go, I refocus on our case. "In other news, I had an idea about how to encourage people to stop taking Second Sight."

Rene's brows arch. "Oh? What's that?"

"You should hold a press conference with Police Chief Monet and Mayor Tremblay. We could explain to people about the recent deaths and show them pictures of the weird spider veining in the fingers. We know the fae mutations begin after two weeks, and people die by two months, so maybe we can scare people sober."

Rene scrubs a hand over his face and rubs under his chin. "A press conference won't convince anyone caught in their addiction."

"No, but maybe someone who recognizes those symptoms in themselves or others could be encouraged to contact your squad for help. This stuff is associated with the party scene, so if we can scare some more casual or curious users off, it's worth a shot."

Rene pulls out his phone and scrolls through his contacts. "Do you want to be center stage for this?"

"Very much, hells no. I'm happy being an anonymous contributor, especially now. The more attention I attract, the more eyes fall on me. As you said, I can't endanger my family."

Rene and I work the rest of the day getting things for the press conference together. Mayor Tremblay and Police Chief Monet are both on board and agree to have their liaisons coordinate the local media tomorrow morning at City Hall.

"Will you be coming?" Rene asks when he gets ready to leave.

"I'll be there. I'll be the one with my head down in the back row."

"You do you, Jules."

I always do. "Look at us."

He laughs. "What about us?"

"I'm expected home for dinner, and I'm going to be there on time."

Rene scoffs. "On time? What's that?"

"I know, right?"

Rene shrugs into his blazer, tucks the file folders we've been working on under his arm, and grabs his keys. "Enjoy your dinner. I'll take care of the rest of the press conference details, and we'll regroup tomorrow with fresh eyes."

I put on my leather jacket, grab my helmet, and walk out with him. "Have a good night."

CHAPTER SEVENTEEN

Thanks to some magical miracle and a few somewhat creative traffic maneuvers, I make it home early. I get home before Charlie and the kids arrive, which should significantly reduce my siblings' stress.

When Scarlett's engine falls silent, I toe her kickstand and tuck her in for the night. Helmet on the shelf, keys on the hook, boots against the wall. "Honey, I'm home!"

Kenzie peers down the pole opening from the second floor. Her hair is twisted in elaborate braids with glittering beads woven in. "Impossible. Juliette Gagne arrived at a family event on time? Call the media. We need this documented."

"Not only on time," I correct her. "I'm early."

"Must have been a zero-crime day," Zephyr calls from the kitchen. "First time in Montréal's history the attentions of our brave sister have been released at a reasonable hour."

I crest the top step and shrug out of my backpack. "Hey, if I'm not living up to expectations, I can head back to work and keep my reputation intact."

"No!" Kenzie appears again. "If you're not here when Charlie gets here, she'll rant. Stupid police work. Stupid motorcycle. Stupid criminals."

I laugh, passing through the kitchen to drop my jacket in my room and change into comfy clothes. When I get back, Zephyr looks all kinds of awkward in the kitchen. "I wasn't made for this."

The counter is covered in smears of grease and spilled flour. "This looks like a crime scene. What's this supposed to be?"

"Homemade tortillas." Briar snickers.

"Isn't Charlie bringing dinner?"

"She is," Zephyr confirms. "She's making her chiles rellenos, and I wanted to surprise her with fresh homemade tortillas as the side."

I brush off the front of Zephyr's T-shirt and try not to laugh. "Well, she'll certainly be…surprised."

Kenzie rolls her eyes. "I say we forget the tortillas and try to get this cleaned up before she gets here."

"No tortillas?" Zephyr looks crestfallen.

"I bought a package at the store," she sheepishly admits. "Just in case."

Zephyr lifts both his mucky hands and gives her two middle fingers. "You suck, Kenz, and your lack of faith wounds me."

Kenzie ignores the insult and opens the fridge, grabbing herself and me a cooler. "You tried. You failed. Now, clean up before the company arrives or the twins will never let you live it down."

Zephyr grunts. "Dumb kids."

Poor Zephyr. He tries hard and has the best of intentions. There's no escaping the reality that he's a natural hot mess disaster waiting to happen.

I step in to help my brothers erase all evidence of the tortilla-tastrophy. Kenzie giggles as I wipe a thin layer of flour from the edges of the cabinets, wondering how he made such a mess. "I have an idea. Jules, step back."

I do as she says and she sweeps her palms across the breakfast bar countertop. As she moves along the sullied surface, a thin layer of water swirls under her palms, gathering the mess.

When she gets to the counter's edge, she reclaims all the water and leaves the baking debris in a little pile ready to be scooped up.

"Zephyr, collect the mess with a cloth, and Jules, you can give the counter a wash of hot air to dry the surface."

The two of us take care of that, and Briar tosses Zephyr a shammy cloth.

"Now buff it with a bit of wind and some elbow grease."

I laugh. "I wonder what Azland would think about us using our elemental powers to clean the kitchen."

Briar shrugs. "He's not around so he doesn't get an opinion."

True enough.

We finish in the kitchen, leaving it sparkling clean, and head into the living room to relax before the party gets started.

Hanging out with my brothers and sister reminds me of Luc's request, and I grab the DNA kits out of my backpack. "Hey, guys, since you're all here, I've got a favor to ask. I'm working with Luc to better understand the molecular stuff happening with magical awakenings, both natural and under the influence of Second Sight."

Kenzie laughs and takes a drink from her cooler. "The molecular stuff? Is that the official scientific term for your study?"

"Hey, I'm not the lab rat part of the equation. Anyway, Luc asked if you guys would volunteer your samples to help with his research."

Briar puts up his massive hands. "Hell no. Have you forgotten what happened the last time we sent something like that away for testing?"

"No, I haven't. This won't be like the MyAncestry DNA testing. It's only for Luc, who already knows about us, and he'll code the samples so it doesn't have any indicators of who they came from."

"And you're sure of him?" Zephyr asks.

"A hundred percent. No one knows about his research except me. He wants to create baseline studies for the four of us to use for our health and benefit moving forward and to compare to what he's seeing in the mutation of cells in bodies showing up at the morgue."

"Wow, he sounds like a laugh riot of a friend to have around," Kenzie snarks.

"He's hilarious, but that's irrelevant."

Zephyr nods. "Yeah, I like him. I've only met him that one time, but he seemed cool."

Briar snorts. "That's because the two of you bonded over tentacle porn."

Kenzie's eyes blow wide. "Okay, stop. I will agree to the samples on three conditions."

"You're such a lawyer." Briar laughs.

Kenzie doesn't care. "One, all talk of tentacle porn ends now. Two, I'd like to be kept in the loop about his study. Three, I get ten minutes with your hair before dinner. I swear you washed it and rammed your helmet on."

"Annnd? What's your point?"

She groans. "You kill me."

Briar laughs. "Charlie will kill us if she finds out we're going the DNA route again."

I wave away his concern. "That was to keep our heritage a secret. That ship has sailed."

Zephyr chuckles. "My bad."

"You think this will help other empowered people?" Briar asks.

I nod. "That's the hope. People are dying, and we're trying to figure out why and who's behind it."

They consider it for a bit and Briar nods. "All right. If you trust the weird guy in the morgue, I'll trust your judgment, sista."

Kenzie nods. "If it helps the empowered community, I'm in too."

"Thanks so much, you guys." I pull out the sample packs from my bag and show them how to take the samples—the finger pricks, the hair samples, and the cheek swabs.

Zephyr balks at pricking his finger, insisting he needs his hands in top shape to play guitar. Briar taunts him about being a wuss, and suddenly they compete to see who can squeeze the most blood out of their fingertips.

"Guys, I only need a drop." I sigh.

Zephyr replies by trying to smear his bloody finger on Briar's shirt, and the two end up rolling on the living room floor, grunting and cursing like idiots.

Once all the samples are collected and labeled Two, Three, and Four—representing our birth order—I put them in the white paper bags and tuck them safely into my bag.

"Now, for your hair." Kenzie grabs my wrist and drags me toward a seat at the kitchen table. "One day, you'll thank me for being invested in your hair care."

I laugh. "Are you sure about that?"

"Yes. Your hair is horribly dry."

"Isn't hair supposed to be dry? You know…when it's not wet?"

Kenzie sighs and scowls at my head as she touches my hair. "I bet all that time in Gareth's fireplace did it."

"I can't help that. I'm a fire elemental."

She runs her hands through my hair, and I feel her healing power activate. The soothing energy of her water moistens my hair through the ends of her fingers until she's satisfied. "*Et voila*, healthy hair."

I know better than to dismiss her efforts. Even though deep moisturization might not be important to me, it's important to her *for* me. "Thanks, Kenz."

She stands me up, and I turn my head back and forth in the mirror, taking in her work. She wasn't wrong. My hair is now glossy and looks like something you'd see in a magazine ad.

I reach to touch it, and it's soft and smooth. "It looks nice, but I can only be a beauty queen at home. Perps won't take me seriously if I'm bougie and gorgeous."

She rolls her eyes. "You're hopeless."

I'm still laughing when a chorus of voices enters the main floor. Our company has arrived.

"Here comes trouble," Zephyr calls.

"We heard that." Micah laughs as he, Anna, and Sammy come upstairs carrying fabric grocery bags of food.

My gaze locks on the pixie with pink hair. "Hey, it's good to see you again, kiddo. How are you?"

She looks at me shyly and smiles. "Better. Thanks."

Good. That's good. "Guys, this is Sammy," I say by way of introduction. "I met her the other day on a call and referred her to Charlie's care while she adapts to being empowered. Sammy, these are my other brothers and sister, Kenzie, Briar, and Zephyr."

Cue the nods and warm smiles.

"Welcome." Kenzie steps over to hug the girl. "We hope everything works out for you."

"Yeah, we do," Briar agrees.

Zephyr chuckles. "Play your cards right, and Charlie might trade up, and you can take Micah's place."

"Dude, be nice, or we'll take this food and go home."

Micah makes a show of hoarding the bags in his hand, and Zephyr laughs. "You're assuming you'd live long enough to get to the door. We're very protective of our chiles rellenos."

Charlie and Azland come up the stairs next. He's carrying the large catering tray, leaving Charlie's hands free to touch my hair. "Who are you and what have you done with Juliette Gagne?"

"Har-har." I make a face.

The screech of a bird of prey brings my attention to the hole in the floor where the brass pole drops to the garage bay. In a move so graceful and dexterous it takes my breath away, Aurora bullets through the opening and spreads her wings, swooping through the living room before landing on her perch by the window.

"Whoa, you got a pet falcon?" Anna shouts, her jaw dropping open. "When?"

Aurora shrieks and clacks her beak at our little sister.

Kenzie shakes her head and stops Anna and Micah from approaching. "She's not a pet, and she's not a falcon. She's a kestrel."

Tad *poofs* in and grins. "Hello, everyone. What's the craic? Hope we're not late."

Kenzie kisses his cheek and gestures at the bird. "Where have you two been?"

"We went to the Tower of the Guild of the Laurentians to check on Kess, the injured faery from the warehouse fight."

"How is she?" I ask.

"She has a long road to recovery, but the healing charms seem to be working."

"She'll live?"

"Most likely. She won't have an easy time of it with her wings plucked off and all, but she'll live."

"Thanks to the two of you," Kenzie adds.

I exhale the tension I've been holding since I saw her being tortured in that warehouse. "I'm so relieved. Thank you for following up."

"My pleasure."

"You saved a faery?" Anna asks.

"Tad and I did."

Charlie's gaze has narrowed on me. "How dangerous was that rescue?"

I don't see any advantage to telling her the whole truth, so I simplify. "Tad and I discovered the situation, called for backup, and got an innocent faery the help she needed."

"And?" She pegs me with a look.

I hold out my hands and twirl. "I am healthy and strong and have better hair than ever. No cause for alarm."

She studies me as if looking for defects to prove I'm lying, but I'm not. I am strong and healthy. I feel better than I have in weeks. "On that note, Azland says you haven't been training as much as the others, and he's concerned you're not taking things as seriously as you need to in order to stay safe."

I send him an ocular fuck you and meet Charlie's gaze. "That's one man's opinion."

"One man's highly educated opinion."

"What's your point?"

"My point is, you have time before we eat to go outside and work up an appetite. If you don't want me worrying about you, put in the time and the effort to make sure you're as prepared for what's coming as you possibly can be."

There's no point arguing.

"Yeah, sure. After a full day at the station, working out is exactly what I want to do."

Azland laughs. "Your objection would only hold weight if opposing forces only attack when you're rested and feel like fighting."

I throw a palmful of flame at him, and he bats it away. "Fuck you, dog boy."

That only makes him laugh harder.

"Juliette Marie, what's gotten into you?" Charlie snaps in French.

"Me? What's gotten into him? He totally threw me under the bus, and now he's laughing? Azland doesn't laugh. He's broody and dire and—"

It hits me then…the two of them getting closer, him carrying the bags, him informing on us to her. "No way. You two are sleeping together?"

"What?" Kenzie is suddenly invested in the conversation. "Is Jules right?"

"Of course, I'm right."

"Are you?" Anna asks.

Charlie scowls at me as her cheeks mottle pink. "Back yard, now. Go train. This conversation is over."

I laugh and hold up my hands, grinning. "The detective of the year award goes to—drumroll, please—Jules Gagne."

"Out," Charlie sputters, pointing. "All of you out now before I drug your food."

We all head out to the back yard. Tad tugs Kenzie along under protest. Micah and Anna whisper to Sammy, catching her up on the gossip. Zephyr and Briar look worried, and Azland looks much less smug than he did ten minutes ago when he was laughing at me and stirring up shit with Charlie.

"It wasn't nice to embarrass your aunt." Azland gives me a dirty look.

"What goes around, comes around, dude." I grab my leather whip from under the back awning. "If you throw me under the bus, you gotta know I'm dragging you down to get munched under the wheels.

"Besides, Charlie will be fine. Before all this elemental drama, she was one of the funniest, coolest people going. This Poreskoro shit has her wound up so tight she needs a kick in the pants."

He shakes his head. "You're the last person to be giving advice about being a well-adjusted adult."

Rude. "You're stewing for a fight, aren't you?"

He flashes me a cocky grin. "You give yourself too much credit. Maybe you're right, and I'm broody and dire."

"I stand by that. Even as a dog you were growly."

He pulls his shirt off over his head and tosses it. Yeah, I see why Charlie went for the guy. Dark shoulder-length hair, deep teal eyes, and enough planes and ridges to keep the most dedicated topographer busy. "You're mouthy and lazy. You almost got yourself killed yesterday and don't want Charlie to know because you know it'll devastate her. Yet, you still slack off."

I tighten the drawstring in my sweats as my cells fire with energy. "Dude, you're a squatter. You don't get an opinion on my life."

"Do you think I *wanted* to lie on your floor and eat dog food for the last twelve years? Do you have any idea what I've given up for your family?"

I flex my palms and stretch my neck. "You stayed because you felt guilty about getting our parents killed. If you don't want to be here, leave."

"If I didn't think you'd be dead inside of a week, I would. Luckily for the four of you, I give a shit."

My laugh is harsh. "Yeah, lucky us."

He swings his hands across the front of his body and the air at his hip ripples. As he draws his hand back, he's gripping the end of a staff. "I'm coming for you, Jules. Ready your defense, not offense."

"Bring it."

He does.

Whatever bug is up Azland's butt has his boxers in a bunch. The air around me ripples and makes me feel like I'm jogging through water as I defend against his staff.

I singe his hair with a quick volley of fireballs and catch his staff on fire once. He gets more hits than me. He knocks my whip out of my hand, and I have to dive for it. When I rise, I send a wall of flame at him.

"Defense!" he shouts.

The wall of fire extinguishes and he comes at me again. When he's close enough to launch at, I wrap my legs around him and use my searing skin to burn him.

He throws me to the ground and winces at the welting blisters on his bare arms. "For fuck's sake, Jules. That was offense. I said defense."

Kenzie rushes over and heals his burns before he comes at me again. He's so pissed that his eyes are practically glowing. "Stop trying to destroy your enemy. For once, try keeping them away from you."

"Why?"

"Because it's an important skill."

"So is taking down the assholes trying to kill me."

"It's reckless to rush into battle to win at all costs. One day soon, the cost will be too high. You have to know when to fall back and focus on safety."

I stomp to where my whip is lying abandoned in the grass. "That's not how I'm wired."

"Then work on rewiring. If not for yourself, then for the other members of your quartet who are vulnerable when you fight like a banshee instead of a team player."

Seriously? Does he think I'd ever do anything that puts one of them in danger? If he does, he *really* hasn't been paying attention.

I shake out the tension in my arms and grip the whip's hilt. When I untangle it, I send a line of flame down the eight-foot length. It ignites like the wick of a candle and roars and dims at my will.

When Azland comes for me this time, I use my flaming whip to keep him back. "I genuinely don't see the point of this. In a fight against skoro or Poreskoro, retreat weakens our position."

"No. Retreat is a critical skill. It can give you time to get your bearings, make it to Kenzie for healing, or allow you to escape a dire situation."

"What if I don't want to escape?" I demand. "Running from battle isn't my thing."

"Try it sometime. Maybe you won't end up with your essence extracted and lying dead on the sofa." I see the fury in Azland's gaze, but I don't understand it. No matter what self-appointed guardian position he's given himself, my survival is not his problem.

Maybe I need lessons on when to quit, but my fate is not his responsibility.

Before I think of something to say, he rams his fighting staff into the ethereal pocket at his hip and stomps off. "So fucking stubborn."

"Yeah, well, look in the mirror, buddy."

The twins are sitting there with Sammy, mouths open and eyes wide. I wave away their concern before they get upset. "I'm fine. I'm not dead or almost dead. There was a situation, but I couldn't take the safe route while two innocent faeries were being tortured. I'm not going into details with Charlie because it will upset her, and the less you three are dragged into the drama of the empowered world, the better."

They accept that without argument.

"All right, let's do another defense drill." Tad joins me in the open area of the back lawn. "If Azland wants ye to work on retreat and regroup, I'll work ye toward that."

I'm not sure what he means by that, but I don't get a chance to figure it out.

He raises his arms to the side, speaking in Irish tongues. A long vine creeps across the grass from the treed area at the back corner. The green rope whirls and whips around him, slashing thorns at me.

I duck beneath the vine and snap my whip. The vine and the leather tangle and Tad yanks me close. I grapple him to the ground, where I pin him and would have roasted him if this wasn't a training exercise.

Tad chuckles. "Ye have a hard time with the word defense,

don't ye? If I end up on the ground with ye straddlin' my hips, yer still on offense."

"Yeah, well, if a bad guy is trying to take me down and I beat the crap out of him, I'm better off, aren't I?"

"Maybe, or maybe he lured ye in, and now yer in big trouble." Tad's magical signature flares and we're at the top of the Olympic Stadium's mast tower, and I'm dangling five hundred and seventy-five feet in the air.

Wind hits my face, and I clutch Tad's arm around my waist as my stomach drops. He's leaning against the tower's top rail, and I'm outside with my feet dangling in the open air.

"*Tabarnak de câlisse*, get me down."

"If I were your enemy, you'd be dead right now, Jules." In the next second, the two of us portal to the back yard and are on the grass.

I fall to all fours, trying to catch my breath, my pulse thundering in my veins. "Not cool, Irish."

He has the good sense to look abashed. "The point is that if ye come at me, I can use my powers against ye. If ye don't want that, stay outside my reach."

When he lurches forward, I roll out of his way and get to my feet. He comes at me again, and I evade.

Stay out of his reach.

It makes me sick that Matthias and those two skoro got the better of me, but what could I have done to stay out of their reach? In that warehouse, I had no powers. Should I have retreated as soon as I knew that?

Maybe.

Here, I *do* have powers so what can I do to keep him away from me? A fire wall? I tried that against Azland. It would have to be bigger than that.

I call to the flame burning in my cells. I can practically feel the fire inside me crackling with potential energy. Focused on the end game, I command my elemental powers to send the most "get the FUCK away from me!" signal they can come up with.

The eruption of flames feels incredible...

Then I hear pained groans.

I glance down, not surprised that I'm fully aflame. Then I see everyone twisted away and shielding their faces. "Shit. What did I do?"

"Ye feckin' blinded me," Tad yells, doubled over on his hands and knees. "Feckin' hell."

Kenzie runs over and takes his face in her hands. "Stop squirming. I'm here. Let me help you."

"Micah, grab the fire blanket from the garage." Briar points.

"I'm sorry, Irish. I never meant to hurt you."

Sitting back on his heels, he's wincing at the pink sky, blinking as Kenzie's healing water washes his eyes. "Och, I know that, Jules. Give me a moment fer the pain to fade, and I'll forgive ye."

I exhale, grateful he understands.

"Is everyone else all right?" I study the girls and my brothers.

Zephyr nods. "You made the brightest flash of light I've ever seen! It was damn impressive."

"It was like staring at the sun," Briar agrees.

Tad's face is wet and dripping, and pink rims his eyes, but he smiles and gives me a thumbs-up. "That'll get the enemy off yer back for sure. What did ye do?"

"I don't know."

He chuckles. "Aye, ye do. Intention is everything in magic. What were ye thinkin' or feelin' right before ye went supernova?"

I try to focus on the specific seconds right before the big flash. "I felt my fire building, and my temper got away from me. I focused my power on getting you away from me."

Tad chuckles. "I'd say ye did a grand job of it too. Well done, Jules. Ye connected with yer power in a very effective way."

"Here you go." Micah holds up the fire blanket. "Do we need it to put Jules out?"

I laugh. "No, kid. I can put myself out. We need the blanket because I burned up my clothes and once the flames die down, I'll be naked."

He makes a horrendous face, which is also hilarious. "Hard pass on naked sister." He hands Briar the blanket, and he and the girls bolt into the house.

"Come wash up for supper!" Charlie calls. "FYI, we have a guest."

CHAPTER EIGHTEEN

A *guest?* Briar holds the blanket up for me, and as he wraps it around my shoulders, I release my flame.

Kenzie helps Tad up from the grass, brushes off his knees, and slings her arm around his hips.

"I'm so sorry."

Tad blinks and smiles at me. "Don't be. Ye did exactly as I asked and ye did it well. Yer stronger fer it, and that means yer quartet is stronger. S'all good."

He leans to the side and kisses Kenzie's forehead. "I'll never complain about gettin' a little private healin' from yer sister."

Kenzie's laugh is exasperated. "Please don't antagonize Jules into blowing up so we can play doctor. It'll be way sexier if I'm not scared to death."

Tad chuckles. "Point taken."

We head inside and climb the stairs. The spicy seduction of Charlie's chiles rellenos draws us to the kitchen with a buzz of excitement.

Then I see him.

Gareth stands at the window overlooking the backyard

looking all kinds of awkward. He takes in the fire blanket wrapped around me and frowns. "Hey."

"Hey."

"Could I have a moment?"

"Yeah, of course. Do you want to come with me while I find something to wear that won't burn?"

He nods. "Of course."

I lead him past the kitchen to my suite and close the door behind us. Now that he's in my space, I scan my rooms, ensuring there isn't anything overly embarrassing lying around.

Then again, I lay naked in his fireplace for almost sixteen hours. Thinking of that, I turn to him and try to express how much his help means to me. "Thank you. I owe you my life. I realize you don't know me and didn't owe me anything, so I appreciate what you did."

"I was glad to help." He licks his lips and swallows. "That's also why I came."

I sneak a hand out of the seam of the fire blanket and open my closet door, searching for anything that might work. "I'm sorry if my Aunt Charlie embarrassed you. Don't feel like you have to stay for dinner if you have other plans."

"Don't worry. I don't do anything I don't want to."

I give up looking in my closet and stare at my dresser, wondering if I'll have any better luck. "Maybe I'll cut a hole in this blanket and wear it like a poncho."

The corners of his mouth twitch as if he's fighting not to laugh. "There's no need to go poncho."

He unbuttons the black dress shirt he wears over a black T-shirt, and I watch in fascination. What are we doing here? Whatever it is, I can't bring myself to object.

When the buttons are all free, he grips the two sides of the shirt and pulls them free from the tuck of his black jeans. Then, gripping the hem of the T-shirt stretched over his shoulders and chest, he pulls it over his head and hands it to me. "Consider it a slip dress."

I laugh, impressed he knows what a slip dress is.

"Your sister mentioned you haven't sourced out clothing yet. I'll give you the name of my guy."

I chuckle and take the shirt into my bathroom.

Closing the door all but a crack so I can still talk to him, I drop the fire blanket onto the tile floor. The first thing I notice after pulling on his T-shirt is that it's incredibly warm. The next is… "Wow, this fabric is hella soft."

"Soft is nice, but the important thing is that it doesn't burn off your body."

True story.

I free my hair from the T-shirt's collar and flatten the hem against my thighs. It's a little risqué but covers all the bells and whistles.

When I return to my little living room, I meet his gaze. "Now you've had your home invaded, been pressured for dinner, and lost your shirt. All this after you said you didn't want to get involved with my drama."

Gold and scarlet flecks spark in his dark eyes. "That's not what I said."

I'm pretty sure it is, but why argue? "Why did you stop by?"

He draws a deep breath and exhales. "Two reasons. First, I brought the construction materials you need to make your enrichment center in the back yard."

What? "Why would you do that?"

"Because you almost died yesterday and you would have because you're ill-prepared for your new life."

I don't appreciate the edge in his tone. "Like you said, you don't want to get involved."

"That's *not* what I said."

Whatever. Damn it. I feel way too exposed standing here wearing nothing but his T-shirt.

"Not everything you need is available in human construction circles. I have a guy. It was presumptuous of me to move ahead on that for you, but after watching you lie in my fireplace for sixteen hours, I think I've earned an opinion."

It strikes me then that Gareth was alone in here with Charlie. "You didn't mention anything to my aunt about what happened, did you?"

"No. I barely got a word in edgewise, honestly."

Good. Let's keep it that way. "Thank you for the materials. Briar is in construction and has the plans you left us. Let me know how much you spent on the supplies, and I'll reimburse you."

Gareth shrugs. "Whatever. Whenever. I didn't do it to jam you up—"

I sigh, realizing we're pissing one another off. That's not what I intended. Holding up a finger, I draw a deep breath. "Sorry. I'm not the best at peopling, and I'm terrible at accepting help, trusting people, and owing people."

He exhales and shakes his head. "I understand those traits more than you know. You don't have to worry—"

"No, no, I'm not worried. Thank you for going above and beyond. I will pay you back. Now, you said you came for two reasons. What's the second?"

"Come outside, and I'll show you."

I follow him out of my suite, through the kitchen, and down the stairs. I'm about to tell him the shortcut is to use the fireman's pole, but I think better of it.

Gareth doesn't strike me as a pole slider.

I avoid making contact with my family as we pass. When we get outside, he opens his truck's passenger door and points at a large square crate taking up most of the front seat.

A colorful blanket covers the crate, and a muffled shuffling sound comes from inside.

"What on Earth is in there?" I ask.

Gareth looks around and ensures our conversation is private. "This might be way out of bounds, but I brought you something. You read my note about Jinx and her puppies?"

"Yeah, wolfhound on bath salts. I remember."

"Well, I thought since your dog is now your trainer and you're living the shitstorm you are, having one of my pups might be good for you. For all of you."

"You brought me a puppy?"

He lifts the corner of the blanket so I can see a black puppy, about a quarter as big as Backup. His fur is scraggly, and he's a bit wild looking with silver eyes and long matching whiskers.

"He's very cute."

"His name is Onyx. He's a hellhound." My mouth drops open, and he holds up his hand. "Before you say anything, he's not a demon dog or possessed. Not everything from the Hell realm is evil or demonic."

Based on my experience with the skoro and the Poreskoro, I'd have to disagree.

"Hounds are naturally occurring magical creatures that populate certain natural habitats within Hell."

The pup whines and I give him my palm so he can sniff me. His nose is warm and wet, and his tongue is even warmer on my skin.

Gareth is watching intently and exhales. "Good. He likes you."

"And if he didn't?"

"Then giving him to you would be a moot point."

"Why are you giving him to me?"

"Hounds are very protective of their masters and intuitively assess the power signatures and intentions of anyone coming into their territory."

Onyx is on all fours now and is pushing at the cage, his tail wagging. He wants to get out.

"As a creature of the underworld, he can be trained to protect against demons. He would be another line of defense between you and those who threaten your family."

I scrub his wiry face and chuckle. "This little guy is going to defend me against demons?"

"He's not like a human dog, Jules. Hounds are like magically possessed guard dogs on steroids. He'll fight to the death at your side when he's trained, but he'll need a strong hand to train."

"Are you volunteering for the job?"

"I'm not ingratiating myself in your life. I wanted to help you survive what's coming at you."

"You don't want to share your fireplace."

He pegs me with a smoldering look. "It was no hardship to watch over you. I'm only concerned for your safety."

"Why?" I shrug when his brow tightens. "Why do you care what happens to me?"

He bristles at the question. "My reasons are my own. Do you want the pup or not?"

"Of course I do." I open the crate and scoop the bouncy puppy into my arms. "I love him."

"I'll warn you now. He'll get a lot bigger. Eventually, he'll be the size of a large black wolfhound."

I snuggle him in and giggle at how wild and squirmy he is. "Do you want to go meet your new family, Onyx? You do? Of course, you do."

Gareth reaches into the truck and opens the glove box. When he pulls out a pocketknife, I'm not sure what he's thinking.

"What's the blade for, big guy?"

He arches his brow and almost smiles. "A hound is bound to its family by blood."

"Is he part vampire?"

"No, but blood magic is a very common and powerful part of the Hell and Fae realms." He flips the blade open and gestures for me to hold out my hand. I set my hand in his, and he takes it gently but firmly. After making eye contact with me to get my permission, he slices a thin line along the meaty pad of my palm. "Come here, sweet boy."

He guides the dog to my hand, where Onyx laps the wound. Something twinkles in the puppy's silver eyes, and his tail wags as he looks up at me.

When that's taken care of, Gareth runs a hot finger over the cut, and it sizzles as it's cauterized closed. "The rest of your family should do the same. If they are here often or near you, they should become part of Onyx's circle of family."

I look into the dog's swirling silver eyes and wonder what tasting my blood did to secure our bond.

Magic be crazy.

I turn and start for the open door to the garage and turn back. Gareth pulls the crate out of his truck and fills it with a bunch of dog stuff. "Go ahead. I'm right behind you."

I don't need to be told twice.

Barefoot and as excited as a little kid, I pad upstairs. Everyone is standing around, hilariously nonchalant and acting all surprised that I'm back and holding a puppy. "You guys suck. I wanted to surprise you. You were watching us out the window, weren't you?"

Micah has the best poker face, but the rest fail miserably at denying it.

"Fine. This is Onyx. Gareth's hellhound had puppies, and he's going to help us train him to defend our family from evil intent. He's little now, but he'll grow to be another defender of our family."

I kiss the puppy's nose and bend to set him on the floor, realizing too late that Gareth has come in behind me and I've now flashed him my bare ass. Straightening quickly, I spin and pull the hem of his T-shirt down my thighs. "Whoops, sorry about that."

Zephyr snorts. "How's that for a thank you?"

Gareth blinks and clears his throat. "Where do you want his crate set up?"

"How about the reading nook in my room? There's an empty wall, and I could see him from my bed."

"Welcome to the family, Onyx." Anna lifts him to snuggle him.

"We might want to roll up the carpets for a few weeks until he's housebroken," Kenzie observes.

"I can bake him homemade biscuits." Charlie rushes over to get in on the puppy love.

I'm touched by Gareth's thoughtfulness and excited to have a dog again—a real dog this time.

Then something occurs to me.

"How is it that you have a hellhound?"

He strides off with the crate, ignoring my question. I start to follow to ask about Jinx and the other puppies. Then I realize this is a bad idea.

I have to stop asking Gareth questions about his background because he responds badly every time.

Everything he has shared with me proves he's a decent guy, so why do I need to know all the dirty details of what he is and where he's from?

Leaving the puppy fun behind me, I meet him in my room. "Sorry. I don't mean to be a detective all the time. Thank you for helping me. I love my puppy and promise to take good care of him. If you want the boys to help you unload your truck so you can be done with the Gagne hoopla and go, I'll make that happen."

He looks at me, a war of indecision in his gaze. "Am I still invited for dinner?"

"One hundred percent. I don't want you to feel trapped because we need to unload your truck."

He looks at me and nods. "Then we should eat while everything is hot and ready. I'll make sure Onyx settles in and is behaving, and we can unload after dinner if that's all right."

I grab a pair of yoga pants from my dresser and pull them under Gareth's T-shirt. "Sounds perfect."

Dinner is amazing and awkward, and Gareth is as well. When everyone has a full belly, and the dishes are clear, I ask Gareth about feeding Onyx table scraps.

"Hounds can eat dog food from the store in a pinch, but they do better on a carnivorous diet. Food scraps are good, bones, hamburger, whatever you're cleaning out of the fridge that used to be an animal, or…don't be alarmed if he catches squirrels and rabbits in the back yard and eats them."

Kenzie makes a face and glances at Tad's kestrel. "He won't try to eat Aurora, will he?"

Gareth follows her gaze. "No. He'll consider Tad's familiar as a member of the family. He won't eat her."

How crazy is it that we're discussing what my hound puppy will eat in the coming days?

"Thank you for the meal," Gareth says to Charlie. "It was delicious."

When he grabs his keys, I recruit Briar, Tad, Zephyr, and Micah to help us unload his truck. I'm pretty sure Gareth carries twice as much as everyone else, but Tad uses his wayfarer magic and portals things into the backyard super quick.

"Man, there are a shit ton of supplies," Zephyr observes.

Yeah, I'm astounded by everything he brought.

Based on the sanctuary construction plans, this could be everything we'd need.

Man, my earth, wind, and water siblings will be jealous when I have a personal spa all to myself.

I walk him back to his truck when all that is taken care of. "Thank you again."

"Not a problem."

"I'm sorry if I offended you earlier."

"What makes you think that?"

"Because I know I tend to poke at unanswered questions and can tell it's not cool from your end. I'm trying to stop and decided you're not a mystery I need to figure out."

Gareth smiles. "I appreciate that."

"Don't get me wrong. I'm still supremely curious. I have theories, but I'm filing them away until we get to a place where you trust me with your story."

Gareth chuckles and shakes his head. "You're such a detective. The inside of your mind must be a bunch of file cabinets and manila folders."

I grin. "There are some bulletin boards with red string connecting facts too. And probably some childhood memories stuffed in a box somewhere."

"You're so odd." Gareth makes that sound like a good thing.

"Hey, I'm part of an elemental quartet that was hidden and lied to my whole life. Now a rich family of demon hybrids and their black-eyed lackeys is hunting me. Weird doesn't begin to cover it."

"At least your life will never be boring."

I'd take a little boring right about now. "Well, I'm glad we're sorta friends, and I'm grateful for everything you've done for me. I'll try to pay it back by being cool and not trying to dig for stuff you don't want to share."

"Thank you. That means a lot to me." I hear the truth in his words and see it in the muscled frame of his body. His usual stressful aura of being a trapped animal has eased.

"Did you want to come back in for a drink? I should probably change out of your shirt."

He shakes his head. "Keep it. I have a feeling it might come in handy to have something to wear after you flame up."

I'm not about to argue.

He steps around the front of his truck and climbs in. The

engine lets out a throaty rumble, and he lowers the window. "Have a good night. If you have any problems with Onyx, feel free to call me. Your sister has my contact information from when I found you beaten in the park."

I step back as he shifts the truck into reverse. "Okay. Thanks again."

I wave as he drives down the laneway and off the property. One of my favorite parts of the firehouse is having enough land that with the high fences and the shrubs along the front of the property, it feels like we're in our own little world.

When I get back upstairs, Anna and Micah are rolling on the floor with Onyx while Sammy watches. Charlie and Kenzie are playing checkers, and Tad is showing Briar and Zephyr something with his powers and one of our potted plants.

"King me." Kenzie grins.

"Nope, I'll trade you a diagonal instead."

"Why would I want to do that? You already have two kings, plus a queened piece and a court jester."

I laugh. Charlie and Kenzie have their own strange and made-up rules for checkers.

I join the twins, and we take Onyx outside to pee and run off some energy. "Gareth said we'll need to be firm with his training, teach him commands, and get to know his behavioral quirks. Once he's big enough, we can do fighting drills with him in case we end up in a battle together."

Onyx jumps on me, and I fall back, giggling.

It's hard to imagine such a precious little puppy being a killer warrior in a battle. Then again, nothing in the empowered world is ever what it seems.

"Hey guys?"

"Yeah?" Micah pushes Onyx toward Anna.

"You know how things around us are dangerous right now, yeah?"

"Yeah."

"Well, Onyx being a guard dog for our family is based on him bonding with us. Gareth said the best way to ensure he recognizes us as *'his'* is to form a blood bond."

"Like a vampire?" Anna says.

"That was my response too—and no. It's an empowered world thing. So, if you're cool with it, we need everyone to prick their finger and give Onyx a taste."

"That's dark." Micah grins. "I'm totally in."

Anna nods. "Me too. If creepy demon guys come after us, I want Onyx to save me."

"Kid, if creepy demon guys are coming after you, we'll all be there to save you."

She smiles. "I know that."

The three of us get up and run for the back door. Onyx gallops behind us, his massive paws all floppy and awkward.

We race to the top of the stairs like a herd of elephants. Onyx trots in behind us like he's lived here all his life. "Okay, family meeting. Gather 'round. Oh, and Zephyr, can you get your penknife?"

Briar makes a face. "What kind of family meeting needs a penknife?"

I hold my palm out for him to see the sealed cut on the palm of my hand. "The kind that bonds us to a hellhound. Onyx is family now. A family that slays together stays together."

Micah laughs. "We are so weird."

I flash him a smile. "Would you rather be normal?"

"Hell no. Weird is the new cool."

I nod. "Good then, let's welcome a hellhound into our family by sharing our blood with him."

Anna laughs. "We're so freaking cool."

CHAPTER NINETEEN

My alarm goes off too soon, and even though Onyx slept through the night like a champ, I kept waking up to check on him. Honestly, I half expected him to whimper and cry, missing his *maman*. Maybe things don't work like that in Hell.

My bad. I give Jack and Jack their morning fish flakes and check the crate. Onyx is still snoring away, his snowshoe-sized paws twitching with his dream hunt.

So. Damn. Cute.

Last night, my little hound spent a few minutes making noises as he shuffled around in his crate getting comfy with his toy, then he settled into a soft snore.

I take a quick shower, get dressed, and open Onyx's crate. "Are you ready for a quick trip outside and some breakfast, puppy?"

Onyx offers me a jaw-cracking yawn and stretches his paws. Then, he gets up, and the two of us are off like a shot out of a gun.

The first order of business is to run the fence line of the back yard and confirm that everything is where he left it last night. When that's done, he makes a second round and marks his territory. After the third round, I call him back inside and upstairs for breakfast.

Gareth left some puppy chow and a couple of pounds of hamburger, so I read the label on the food and put down what I think he'll eat.

He gets his long, scraggly ears in the food and makes a huge mess spilling it all over the tile, but even that is adorable. Suddenly, Tremblay's stories about his dog make much more sense. Could Tremblay love Oscar like I love Onyx?

In answer, my boy lifts his shaggy muzzle out of his water bowl and waterfalls puddle all over the tile.

No way. Onyx is one of a kind.

Once we've both had our breakfast, I take him out for another ten minutes in the back yard before I go to work.

Tad is out doing Tai Chi with Aurora. As he stretches and moves in the controlled positions, his long limbs flowing over the grass in slow, graceful sweeps, Aurora swoops and dives around him.

Onyx interrupts by barking and running beneath the bird. Aurora disappears into a tall tree with an angry squawk.

"Sorry we disturbed you."

Tad chuckles. "Ye didn't. I sensed yer wee lad comin' before ye got here. He's got quite a strong spirit."

It's crazy that I'm already a proud *maman* and I've only had him for twelve hours. "Hey, I've got to go to work. I can put him in his crate, but if you're going to be around today would you mind if I left him out?"

"Are ye askin' me to watch the pup because I'm a druid or because I'm the only one awake right now?"

"Both. If it's a problem, I can put him back."

"Och, no. It's no problem. I'll keep an eye on the pup fer ye. Make sure to watch yer back on the streets. Safe home, lass."

"Thanks, I'll do my best."

My first stop is the morgue to drop off the sample kits to Luc. He's delighted my siblings agreed and excited to start his side hustle experiments. So much so that I'm glad I'm not waiting for any pathology reports today because Luc is focused on elemental biology.

My next stop is the press conference at City Hall.

Even though it was my idea and I helped make all the arrangements, I'm happy not to be in the spotlight on this one.

"Hey, you look good," Rene observes as I shuffle to my place in the back of the crowd. "Did you do something to your hair? It looks different."

I touch my hair, remembering that Kenzie used her healing waters to make it all healthy and shiny yesterday. "Oh. That was my sister and one of her special water treatments."

Rene's brows arch, and he gives me an approving smile. "You can tell her it turned out well."

I tousle my hair, now self-conscious about being looked at—especially by Rene.

Someone wearing a headset and carrying a clipboard shushes me and takes Rene by the arm, leading him up to the podium.

Mayor Clarissa Tremblay—a cousin to Guy Tremblay in my office—stands at the podium looking distinguished in a deep purple skirt and jacket with a pale ivory blouse. When the awakenings started happening, some officers in the department doubted she had the balls to ride this out.

When her adopted daughter had an awakening, she became as devoted to fae empowerment as anyone could've hoped for. She was the one who first invited Fiona Cumhaill and her team to Montréal.

If not for that, who knows how different my life would be right now?

Rene shakes hands with Police Chief Thomas Monet, and the two of them strike a formal pose, standing behind the mayor.

The chattering of reporters and the *click* of their cameras become a mashup of white noise as everyone waits for the press conference to begin.

I scan the logos on the microphones and cameras assembled, pleased that this message will be airing on all the local television networks and radio channels in Montréal as well as the surrounding regions of Quebec.

Hopefully, that will save at least a few people.

One of Mayor Tremblay's aides raises her hand. *"Bonjour, tout le monde.* Hello, everyone. We're ready to begin."

The crowd hushes.

Mayor Tremblay smiles at the audience here and through the cameras. "Good morning, everyone. Last night, Police Chief Monet's office contacted me to inform me of an alarming discovery affecting our fair city's citizens."

She lifts her chin, staring directly into the camera lenses. "Five bodies have been flagged in the coroners' office within the past four days. In each case, the cause of death has been conclusively attributed to the currently popular feel-good drug, Second Sight."

She pauses while the crowd's rumbling dies down. "While the drug was rumored to be safe, our labs have now proven that repeated use causes cumulative damage on a cellular level. Our scientists are seeing unnatural fae mutations that are resulting in death."

A reporter's hand shoots up. "When you say fae mutations, are you talking about awakenings?"

"No. This is something entirely different. The drug is physically altering human cells until the host body dies."

There's a rush of questions, and she holds up her hand to stop the barrage. "In each of the five deceased, the coroners have found these bright pink striations on the victims' fingernails. If you or anyone you know has these markings, we encourage you to call the fae task force and ask to speak to a liaison."

She gives out the number and introduces Police Chief Monet to speak. "We take this threat very seriously and urge everyone else to do the same. Second Sight is not only an illegal narcotic. It is killing our citizens. Help us stop the distribution and sale of the drug. Help us save lives. If you have any information that will help us, we urge you to come forward."

I'm not hopeful anyone will, but you never know.

"Your city's leadership remains committed to addressing the complex issues of drug addiction as well as the integration of newly empowered citizens within our community," Mayor Tremblay finishes. "If you have any questions, Police Chief Monet and Inspector Rene Michaud of the Fae Liaison Task Force will be able to give you more information. Thank you. *Merci*."

As the room bursts into questions from the audience, I slip out into the hall. It's good that there are people like Rene who don't mind being in front of the camera.

That's not me.

Even before wanting to stay out of the spotlight I never wanted to be the center of attention.

"Inspector Gagne!" Mayor Tremblay's voice echoes in the open atrium of the City Hall. She waves as she approaches. The *clack, clack, clack* of her high heels beat out a steady rhythm. "Could I have a moment?"

"*Oui*, Madame Mayor."

She gestures for me to join her and we walk into the reception area for the post-meeting debrief. "It's nice to see you again, Inspector. Come, grab yourself something to eat."

The mayor selects a set of stainless steel tongs and moves a turkey club and some vegetables onto a plate. "How have you been since last we spoke?"

The last time we spoke was a couple of weeks ago when I phoned her late one evening while pressuring a guy on the street to talk. Using my connection to the mayor's office was the leverage I needed to get one step closer to tracking down the manufacturing plant of Second Sight.

Is that what this is about?

"I'm sorry about that, Mayor. I shouldn't have called your direct line so late. I was…"

She shakes her head. "No, no. That's fine. I could tell you were working an angle. I hope having me on the other end of the phone helped your cause."

"It did, thank you."

"I hear you've been an integral part of the investigation into Second Sight and its effects on the city's citizens."

"It's a team effort, but yes, we've been chasing down leads with the help of the coroner's office and Rene's team."

"Yes, Rene mentioned you've been collaborating with the liaison task force, but you haven't officially joined them. Is that correct?"

"*Oui, Madame.* I remain a detective of the Twenty-Third Precinct."

"Have you considered making this collaboration permanent? Rene mentioned he's spoken to you about the idea. I'd love to see you two working the task force full time."

"He has spoken to me about it, yes."

She's studying me as we speak and nods. "Then I'll leave you to think about it. We'd love to have you."

"*Merci, Madame.*" I nibble the edge of my peanut butter cookie. "Thank you for helping us get our message out. It was the best way we could think of to reach the people."

"Now to see if anyone was listening."

I smile, and her assistant sidles up to us with a man in a suit at her side. "Madame Mayor, may I interrupt?"

I nod and step back. "Of course. Lovely to speak with you as always, Madame Mayor."

As much as I love my team and the work we do at the

Twenty-Third Precinct, I've been thinking more and more lately about joining Rene's task force.

The more I realize the dangers of what's out there against the citizens of Montréal, the more I feel like the constraints of our human police force can't straddle that expanse.

"Whoa," Luc says when I push through the double doors into his lab. "I was about to call you." Then his eyes go wide. "Wait! Are you getting psychic powers now, too? What am I thinking?"

"I shudder to guess. No, I left the press conference at the City Hall and thought I'd stop in on the way to the precinct to let you know you might get calls from reporters wanting to expand on our findings on Second Sight."

"What you're saying is that I'm a celebrity now."

"Nope. I wasn't saying that at all." I yawn and wander past the two bodies on Luc's tables. "Either of these Second Sight?"

"Not unless the fae drug inspired him to shoot himself with a harpoon gun and her to be standing in a puddle of antifreeze while fiddling with an electrical short in her garage."

"Ouch."

"Yeah." He peels off his gloves and grabs a file off his desk to bring to me. "Wait. Why do you look so tired? Are you on the stride of pride?"

"The what?"

"It's like the walk of shame, but hello—why be ashamed—so, it's the stride of pride. You look like you were up all night."

"I was. Just without the sex."

"Disappointing."

"For you and me both."

He chuckles. "What kept the sandman at bay?"

"I am now the proud owner of a baby hellhound and last night was his first night in our home."

"A hellhound?" Luc seems as excited about that as when he thought I was psychic. "Tell me everything. Where do you get a hellhound? Did you go to Hell? People have told me to go to Hell and that I'm going to Hell, but if they give you puppies, how bad could it be?"

Only Luc. "He was a gift from a friend who wanted to help protect my family from a demon attack. Hounds are protective and make good guard dogs."

"How could they not?" He stands there for a minute, staring off into the distance, and I can see by his expression that he has mentally checked out completely, dreaming up some craziness in his mind.

I wave in front of his face. "Hello, Luc? You said you were about to call me about something. Does that mean you have something to tell me?"

He blinks and shakes himself back to the moment at hand. "Right. I was spending some quality time with Teresa and your lab samples, and I noticed something super cool yet unique."

"Awesome. Try to keep the science babble to a minimum. I'm tired and cranky."

"Got it. Please pull up your patience panties. I promise it'll be worth it in the end." Without awaiting a response, he grabs a pile of glossy photos and lays them across the white sheet covering the dead harpoon victim.

I stare at him. "He's not a table."

"He's also not going to object. Now, hush your face and learn something."

There's no arguing, so I let him do his thing.

"Okay, so to dumb it down for you, the cells of a healthy fae have these extra little fringy bits on the edges there. Non-magical human cells don't have nearly as many of them. See?"

"Uh-huh. What are they?"

"We call them chemoreceptors. They sense chemical signals from the environment around them. These other little guys in between them are called signal cells. They create and send out chemical signals."

"What do you mean, chemical signals?"

"You know about pheromones?" Luc asks.

"Sure, it's a chemical released by the body that elicits a biological response to others."

"Very good, sasshopper."

"Yeah, Kenzie read a girly magazine about how to choose the right perfume for your pheromones and was spritzing and sniffing me for weeks."

"Did she do your hair? It looks nice."

Damn, what's with men complimenting my hair? I might not put much effort into it, but it's always clean and never a rat's nest or anything.

I'm getting a complex.

"Back on topic. What about the fringy bits leads us to the pheromone conversation?"

Luc laughs. "Okay. So, you know how fae prana is flowing freely and is in the St. Lawrence and making the sky pink and everything?"

"Yes."

"Well, I think I've identified the mechanism within a fae's body that radiates the chemical signal of your magic. Does that make sense?"

"I think so. You think you've pinpointed our fae pheromone release thingy."

"Right."

"How and why does that help us?"

"Because I think that's how Second Sight works. We know it's laced with magic, and I think it changes the chemical receptors in a user's eyes so they can 'see' the fae pheromones released from a magical person's body. They see the aura, and they peg them as fae."

"Awesome. You rock my socks, Leclerc."

Luc bows, his long chestnut hair falling into his face. "I also think that's why skoro have such a strong odor of burned cookies."

"Because they have baked pheromones from Hell?"

He makes a face. "No. Because they are conjured through another, more powerful being's fae energies. The Poreskoro Six—"

"Four."

"No, it was The Six that consumed the power of the elemental kingdoms and spawned an army. They aren't the parents of their soldiers. They are the creators."

"And the burned cookie smell?"

"It's the same idea. It's the radiation of their cells emitting the chemical signal, but it's more pronounced because they aren't organically occurring beings."

"You're about to lose me again," I warn.

"Trust me. It's the same yet different. The important part is that whether it's skoro or Poreskoro or prejudiced assholes in the street, Second Sight detects the fae energy coming off you. It allows others to see it visually or sense it in the air, but the result is the same—it allows them to target you."

"What do we do about it?"

Luc grins and waggles his brows. "Thank you for asking, young lady. Luc the Magnificent has figured out a way to mask the energy radiating off fae cells so they are no longer detectable."

"Like a body shield?"

"Nothing as bulky as that. I have come up with what I think could be a fae pheromone inhibitor. It won't prevent you from accessing your magic, but will ensure it doesn't call unwanted attention."

"A fae pheromone inhibitor," I repeat. "That sounds complicated."

"Complicated is my jam." Luc shows me a bunch of graphs

covered in scribbled notes, diagrams, and equations. "I've been working on the science, but I also need a magical component. If I can speak with someone who wields magic, we can make this idea a reality."

"Wields magic how? What kind of person?"

He shrugs. "That's more a *you* question than a *me* question. I'm thinking a witch or a wizard or a sorcerer. Someone who understands the magic side of things."

"I know someone. Back when Rene and I worked with Tad's Toronto team, Fiona introduced us to a white witch named Emerald Moon. She has a lavender farm and a little shop on St. Jesus Island in the rural lands of Laval. She might be able to help."

"Excellent. Make it so, Number One."

I laugh. "What am I making so?"

"For sure a conversation, maybe a meet-up, and if things go well, maybe dinner and a movie?"

I laugh. "If the date goes badly, you'll end up a frog hopping around in someone's koi pond."

He makes a face. "Good point. A phone or video call will be fine."

CHAPTER TWENTY

The next morning, I'm awoken at an ungodly hour by a crashing noise. Thinking that maybe we've been invaded by skoro again, I roll off my bed, press my thumb onto the security pad of my gun safe, and retrieve my Glock.

I race out of my rooms. Fortunately, the mess that greets me is not exactly demonic in origin.

It is, however, demon adjacent.

Onyx is racing around the living room with a package of bacon in his mouth, trying to munch on the pieces that are falling out.

The fridge is open, and Aurora is perched on the top of the door preening herself.

"Onyx! No! Naughty!" I chase him, but he's fast and committed to hanging on to his bacon. It doesn't take long before Briar jogs out with his fist hardened into a club. "A little help here?"

Seeing what's going on, Briar releases his stone fist and joins the hellhound scramble. Between the two of us, we corner him better. Briar rips the package of bacon out of the puppy's mouth, and Onyx goes from defense to offense.

Jumping up and snapping his teeth, I get my first view of what our hound will be like once he grows into his protector role—because right now, he's passionately protective of his bacon.

Briar hardens up again to keep from getting bitten.

Onyx crouches, dropping to his elbows on his front paws. He barks twice, low warning growls rolling out of him as his eyes glow scarlet.

"That's creepy as fuck." Briar hands me the slobbery bacon. "I'm out."

Yep. I'm not gonna sugarcoat it...my puppy might be possessed. Then I remember what Gareth said.

"He's not like a human dog, Jules. Hounds are like magically possessed guard dogs on steroids. He'll fight to the death at your side when he's trained, but he'll need a strong hand to train."

Right. He needs a strong hand to train.

Holding my finger up, I call flame to my hand. "Listen here, Mr. Man. You've made a mess and been naughty about listening. Lay there and be a good boy while I clean this up and I'll consider giving you back the bacon. If you're bad, I'll throw it out."

I have no idea if our blood bond translates to him understanding a word I'm saying, but he settles on his belly, curls his tail around his butt, and stops growling.

"Good boy. Now, stay there and be good."

I set the bacon in the sink while assessing the kitchen mess. "Aurora, did you open the fridge door?"

Aurora flaps her wings, screeches, and flies off to her perch.

"What on earth is happening out here?" Kenzie is awake, her naturally blue body wrapped in a burgundy silk robe. "Did Zephyr have a nightmare?"

"No, the animals were up to no good." I can see Tad draped in the sheets through Kenzie's open bedroom door. "I think Aurora is causing trouble. My guess is she's bored, lonely, and jealous."

"Jealous? I thought she was adjusting well."

"Well, one of them caused this, and while Onyx was enjoying the aftermath, I think Aurora is the brains of the operation."

"Blaming the bird is bad form," Tad shouts from inside the bedroom. "Yer pup is a creature from Hell. Which do you think is more prone to chaos?"

"All of you, shut the fuck up!" Zephyr's voice booms from his bedroom. "Some of us need beauty sleep!"

I laugh. "You could sleep for days, and it wouldn't help your ugly mug."

A freezing wind blows through the house, raising the hair on my arms and rattling the windows.

Zephyr isn't amused.

Kenzie and I get the kitchen cleaned quickly enough, and she goes back to bed. I take the mangled bacon to Onyx's bowl and forgive him for his primal impulse to covet the meat.

"You stayed a good boy while I cleaned up. Here's your reward. Next time, let's do without the demonic eyes and growling."

I leave him chomping up the raw bacon and wash my hands in the kitchen sink. Since I'm up, I might as well get started with my day.

After a quick shower and an extra treat for Jack and Jack to thank them for never making a mess of the house or waking me up, I check my phone.

There's a message from Rene.

I check my watch, and while it's still before seven, he sent me a "Are you up?" ten minutes ago, so he's up and working.

I hit the phone icon and call him. "Good morning. It looks like the early birds are getting all the worms today. What can I do for you?"

"Good morning to you too." His voice is deep from sleep. "I got an email during the night from the cryptologist working on those codes we found on the edge of the maps you and Tad recovered from the food truck warehouse."

"Oh great! What did they find?"

"Unfortunately, nothing conclusive. They think they represent numbers, but without the key code, there's no way to know what numbers or what they mean."

Disappointing. "Not the best way to start our day."

He chuckles. "Sorry about that. I'll try harder."

"Do that. Otherwise, we should go back to bed and call it a day before it even begins."

"That sounds a little defeatist. I'm sure we can turn things around."

I chuckle. "All right. I'll hold you to that. Are you heading in early?"

"Yeah. I'm leaving in ten."

"You going through the Tim's drive-through?"

"Yep. What do you want?"

"Green tea and a breakfast sandwich on a biscuit."

"You got it. See you there."

When I arrive in the small meeting room, Rene is already there, my tea and biscuit are on the table, and he's lost in the paperwork spread around the room.

"Anything new popping out at you?" I pull my breakfast sandwich out of the brown paper bag.

"Nothing earth-shattering, no. How do you feel about running down some fae liaison stuff today?"

"Is this your way of luring me to the dark side?"

"No. Once this Second Sight bullshit is over, I promise I'll let you go back to your regular precinct work. For now, I'd love to have you on this instead."

"What's the assignment?"

"I have two things I want your attention on, both related. First, about your idea to make a private fae website where other magical folks can connect. I think it would also be a great resource for the task force. Are you still planning to make that happen?"

"Yeah. I meant it to be a personal side project for elementals, but if you want to expand the objective and put me to work on it while I'm on the clock, I won't complain."

"Excellent."

I pop the last bite of my sandwich in my mouth and reach for the stack of napkins. "And the second thing?"

"That relates to the other elementals in the area."

"Yeah? What about them?"

"Have you reached out to any of the names on the list I gave you?"

"No. I haven't had a chance. Kenzie and I were going to contact them when we had the website up and running so we could connect. Tad was concerned that having too many elementals in one place would invite skoro violence."

"I hear what you're saying, but leaving them alone in the city without connecting them and explaining the skoro and Poreskoro situation is equally dangerous."

Yeah, I suppose. "I don't suppose you have another copy of that list, do you?"

He snags a piece of paper off the top of a pile and hands it to me. "Take your sister too, if you'd like. She's engaging and disarming."

I snicker. "And the subtext there is that I'm not? Is that what I'm hearing?"

"I never said anything like that." He flashes a teasing smile.

"Fine, I'll ask her." I fold up his list and stick it in my pocket, then text the family group chat, letting them know we have a Team Gagne project to get started on.

After making sure Marx, Reese, and the guys know I'm on loan to the fae liaison squad, I zip home to find Tad and Zephyr in the living room waiting for me.

Zephyr has his old gaming computer set up on a card table against the living room wall. He's brought out two monitors, has his light-up keyboard plugged into it, and a rat's nest of wires cascading onto the floor.

"What's the plan?" Tad untangles loose cables.

I explain to them about the website and how it needs to be easy for folks with magical powers to navigate once they're there but secure enough to keep it from becoming an accidental fae honeypot.

"We'll get started." Zephyr taps away on the keyboard. "You might want to go check on Briar in the yard."

"Why? What's he doing out there?"

"He's laying out the plans for your magma pit."

"Oh, awesome. Yeah, you boys get started, and I'll be back." I clap and call for Onyx to come, but he must already be outside because he doesn't respond.

Briar and Gareth discussed the positioning of my sanctuary while we unloaded his truck last night. My brother has taken that to heart and then some.

"Wow, look at you go." I scan the massive change in landscaping already completed.

Briar grins at me and waggles his eyebrows. "I fucking love my powers."

I can see why. He's created a ten-foot-by-twelve-foot pit in the lawn and piled the displaced dirt around the back half of the empty pool like a retaining wall.

"Onyx seems to be enjoying them too." I laugh at our puppy chest deep in dirt, digging and flicking soil in the air, having the time of his life.

"He's going to need a bath."

"Maybe Kenzie can give him a power bath."

Briar grins. "Nice. I bet she'll love that."

"That lets us off dog-washing duty."

"Even better."

The two of us watch him having fun for a few more minutes before I get back to it and point at the work Briar's been doing. "What are you thinking here?"

"Honestly, we could do a lot with the plans Gareth gave us. You could have a lavafall over rocks back there and maybe some stone pillars and a wooden trellis above for privacy."

"That sounds great, but I don't need it to be crazy elaborate. I need a way to recharge my energy so I don't end up naked in Gareth's fireplace every ten minutes."

Briar chuckles. "I didn't hear him complaining."

I roll my eyes. "He said he wasn't interested in me and my elemental drama."

Briar shakes his head. "Why is it women always hear something other than what a guy actually says?"

"We don't. That's your testosterone talking."

"No, it's the fact that I was listening when he stormed off the other night. He said that something about what was going on between the two of you was a mistake and that he *couldn't* get involved. He didn't say he didn't want to get involved but that he couldn't."

I meet Briar's blue-green gaze. "Why couldn't?"

"How am I supposed to know? You're the detective."

"Well, one of the last things I said to him last night was that I was done trying to solve the mystery of him."

"How did he respond to that?"

I think back to that conversation and my curiosity amps up another couple of notches. "He was relieved, actually...like, really relieved."

Briar studies the palm of one of his massive hands and brushes off some imaginary dirt. "It's your business, Jules, but I think there's a lot more in the column of things you *don't* know about Gareth than things you *do*. Maybe that should be an indicator for you to keep your guard up. Papa always said rushing makes for ruin."

Yeah, that was one of his go-to fatherly phrases.

"I admit, the idea that he has fire powers and knows things I don't about how to survive is a huge draw, but I hear you. I have my shields up."

Briar chuckles and shakes his head. "There go your woman listening skills again. That's not what I said, but what you think I said."

I wave it off. "Back to the topic at hand. Sure, add cascading lava and pillars and whatever you want, but please consider how long it will take to finish if you do. Danger seems intent on stalking us, and I'd like my elemental spa up and running so I can be in top form when it comes to breathe down our necks."

"I hear you loud and clear, sista." Briar makes a few notes, crossing things out and comparing them to Gareth's plans. "Fast and fabulous, coming up."

I pat Onyx, tell him I love him, and leave him and Briar to their work.

"Everything all right out there?" Zephyr asks when I return. Neither he nor Tad looks up from their screen, intent on what they're doing.

"Of course. Briar rocks. He made this whole firehouse into a great living space for us, and with his powers, the landscaping part of the project is already done."

Tad nods. "I'll see if I can help him with anything after we finish here."

"Thanks. Hey, do you know what time Kenzie is getting home? I have an empowered errand, and I thought she might like to come with me."

"She's at work until three," Zephyr says. "She said she's coming home early from the courthouse and will finish up with some files here later tonight."

"Okay, that should still work." I step in and look at what they've gotten done. "How's it going?"

"It's still a bit janky, but we decided to use several private

Discord channels instead of a website. The pretty will come later. Right now, look at the channels we built. For the main fae group, we have an awakening chat room, one where we can post empowered news, and one for community resources. Then, we have a private Discord channel for elementals."

I lean close to see what that one entails. "Oh, you've already got training tips and videos."

Zephyr nods. "A few basic self-defense videos and a help room to request help if anyone feels like they're being stalked or targeted."

Tad shifts the mouse and clicks into the resources channel. "We also uploaded the elemental sanctuary designs and subdivided them by fire, earth, air, water, and spirit."

"I wonder if Azland is right and he's the only—or one of the only—spirit elementals left."

"There could be a secret pocket of survivors. Bakkali might know more."

"Speaking of Bakkali, do you think we should let him know we're doing this?"

Tad shrugs. "Maybe. Why don't we set it up first, contact the folks ye know about, work out the kinks, then expand."

"Sounds good. Also, I think we need two more sections. One where they can connect confidentially with the fae liaison task force, and one where we can swap sightings and collect information about skoro and other bad guys."

"Done." Zephyr taps on the keyboard, and I see two new sections pop up on the channel list.

I make everyone afternoon pizza bagel bites while they work. Half an hour later, Kenzie gets home.

"Looking good, Counselor." Tad winks at her.

She leans into her suite, kicks off her heels, and tosses her briefcase onto the chair inside her door. Padding over to us, she tugs on the elastic holding her braids back and lets her chestnut hair fall free.

As she approaches, she drops the glamor that reinstates her human African-Canadian complexion and assumes her true elemental pale blue skin tone.

I'm proud of her. She's getting more comfortable in her true form and is learning to accept who she was born to be.

"How was your day?" I offer her the last pizza bagel.

"Good. Court went well this morning, I got a nod from my boss, and the new case they assigned me seems straightforward."

"Excellent. You deserve a day of wins."

"Thanks. Why are you looking at me like you want a favor?"

"Not a favor, exactly. I thought you might be interested in tag-teaming with me on something. Feel free to opt out."

I spend the next few minutes explaining to her about the other elemental fae Rene is aware of and how he asked us to visit them, knowing how secretive we need to be with skoro and Poreskoro in the city actively seeking them out.

"Sounds fun," Kenzie says.

CHAPTER TWENTY-ONE

As it turns out, Tad accompanies Kenzie and me under the guise of thinking it a proactive measure to have visited the homes of the other elementals in case there is ever an emergency, and he needs to portal us. There's no arguing that, so the three of us zip off in Kenzie's electric car toward the first address on Rene's list.

"Gabrielle Turell," I read out loud. "She lives with their mother near Shaughnessy Village."

"Wait a minute." Kenzie glances sideways at me. "Gabrielle Turell—I know her."

"You do? How?"

She shakes her head. "I don't mean I know her personally, but I've heard of her. Remember? The Montréal Miracle?"

I haven't the foggiest idea what she's talking about. "Nope. I've got nothing."

Kenzie rolls her eyes at me. "You really ought to read more. Years ago, probably around the time *Maman* took me in, someone left a baby at the Notre Dame Basilica. No note. No nothing. She was left in the church during the funeral of Jean-Claude Turell, a wealthy businessman."

"Abandoned during a funeral?"

"Yeah. Well, the widow took it as a sign from her dead husband that the child had been left so she would never have to be alone. The couple had tried for years to conceive, but they weren't able to have kids. Don't you remember?"

"If it was when you came to live with us, I wasn't even two. No. I don't remember."

Kenzie groans. "Obviously I don't remember *Maman* watching it on the news, but every few years, the local media does an update on the Montréal Miracle. Last I heard, I think the mother needed heart surgery."

"This is why I pay no attention. They're two people living normal lives. Sure, it's great that they found one another and the child got adopted, but if that makes them newsworthy for the next twenty-five years, aren't the four of us Montréal Miracles too?"

She shrugs. "I'm just saying she's famous."

"Let's hope not too famous to speak to us."

We pull up to the address, a lovely estate home in an older part of Montréal. It doesn't scream famous kid rescued from a church or anything. It's a well-kept home in an affluent neighborhood.

Hopefully, that's an indicator that they are ordinary people and this isn't going to get weird.

Kenzie parks along the curb and the three of us get out and walk the long driveway before taking the stone path toward the front door.

"Check out the door knocker." Kenzie points at the elaborate silver snake perched on the door at eye level. It's coiled around a silver plate mounted to the door, its tail looping down to form the handle of the knocker.

"Creepy AF." I lift the metal ring and—*"Tabarnak!"*

I wrench my hand back as the snake strikes. Its fangs have dropped, and it's poised in the air, hissing and ready to attack.

Flame bursts out of my palm and I smack the stupid thing against the door. It *clunks* against the strike plate, hissing and flicking its silver tongue at me.

Tad steps in beside me and says something in Irish, a rush of energy hitting the snake as he holds his palm out to cast.

The creepy accessory has the good sense to retreat, curling into the shape of a door knocker once more and going motionless.

A moment later, the door opens, and a woman in her midsixties looks out at us with suspicion. "Who are you?" she asks in French, staring at my flaming hand.

I release my flames and clasp my hands at my back. "I'm Inspector Juliette Gagne of the *Service de police de la Ville de Montréal*. This is my sister Kenzie, and this is our friend Tad McNiff. Are you Madame Turell?"

The woman glares at me and scans Kenzie and Tad. "Why do you want to know?"

"Because as you might know, there are a great many dangers in the world of fae awakenings, and we were sent here to speak to your daughter to ensure she is safe and well-informed."

She turns her head and frowns. "You're from the Guild of the Laurentians, then?"

I shake my head. "No, Madame. I'm representing the fae liaison's office, the task force run by Mayor Tremblay."

She looks me over and sighs. "All right. Come in."

The inside of the house could double as a museum. She leads us to the living room. The blue velvet couch is surrounded by, among other things, two antique end tables, a stained glass floor lamp, a massive oil painting that looks like it might be one of the masters, and a marble-topped sofa table with crystal decanters of booze.

I take out the card with the contact information for the fae liaison task force and hand it to her. "We came to speak to your daughter about being an elemental, but if you're aware of the

Guild of the Laurentians, perhaps you've already had a visit about her safety?"

The woman nods. "When Gabrielle fell ill last month, a close friend of mine realized she was suffering from an awakening in distress. He called a leader of his community, and a man named Bakkali visited with two colleagues. They helped Gabrielle through her difficulties, set us up with protection, and have been mentoring her on her heritage and its dangers."

"They set up the magic snake door knocker?"

"*Oui*, among other things."

She leaves that hanging. I get the sense I'm supposed to find the mystery of possible security measures intimidating. I don't, but hey, I'll give her a point for effort.

"Is your daughter home? We'd love to meet her."

"Why?"

I hold up my hand and release my flames again. With a look from me, Kenzie releases her glamor, and her skin goes blue. "Aside from working with the fae liaison task force, we are also elementals, like Gabrielle. We simply want to talk to her about what that means and what she might face."

After another scrutinizing once-over, Madame Turell presses a button on the wall next to the room's entrance. "Gabrielle, would you mind joining me in the living room, *ma chère*? You have guests."

An athletic blonde woman Kenzie's age joins us a moment later. She has her hair pulled back in a sporty ponytail and is wearing capri jeans and a cute knit top.

Upon seeing Kenzie, she raises her eyebrows. "You're blue."

"And you're Montréal Miracle," Kenzie shoots back.

Gabrielle nods. "My apologies. I didn't mean to ruffle your feathers. How can I help you?"

I take the lead on that. "We wanted to introduce ourselves and leave you with some information about being elementals in the city. I'm Jules, and this is Kenzie, my adopted sister."

"You're elementals as well?"

I nod. "I'm a fire elemental from the kingdom of Lasair, and Kenzie is a water elemental, originally from Uisce."

She smiles politely and turns to Tad. It's not surprising she noticed him. He could seriously be a European runway model. "And you are?"

"I'm Tad McNiff."

"Which element do you represent?" A warm, honey tone fills her question.

"Och, I'm not an elemental, lass. I'm a druid. I'm here as a friend and to lend a hand if any difficulties should arise."

It's hard to say whether him talking about difficulties or hearing him speak in his Irish lilt has her swooning.

She sits and gestures for us to do the same. I perch on the edge of the museum furniture, and I'm suddenly worried about whether or not my butt is clean or if I might have dog fur on my pants.

"Have you had any trouble since your powers awoke?" I ask.

"No. Nothing beyond becoming accustomed to such a bizarre twist to my life. Taryn, my trainer, warned me about the men who feed on fae energy, but I keep to myself and haven't had any issues."

"Which element are you?"

She extends her finger toward the crystal vase of cut flowers on the side table, and the blooms expand and become even more full and colorful. "Earth."

"Ye have a fair grasp on yer gift," Tad notes. "I felt yer intention there. The strength of yer energy signature is quite pure and strong."

"Thank you. It's sweet of you to say so."

I can practically feel the air getting cooler around us.

Kenzie offers her a sweet smile. "Jules and I are sisters, and we have two adoptive brothers who possess wind and earth."

"There are four of you?"

"Yes. From what we've learned, although elementals are rare, the magic of our existence seems to gather and build groups of us. There were originally five elemental groups, so some are quintets, but since there are almost no spirit magic elementals surviving, quartets are more common.

"Have you found you're drawn to anyone else that's had an awakening?" Kenzie asks.

She shakes her head, her ponytail flipping from side to side behind her as she moves. "I've always been private. I don't go out much, and I don't have a large circle of friends."

"That's fine. The important thing is that you have a mentor, you're aware of the dangers, and you're training to defend yourself."

"My training only started three weeks ago. I'm not sure I could say I can defend myself," Gabrielle admits.

Madame Turell clucks her tongue. "Maybe not yet, but you work hard, and soon you will be."

Gabrielle chuckles and waves away her mother's praise. "I'm fine if I never have to test that theory. I work online, and our cook buys most of the groceries. I don't need to leave the house much."

Being a shut-in elemental is a great way to stay safe.

"Did your mentors tell you anything about the benefit of having a recharging station?"

She nods. "The guild sent over a sanctuary designer. We picked out a few things to build in the backyard. They broke ground a couple of days ago."

I look at Kenzie and shrug. "Well, all right. It sounds like you've got things well in hand. I gave your mother a card for the fae liaison, but I'll give you mine as well. My brother and Tad have been putting together a private Discord server for elementals so we can share experiences and alert one another if anything dangerous comes up. I have your email. If it's all right with you, I'll have him send you an invitation."

"*Oui, merci.* That sounds interesting."

"Well, it was wonderful to meet you. Let's stay in touch, and if you ever need help, call my cell and we'll be there."

The next address on Rene's list is The Grey Nun Café. It has a hipster vibe with flower boxes and outdoor lounges out front and jazz music playing softly over the speakers. The interior smells like pumpkin spice lattes and freshly baked cookies. If we weren't here for a purpose, I'd grab a table and order something.

Guaranteed it would be better than pizza bagel bites.

"Do they work here?" Tad asks.

"According to Rene's notes, the person or people we're looking for live upstairs over the café. He's guessing two or maybe three elementals based on the information his team pulled together."

Kenzie grins. "Do you think if *Maman* hadn't gathered the four of us together, we'd have gravitated together naturally?"

Tad shrugs. "Magic is a funny thing. Like energy attracts. I was surprised Gabrielle doesn't have any other elementals in her life."

"I don't think Gabrielle has any other people in her life. She seemed quite anti-social."

"Maybe being Montréal's Miracle isn't all it's cracked up to be."

"Yeah, maybe."

The line at the counter is long, but that's more about the volume of customers than the efficiency of the baristas. These people are working full-tilt, taking orders, handing out coffees, and moving on to the next person in line.

Rinse and repeat.

The pastry case is nearly empty, and I don't want to be here when things run out. The muffins and cookies are gorgeous and perfectly baked. I bet when they're gone, the crowd will turn ugly.

"There must be private access around the side or back, and they look too busy to bother."

"Agreed." Kenzie takes in the buzz of the crowd.

We slip out the back door, finding a wooden gate with a sign that reads Private Residence.

Making sure I have my police badge handy, I reach over and unlatch the gate. Around the back of the building is a staircase that leads up to a door above the café.

Thankfully, there's no snake knocker here.

I rap a few times with the meaty side of my fist.

There's rustling inside, and the door opens. The guy looks like death warmed over. His green dreadlocks are hanging limp, his dark skin is chalky, and his eyes are bloodshot, telling me he hasn't slept in days.

Instead of a greeting, he looks at us and grunts.

"Are they here?" a moaning voice comes from inside the apartment.

"They who?" I wonder if Rene or his people called to let them know we were coming. Hell, maybe Bakkali or someone from the guild is coming.

"Not they who," green dreads guy says. "They what. We ordered cough drops and cold tablets to be delivered from the pharmacy."

Kenzie shrugs. "Sorry. We're not delivery people. We wanted—"

He turns in the doorway and starts to close the door. "No offense, but no thanks."

I stick my boot against the jamb of the door frame and meet the guy's annoyance. "Let me guess. You and your besties feel like absolute shit."

"Like we got hit by a train," green dreads guy agrees. "You shouldn't be talking to us. We seriously might have the plague."

The groaning, miserable voice comes again from the back room. "Do you have the cough drops or not?"

"No."

"Then tell them to fuck off."

I chuckle. "I know exactly how you feel. I had this plague about three weeks ago. I did the whole hospital routine and everything. Let us in, and we can have you on your feet within a couple of hours."

His bleary-eyed gaze narrows on me. "Seriously?"

"Yep. All I need is ten minutes to explain what you're suffering from and to phone a friend to fix you up."

"If your friend is a drug dealer, you can fuck off. We don't touch that shit no matter how awful we feel."

"Glad to hear it. This has nothing to do with drugs." I pull out my phone and text Azland. His reply *pings* me back almost immediately. "He's at Charlie's house."

Kenzie chuckles. "Shocker."

"Right?" I glance at Tad. "Would you mind? I have a feeling we have some binding spells to remove."

"Aye, be right back."

When Tad vanishes, the green dreads guy's eyes bug wide. "What the fuck? Now I'm hallucinating."

I laugh. "No. You're good. Tad has powers and can portal. He went to get that friend I mentioned." The two *poof* in and stand next to us a moment later. "Now we're ready to get you guys on your feet again."

He considers that for a moment, shrugs, and heads inside. "It's your funeral. If you get sick, don't say I didn't warn you."

The four of us follow green dreads dude into the living room where three others are sacked out on the couches and chairs, all of them looking like death in pajama pants.

The room is a demonstration of barely contained chaos. Standing in one spot, I can see a keyboard piano, a photographer's tripod, a duffle bag overflowing with hockey equipment and lacrosse sticks, and a desk with a massive computer set up on it. There's also a music stand, several stacked crates of Girl Guide cookies, a game console, half a dozen controllers, and an easel with a half-finished painting.

These guys are busy.

"Hey, everyone. My name is Jules, and this is Kenzie, Tad, and Azland. If my suspicions are right, you four feel like you're nursing the mother of all hangovers. I know this because I went through the same thing a few weeks ago. Aches, fevers, all around hating life."

"Sounds about right," the guy sprawled across the couch agrees. "Are you from the health department?"

"Not exactly. The four of you have heard about fae awakenings, haven't you?"

Two of them groan, one glares, and green dreads curses. "That's not what this is. We're sick. No one is sprouting gills or wings or getting scales."

"Well, you're partially right." Azland holds his hand up and sweeps his palm toward them one at a time. "No one is transitioning because you have a binding spell keeping you from accepting your fae form."

"That's what's making you feel so rough," I add. "Your body wants to claim its powers, but it's locked out."

The four of them blink at me like I've lost my mind. I lift my hands into the air and create a ball of fire in each of my palms. "Three weeks ago, I found out I'm a fire elemental. I felt as bad as you all do until Azland removed the block on my powers. Then I felt better."

Green dreads guy stares me down. "You're serious. You honestly think we've got powers?"

"We know you do." Azland points them out. "You're earth, fire, water, and wind."

The four guys stare at us with a mixture of brain fog confusion and disbelief warring in their expressions.

"Here, I'll prove it," he says to the guy who opened the door for us. "Sit up and lay your hands in mine."

Green Dreads groans and forces himself to sit up.

Azland takes his hands and speaks in tongues, repeating the same process with this guy he used on us a few weeks ago.

While he does that, I get Kenzie a bowl of water from the kitchen, ignoring the empty soup cans and three or four days of dirty dishes.

When I get back in the room, Azland is moving on to the second guy, and Kenzie and I help the one he finished with. "What's your name?" I ask.

"Keith Moss."

I set the bowl of water on the ottoman in front of him and tilt my head toward my sister. "Kenzie is a water elemental. Now that the glamor blocking your powers is gone, she'll heal you and get rid of all the lingering oogies from the block. Ready?"

He still looks like he thinks I'm a few bricks short of a load, but he either hasn't got the energy to say no, or he feels so shitty he doesn't care if we are nuts.

Kenzie smiles, then passes her hands over the water. The orb on her bracelet enlarges and leaves its setting, lifting into the air. As she weaves her hands in small circles, the water from the bowl rises and creates an infinite wave flowing in the air before him.

"Either I'm completely fever fucked, or this is real." Keith glances at his buddies.

"It's real." I return to the kitchen to pour a glass of water. "I promise. You'll all feel better soon."

Keith is glaring at the glass in my hand. "What's that for?"

I chuckle and offer it to him. "To drink. You've been wretchedly sick and are likely dehydrated."

He blushes as he accepts the glass, tips it back, and drains it. For a moment, nothing happens. Then his dreadlocks go from a drab green to the healthy, bright green of a freshly unfurled fern. His posture straightens, and the redness in his eyes recedes.

"Whoa." He flops backward onto the sofa, rubbing his hands over his face. "What was that?"

"The magic of letting your true self free," I say.

Azland moves to the third guy, and Kenzie goes to the second. "It was a necessary evil to keep you safe from predators to your kind."

"What exactly is our kind?" The fourth guy still looks skeptical.

"We're elementals," Azland repeats. "You are each the embodiment of one of the elements. We're rare and stand as the last of the most powerful bloodlines in each realm."

I see the confusion in their eyes and totally understand. "I know, it's trippy, right? The truth is, you felt like cat hack because your body wanted to break free of the binding spell keeping you from tapping into your powers. The same thing happened to us."

"If we're so rare, how did four of us end up living together in one dorm building at Concordia College?" the second guy asks. He's tall and lanky with wild, curly hair. I get the feeling the crazy fly-away scare-do has less to do with his current malaise and more with the nature of his unruly mop on top.

"Your name?" I ask.

"Sean McNeal."

"Well, that's the crazy thing about magic. People like us tend to gravitate toward one another. The people who know more than us called us one of the Quebec Quartets. Then we found Azland."

"Technically, I found you." Azland moves to the last guy.

"True. Then Azland found us, and we became a quint. You're a natural quartet."

"Will we find a fifth?" Sean asks.

"Please let her be a hot redhead with big b—"

"Hey, now," Kenzie snaps.

"Brains. What? I was going to say brains."

Kenzie arches a manicured brow, and I laugh. "Sure you were."

Sean shrugs. "Will we get a fifth?"

"Likely not." Azland finishes with the unbinding. "As I said, elementals are rare, and my people are rare among that group."

"How did you find us?" the third guy asks. He's short and stout with heavily tattooed arms. "And how did you know which of us will be what kind of elemental?"

"Good one, Morgan." Sean frowns. "Yeah, how did you end up here with all the answers?"

"I was given your address by a colleague who runs the Fae Liaison Task Force for the mayor. How he got it…I couldn't say. You must have been on either his radar or the guild governor's radar at some point."

"Guild Governor of what?" Keith asks.

Kenzie moves to ease the final guy, and it's easy to see that the other three already feel better.

"There is a lot to tell you, but the most important thing is that while it's amazing to have elemental powers, it's dangerous too. Other non-human beings in the city consume our powers, and we have to get you four ready to defend yourselves if anyone like that comes after you."

"Consume our powers? That doesn't sound good."

"It's not," Azland agrees, ever the voice of doom. "They are the ones who destroyed our elemental kingdoms and got you sent into the human realm to be adopted."

"Adopted?" Sean says. "I'm not adopted."

Oh, dear. "There's a lot to take in all at once. Let's focus on getting you four all on the same page. We need to talk to you about training, safety, and everything we know about our heritage."

We hang out for a while, explaining everything we can about what it will mean for them to be an elemental quartet. Keith is earth. Morgan is water. Sean is wind. Nazim is fire. We tell them about the Poreskoro family and their skoro thugs, the Guild of the Laurentians, and the fae liaison task force.

They make plans with Azland to start a training schedule. We get their contact info and log them into the fae website and the private elemental Discord group.

We learn that the four are equal partners in The Grey Nun Café and split the tasks downstairs. It's great that they have a small business, and by the lines downstairs, are making a go of it, but the downside is that they're easy to find and pin down.

They live and work here.

I ensure they understand the threat they're facing and give them a card with the fae liaison task force's information. "If you think there's trouble, reach out to us any time, day or night. I mean it. Four in the morning, you wake up and have a bad feeling, I expect a call."

Keith nods. "Yeah, okay. Thanks…you know, for setting us free from the binding and all. I really was starting to wonder if we had a plague of some kind."

"Oh, I hear you. I've been there."

The doorbell rings, and we all stiffen at full alert. Azland strides to the door, but there's nothing to worry about. "It's the delivery guy with the cough drops."

"Guess we don't need those anymore," Morgan says.

As we leave, Nazim calls the first shower. He needs to get downstairs and help the staff.

CHAPTER TWENTY-TWO

I slide into the back seat of Kenzie's electric car with Azland and leave the passenger seat for Tad. It's been nice meeting other elementals and seeing how they're similar to and different from my weird little family.

Hopefully, we'll be able to help them. Not only to adjust but also to stay safe and thrive.

I've been thinking about Luc's idea.

"If it really is possible to block ourselves from being picked out of a crowd by skoro assholes, we'd all be so much safer."

Tad twists in the front seat and holds up his phone. "Fi and Sloan contacted the white witch. Emerald Moon's property is heavily warded, and visits to her apothecary shop are by appointment only. She's willing to meet with us if we get there in the next few hours."

"Then that's what we'll do." I pull out my phone and give Luc the update. We swing by the coroner's office to pick him up.

We drive to Laval and Emerald Moon's rural farm property. The sun is setting as we arrive, and the sky around her quaint roadside shop is a brilliant pink hue.

Emerald Moon is returning from a lavender field when we

pull off the road. Her long ebony hair is riding the breeze, and I don't miss Luc's eyes popping wide as we see her ass hugged in skin-tight jeans. "Not a word, dude. Don't make this awkward with any of your freaky fetish talk."

"Judgy much?"

I laugh. "I don't care what you do with your willing participants. I'm saying don't piss off the witch we need to make this happen."

Tad turns and is on my side. "The last thing ye want to do is piss off a witch. Don't let the 'do no harm' motto fool ye. There are plenty of loopholes in that tenet."

Azland nods. "Witches tend to target male parts. From my experience, anyway."

Luc looks horrified. "'Nuff said. Consider me warned."

We park in one of the ten slotted spots against the front of the shop and meet Emerald as she enters the door. She has an armful of freshly cut lavender. Tad jogs forward to catch the door for her.

"Lock up and turn the sign, will you? We shouldn't be interrupted."

The windchimes dance in the breeze, setting off a steady tinkle of a song as we step inside.

Like the last time I was here, stepping across the threshold is jarring. What looks like a relatively simple rectangular board-and-batten store from the outside is an improbably large space filled with all manner of herbs, potions, crystals, and magical items.

"Whoa." Luc reaches out and brushes his fingers over an intricately carved wooden wand. Then he runs his hands over a row of little glass bottles. "This place is amazing. It's like Ollivanders wand shop and Professor Sprout's greenhouse had a kinky liaison, and this is their secret love child."

Emerald Moon bursts out laughing, her voice twinkling in the air around us. "Thank you. I appreciate a man with taste."

"Brains, too." I give him a plug of confidence. "Did Fiona explain to you why we've come?"

She offers me a seductive grin. "I don't speak to Fiona—only Sloan. That accent of his. Delicious."

I chuckle and hand Tad the sheaf of papers that lay out the equations and diagrams of our plan. "Then may I introduce you to Tad McNiff? Also one of the heirs to the Druids of the Ancient Order of Ireland."

Emerald's attention swings to our beautiful blond and her gaze drinks him in. "Well, hello there. Yes, tell me all about your plans."

Kenzie flashes me a dirty look, but I wave her hostility away. One thing I've learned from working with partners and speaking with contacts and informants is that if there's someone they like better, play into that fondness.

It gets you further faster.

Tad spreads Luc's plans out on the glass counter, and Emerald bends to look closer. There's no way the cleavage show is an accident, but hey, the girl knows what she likes and doesn't play coy.

"Kenzie, how about you and Azland go shopping in the back somewhere before it starts to rain on our parade?" I make eyes at my sister.

Azland chuckles and turns Kenzie by the shoulder. "Good idea. We'll be over here if you need us."

"Just you wait, Jules." Kenzie waves her middle finger over her head.

I chuckle as I position Luc into the conversation. No matter how pretty Tad looks and sounds, Luc came up with this plan. "Go ahead, Luc. Explain the science of what you hope we can do."

My buddy steps up like the champ he is, describing what he wants to do and the magical components he thinks it will require.

For once, his audience doesn't seem baffled or bored. Emerald listens intently, asks questions, and occasionally makes surprised noises of assent.

"Might as well let them chat." Tad grins. "Man candy is no longer needed."

I chuckle and pat his back. "Sorry about that."

Tad winks. "No worries. Whatever it takes to get the job done. Besides, an Irishman is always ready to lay on the charm if the need arises."

I point at where Kenzie is glaring from behind a rack of Tarot cards and shove Tad. "My bad. The need has arisen."

Tad winks at me and strides off to calm the waters of my sister. Not that she'll be annoyed. She's far too independent and self-assured. What's bugging her is that she can't assert herself.

We need Emerald's help.

I wander over to a wooden pegboard, where dozens of scarves hang. When I touch one, it shimmers and sparkles, sending out waves of color that stop as soon as I let go of the fabric.

Not really my style.

Continuing, I look at the trays and trays of raw and polished crystals.

"Druids carry crystals on them at all times to enhance our connection to the earth's magic." Tad joins me. "Ye might consider pickin' up a few fer yerselves."

"At the very least for Briar," Kenzie agrees, glancing down at all the cuts and colors. "What would be good for him?"

"Hematite is one of the most powerful grounding stones. Its energy connects you deep into the earth. Red jasper brings strength and stamina to the fore."

Kenzie laughs. "Briar doesn't lack in either of those."

I roll my eyes. "Especially not stamina. I've lived through too many awkward moments sharing a bedroom wall with his room growing up."

"Oh, what about this one?" Kenzie picks up a pretty dark green stone with flecks of red and orange.

"Bloodstone. That would be better fer Zephyr. Bloodstone centers and grounds strong vibrational energy." Tad picks out a good piece. "You could get one too. It's also a great stone for detoxification, purification, and immunity boost."

Kenzie grins and picks through the tray until she selects one that speaks to her. "What else is good for a healer?"

"Well, amethyst of course, lapis lazuli, and turquoise." Kenzie continues to pick as he rhymes off the names of gemstones and points at the trays.

My attention has locked on a different tray, my instincts drawing me to a deep red stone. "What's this one and why do I feel like I need it?"

Tad smiles. "Because if ye think ye need it, then ye do. The garnet carries the energy of passion, creativity, and joy. It exudes vitality and fuels sensual energy because it awakens the spirit of the fire element. The garnet has unique qualities to meet a wide range of energy needs, from improving vitality and health to protecting against negativity."

Kenzie snorts. "Protecting against negativity? Fill her pockets. She needs that badly."

I stick my tongue out at my sister, but I grab a couple. It couldn't hurt.

I glance at where Luc and Emerald Moon are still engaged in a deep conversation, their heads nearly touching as they point at a section of his papers. "Okay, things seem to be going well over there. Let's stay out of their way."

Tad finds a table covered with a silvery blue cloth. On it are dozens, nearly hundreds, of bottles and jars of every different size and shape.

"What are these?" Kenzie picks one up, squinting to read the tiny label. "This says Colorado Hot Springs."

"This one says Bolivian River." I read a different label out loud. "And this one says Romanian Radioactive Waste Site. Yikes."

"They're samples of water collected from different locations worldwide," Tad explains. "Just like the St. Lawrence River is a special conduit for fae energies, other waterways can also be sources of magic. If you do spells involving water, you'll get different effects using water with different magical signatures."

Kenzie picks up one labeled Chicago Puddle. "I wonder if any of them are good for healing."

"This one might work." I point out a squat jar labeled "Roman Healing Baths."

She glances at it but doesn't pick it up. Her hands are already full of the gemstones and crystals we chose.

Emerald Moon must have sensed that because a white wicker basket appears on the table in front of Kenzie's full hands. More appear in front of us.

"I guess that settles that." Kenzie chuckles and sets the jar in her basket with the gemstones. "Are we done, or do you need something?"

I shake my head. "No. I'm good."

"Maybe something for Onyx?" Always one for a shopping trip, Kenzie looks around for anything that might be good for a hellhound.

She finds a rack of collars and leashes, each inlaid with gems, seashells, and other materials. The tags explain that the collars are supposed to protect the wearer or imbue them with a bit of extra patience, wisdom, or viciousness.

"I think we should get Onyx a collar for protection," Kenzie declares. "Look how cute this one is!" She holds up an embossed brown leather collar with glittering copper rings and blue jewels embedded in it.

"I don't think that's his style," I say. My eyes are drawn to a collar in plain black with a row of burnt orange jewels. "This one is perfect."

"You with your orange." Kenzie groans. "Orange fish, orange phone case, orange undies…"

I hold up my hand and roll my eyes. "Do you need to discuss my underwear in mixed company? Neither Tad nor Azland needs to hear it, do you, boys?"

Tad chuckles. "Not really, no."

Azland grunts from the next aisle over and I take that as a no.

I put the collar in my basket.

I'm next drawn to the velvet cushions. According to the tag, they emit a gentle magic that helps relax any pet that sleeps on them.

Onyx could use some relaxing so I get that too.

Luc and Emerald Moon are showing no signs of winding down their conversation, so we keep going. Tad picks out a little leg ring for Aurora with an amethyst jewel, and I get a miniature pewter castle for Jack and Jack.

Kenzie and I pick up a pouch of magical bird treats in case Bakkali's raven visits us again.

By the time we finish walking through the apothecary shop, we all have a nice haul in our baskets. As we approach Luc and Emerald Moon, it looks like we aren't the only ones who found what we're looking for.

Luc is positively beaming.

"How is it going? Is Luc's idea doable?" I ask.

Emerald Moon nods. "It's totally possible to block your detectable fae energy and prevent elementals from being singled out by Second Sight. Given Luc's science, I have a couple of ideas for where to start."

"That's awesome. Thank you," Kenzie says. It seems she has forgiven Emerald Moon the slight of fancying Tad now that her attentions have moved on to Luc.

"Don't thank me yet." She laughs. "I might be a white witch, but I don't work for free. Even though Luc has done a lot of the preliminary research, this kind of custom commission isn't easy, nor will it be cheap."

"What's the charge?" I ask.

"Five grand. That's for the initial spellwork. If it works the way you want, I'll replicate the spell as often as you like at a hundred dollars each time."

I'm about to tell her that she can stick it—there's no way the fae liaison task force has that kind of money to throw around—but Tad whips out an American Express black card. "No problem. How soon can you get it done?"

"Tad. Dude. That's very generous of you, but it's not your responsibility to pay for something—"

"Och, don't fret, Jules. It's only money, and I have too much of it fer my likin'. Besides, if this leads to a way to protect yer lot and the other fae in yer city, it's well worth it. That is my callin' as a druid, aye? To protect the fae folk and the goddess' fair creatures."

I have no idea how this guy ended up being so kind and generous when his father was a maniacal man who grew so power-poisoned he tried to kill his only child.

I'm so thankful Fiona was there to save him.

I kiss his cheek. "You're a good man, Tad McNiff. We're lucky to have you in our lives, and I'm proud to call you my friend."

From what Fi and he told me of what went down with his father, no matter how well-packaged he presents himself as being, he was deeply wounded and needs to hear he has value. I don't mind feeling awkward about putting it out there if it can solidify the cracked foundation of a man like him.

We check out. Emerald Moon gives us a discount on everything in our full baskets. She even hands Luc a starter book for non-magicals who want to understand the relationship between science and magic.

Luc beams the entire way back to his office, chattering about how impressed Emerald Moon was with his knowledge of magical components and the science of fae biology.

"She said she had never seen such a comprehensive breakdown of a fae DNA during the awakening process," Luc is still saying when we pull up to the coroner's office. "Hey, do you think if I learn magic and practice, I could help with the task force?"

He really is the best. "I'm not sure that's a good idea. Being able to combine some herbs or chant the right thing over a crystal isn't the same as having inherent magical abilities."

"We'd hate to see you get hurt," Kenzie adds.

"Maybe I could train with you."

Azland raises his eyebrows. "No."

Luc deflates, his shoulders slumping as he gets out of the car. "Yeah, well, you're welcome."

When the door slams shut, I glare at Azland. "Seriously? Could you have been any ruder?"

I get out of the car and jog after Luc.

"Hey, dude, wait up. Don't let Azland get under your skin. He's a broody ass." I catch up to him as he pulls open one of the double doors. "Really. A month ago he was eating dog chow and licking his balls on my living room rug."

Luc chuckles but still looks dejected.

"Hey, I know the fae thing seems cool—"

"Because it is."

"It can be, but it also sucks on many fronts and puts me and mine in danger." I wait until his eyes meet mine. "Promise you won't do anything stupid, like use Second Sight to alter your DNA or try to trigger powers."

"I won't."

"Promise?"

"Promise."

While we're not hugging friends as a rule, I ignore that for the moment and bring him in. "You were awesome today. Your superpower is your badass brain and you being you."

"It's true. I'm pretty incredible."

"Yeah, you are. Don't let anyone make you feel anything less."

Back at the fire station, loud music draws us into the back yard. It's not like Zephyr's usual stuff, so after we park Kenzie's car in the garage bay, she plugs it in, and I move to the back door to investigate.

Briar and Gareth, both covered in dirt, have lined the hole in the lawn with dark-hued concrete. My magma pit is taking shape. A regular contractor would have taken weeks to get it to this point, but neither Briar nor Gareth are regular contractors.

My brother can shift earth at will and Gareth is crazy strong. Speaking of Briar and his earth powers, he's moved some of the dirt he removed to make my pit to where he plans to build his elemental sanctuary.

Waste not, want not.

I hop down into the pit, examining the concrete. It's darker than typical concrete, almost slate gray with a hint of purple. "What is this?"

Gareth grins. "It's a volcanic rock blend."

"So it doesn't crack once it has super-hot molten lava inside it?"

"Yep. It'll set to become as hard as the inside of a volcano."

"Where on earth do you get something like that?"

He winks. "I've got a guy."

All right, then. Even his magical home improvement store is part of his secret life.

"We'll pour one more layer and break for a beer," Briar declares.

Kenzie and I stick around to help. We sign our names in the

concrete and let Onyx leave little pawprints to commemorate the construction.

Tad encourages Aurora to press her feet into the wet concrete to leave her mark, but she's not having it and flies off.

Afterward, we rinse off under the hose. Kenzie enchants the water to be cleansing and energizing. Then we all head inside, crack open some cold drinks, and relax after a long day of hard work.

CHAPTER TWENTY-THREE

The next morning, I wake with a gasp and the shadow of panic clinging to my ragged breath. It takes a moment to orient myself, but I'm thankful neither my sheets nor my pajamas are on fire. Onyx misses the whole thing with his head nestled into his enchanted purple pillow, sleeping in his crate.

Right then. Nothing to panic about.

Whatever it was, it was only a dream.

After I get moving, I wash up, feed my fish, and let Onyx out. While he runs around the back yard and investigates the changes in the landscape from Gareth's and Briar's efforts, I check my phone.

I sent Keith Moss a text late last night, checking in with him and their quartet. I didn't get a response and none of the Grey Nun elementals have logged in on the Discord channel.

Gabrielle the Montréal Miracle is good, though. She accessed the information Zephyr and Tad have been building on the site and has been clicking around.

I scroll through the discussion posts for a bit and see that Azland has posted about good open spaces to practice magical maneuvers and some tips about how to combat the "awakening headaches."

Zephyr has also posted, but his communications consist of a few silly memes about what life is like as a fae in Montréal. I'm glad to have the site, even if there aren't many people on here yet.

Something about the panic of my dream and not hearing back from Keith doesn't sit well. I call the number listed in the local directory for The Grey Nun Café.

No one answers.

Shit.

After corralling Onyx back inside, I shrug on my slicker, grab my backpack, and hook my ankle around the brass fire pole. "Laters, B. Love you."

"Love you too. Be safe."

"Yep." My phone starts ringing during my descent, and I pull it free from my pocket as I walk over to the cubby where I keep my motorcycle boots and helmet.

"Yo, Rene. What's new?"

"Nothing good."

His heavy sigh and the long silence before he speaks again conjure a ball of anxiety in my gut. "Tell me."

"The quartet tied to The Grey Nun Café."

"Yeah, Keith, Morgan, Sean, and Nazim. What about them? I've been trying to call them, and they're not answering."

"Sadly, they won't. They're dead."

The news hits me, and I stagger back a couple of stumbled steps and steady myself with my back against the concrete block of the wall. "When? How?"

"From the looks of it, they were killed yesterday evening, shortly after you visited them."

"What happened?"

"As far as I can tell, someone drained them. With their elemental essence consumed, their cells dried out like old husks."

"Fuck." Grief and rage burn hot under the surface of my skin.

Then comes guilt. "Do you think we led them there? Is this my fault?"

"Don't do that. There's no evidence the skoro were following you. We know they can track elemental energy. Odds are, they found them when their power signatures started coming through."

I groan. "This *is* my fault. We released their powers and warned them about the dangers, but they weren't prepared. I should never have left them alone—"

"You can't move in with every elemental that awakens, Jules. This isn't your fault. More than likely, it was skoro assholes, and that's why we have to stop them."

"Does Luc have the bodies?"

"I made sure to direct them to him specifically."

"Okay, thanks. I'll call him and stay on top of it."

"Let me know if you learn anything useful."

"Same."

"If you need the day out of office to deal, you have my permission to take the day off."

"Nah, then I'll brood. I need to work."

I hang up the phone, the fire of anger and self-recrimination burning hot in my cells and turning my vision red. My skin is tight over my bones, and I peel off my jacket and stomp into the backyard in my socks.

This isn't right. I'm supposed to protect the people of this city, yet the skoro are sowing death and destruction at every turn.

I think of the boys, remembering the pain and horror of being drained…how the fear and weakness robbed me of any way to fight back. It guts me that they suffered without anyone there to protect them.

"Augh!" I tilt my face up to the morning sky and scream. Rage pours out of me, and my body ignites in a massive *whoosh* of heat and flame.

"Jules! Whoa, Jules!" Gareth shouts, rushing in from the side fence. He drops the supplies in his arms and jogs over to me. "What's wrong? How can I help?"

I raise my arms and shout again, the violent rage inside getting away from me.

"I get it, beautiful." His voice is soft and sweet. "Sometimes it's too much, and you want to raze the world, right? Burn everything to the ground to make it stop, even for a little while."

Yeah. That's it. That's exactly it.

I meet his gaze, and he reaches through the flames and cups my cheek. My fire doesn't burn him. It doesn't even faze him. "Try to calm the fire. Focus on me and know that whatever it is, I'll listen and help you through it."

I scan the back yard and realize I'm in full blaze. Dammit, if I let go of my fury, I'll be naked.

"I'm sorry," I mumble.

He sees me looking down at myself and must grasp my immediate concern. Lifting the hem of his T-shirt over his head, he strips it off and offers me a sad smile. "I've got you covered."

Literally. He's likely the only one who does.

I release my flames, and he turns his back, holding his T-shirt for me to claim. Pulling it on over my head, I cover my body, but now that my flames are out, I feel utterly drained. "They're all dead, and I think it's my fault."

In my lifetime, I've had many occasions that were worthy of breaking down in a fit of tears, but I've never really been that girl. Now, I'm unsure if it's the horror of what happened, the hormonal changes my body's going through, or having Gareth there looking at me like he can read me down to my broken heart. Whatever it is, there's no holding back the firestorm of emotions.

I step into his personal space and collapse against his chest, hoping he can hold me up for a while because I'm too tired.

Between sobs, I tell him about the Grey Nun quartet and promising I'd help them through their awakening. I tell him about waking in a panic and Rene calling to tell me they're dead.

"All four of them. Dead because I didn't do my job!"

The hand gently massaging the back of my head grips my hair and pulls me back so I'm looking up at him. His dark eyes are smoldering a deep red, and I wonder what he is and what the different colors mean. "I understand it feels like that to you, but it's not your job to save everyone from every bad thing in the city."

"Wrong. That's the very definition of my job."

He takes a step back, his hold on me sliding down my bare arms until he captures my hands in his. "You can only be held accountable for your actions. The people around you will do things, and you can try to stop them. You can fight and beg and hope they make better choices—humane choices—but in the end, what they do isn't on you. If you try to take on the weight of the world, all it will do is crush you."

A mental image of Atlas bent and bowed under the weight of the Earth flashes through my fractured mind, and I draw a deep breath. "They were good guys. They met in college, ran a little café, and were genuinely excited about the next chapter of their lives."

Gareth nods. "I'm sorry you lost them, Jules, and even sorrier that the kind of men who do that sort of thing are permitted to walk the streets of this city."

I hate that too, but I'm too burned out—literally and figuratively—to think about it anymore.

Maybe Rene was right, and I should take the day or at least a few hours to regroup.

"Jules? You all right?" Briar has stopped on the back patio, obviously unsure whether to interrupt our intimate moment.

Kenzie and Tad have followed him outside, and my sister rushes forward. "What happened?"

I don't want to talk about it, but Kenzie has a right to know. I extend my hands to her, but Gareth grabs them and shakes his head, reminding me my skin is too hot. "Right. Sorry."

He offers a sad smile. "Jules, there is nothing for you to be sorry about."

So he thinks. He's wrong—but it's sweet.

Turning back to Kenzie, I draw a deep breath. "Rene called. Keith, Morgan, Sean, and Nazim were targeted by skoro last night. There were no survivors."

Kenzie gasps. "Drained? All four of them?"

"Yeah."

"We were just in their living room," she says, blankly looking toward Tad before refocusing on me. "You're sure? They're all gone?"

"I'm sure." I want to hug my sister, but it's still too early since I went supernova. "I'll find out about their arrangements, and we'll pay our respects, but for now, there's nothing to be done."

Kenzie studies me and crinkles her nose. "You're not wired to do nothing."

"No. That's why I'm going to go for a jog."

"I'm going with you," Zephyr declares.

I wave off the offer. "I'm good."

"Tough shit. We discussed this after you got beaten to a pulp. No more jogging alone. At least not until Onyx is big enough to eat a skoro for breakfast."

"When I agreed to that, I had been roughed up. Now, I'm more interested in some time alone."

Zephyr grins at me, unmoved.

Damn. He's as stubborn as I am, and Kenzie and Briar will back him up. I'm not in the mood for a chaperone, but I'm even less in the mood for an argument I know I'll lose.

"Fine. But it'll be a silent jog. My head is spinning."

Zephyr pinches his finger and thumb together, twists them as if he's locking his mouth, and throws the key over his shoulder.

I fight not to chuckle. "Give me five to cold shower my skin so I don't combust my clothes. You grab Onyx and his harness, and I'll meet the two of you out front."

Zephyr winks and flashes me the okay symbol with his fingers.

I roll my eyes and head inside.

Zephyr, Onyx, and I jog the first few miles in silence. I push myself too hard to have a conversation, and Zephyr can tell that his big sister isn't interested in a chatty power walk.

As we approach the river, I slow down. If I keep running at full speed, I'll be too exhausted for work tomorrow. Plus, I like the sights and sounds of the river too much to whiz past it.

Now that we're going at a gentler pace and I've worked off some of the grief of failing Keith and his buddies, I decide to break my vow of silence. "I saw Gabrielle has been commenting in some of the Discord channels."

He nods. "It was a cool idea. I think it'll be fun once we get more people on there."

"Thanks for taking the lead and making it happen. I always knew your nerdiness would come in handy."

"Azland has some good YouTube videos tagged for self-defense. If we can get the stick out of his ass, he might be helpful."

"The stick out of his ass part is the issue."

"Tad and I are working hard on security to keep it from getting hacked. His boss in Toronto, Garnet Grant, is helping to ensure we're super secure."

"Excellent."

We fall into a companionable quiet, winding down the riverside paths. As much as I didn't want him to come, I'm glad to share time with only the two of us.

All four of us are close, but because Briar and Kenzie are the same age, they ended up in the same classes at school, doing the same homework assignments together, and going to the same parties. Zephyr and I ended up spending a lot of time together as kids.

The rhythm of my footfalls falters a beat when I see a gang of asshole skinheads milling around the bench a few yards ahead. They look rough, and I'm betting that besides taking Second Sight, they partake in other pharmaceuticals.

They're passing around a spliff the size of my middle finger. By the brown bagged bottles in their hands, it's a regular day drinking party.

"Fuckety-fuck. Sister-beating dickwads up ahead."

Zephyr glances up and nods in recognition as he sees them. Their shaved heads and anti-magic patches mark who and what they are. "How do you want to play this?"

"Like they're not there. We're two siblings out for a stroll in the park."

As we continue, I notice a streak of white powder on one of their backpacks. As a cop, I'm supposed to look out for every citizen of Montréal, even the nastiest, cruelest thugs.

Part of me thinks I should warn them to stop using so they can avoid the deadly fae mutations.

Then again, it would tickle my payback funny bone for these bigoted knuckleheads to turn into fae mutants in a painful, hopefully fatal way.

I decide to leave them alone, at least for now. Let's see what happens—karma is a bitch, after all.

If they want to keep taking Second Sight because it allows them the targeting they need to assault innocent people, that's their business.

I won't feel bad if they end up on Luc's table.

CHAPTER TWENTY-FOUR

After dinner, I call Rene and check in. "I took your advice, went for a jog, and cleared my head. Now I'm back in the game. If you're free tonight, I thought we could drive out to the Mohawk Territory and back to McGill. Maybe tracing the boys' steps at their class time might stir up something new."

"I'm game. I'll swing by the firehouse in twenty."

Soon I'm in the passenger seat of Rene's sensible sedan as we rumble along the freeway.

"I'm glad you called. It'll do you good to do some police work after the setback this morning."

"My siblings did their best to help, but ultimately, I'm happiest when I'm on the job."

"Some of us were born to be cops."

"Maybe that's why I piss off jerkoffs so easily."

"That's just your personality."

I laugh.

Rene hits his turn signal and takes us off the highway toward the reservation. "Seriously, though, it's always great to work with you."

"Are you coming on to me, Michaud?"

He snorts. "No offense but not in a million, Gagne. The only relationship I'd survive with you is a partnership on the streets—when you join my team."

I sit back and rest my head against the seat. "You don't quit, do you?"

Rene grins. "Nope. I'm wearing you down, aren't I?"

"Maybe."

"Not that I'm complaining, but what changed?"

"Well, I started working in Major Crimes because I wanted to help victims of the worst kinds of crimes. I used to think that meant solving murders and keeping violence off the streets."

"Not anymore?"

"After having my fire sucked out of me and nearly dying at the hands of a magical enemy, I'm starting to think having the essential energy of your soul consumed is about as major as it gets."

Rene's grin lights up his entire face. "Then welcome to the fae liaison squad."

I laugh. "I never said I was on board. I've been at the Twenty-Third for a long time."

"Even more reason to go for a change."

"Yeah, well. Everything about my life is in upheaval right now, so a career shift is a lot to think about."

"Fair enough."

When we enter Mohawk Territory, I check that the dash cam is recording.

Rene pulls into the residential area dotted with low-slung houses, then parks outside the home where the victims of the Second Sight deaths were found. "All right. Ready to go to school?"

"Can't wait."

Rene pulls us back onto the freeway. I peer out the window, hoping to spot something that's changed since the day Tad and I drove out here.

I track the GPS notes the Peacekeeper gave us, ensuring we follow the exact route the boys took each week.

At the university, Rene decides to park in the student lot rather than the visitor one out front. It makes sense since that's where the kids would have parked.

"That's the Leacock building." I point at one of the academic buildings.

Rene pulls the handle on his door and we both exit the car. "Seventh floor, right?"

"Yep."

Unlike the day Tad and I visited, tonight a number of windows on the upper floors of the building are lit and actively used for classes.

"Do you ever think we missed out by going to police college?"

Rene shrugs. "Missed out on drunken debauchery and starting life sixty grand in debt?"

I chuckle. "No one will be coming to you to create campus flyers."

"Fine by me."

We walk along the pathways, lit by yellow streetlamps and dotted with the bright blue lights of safety boxes. Inside the Leacock building, we find a bulletin board plastered with posters and advertisements for various events on campus.

Rene and I scan it carefully, looking for anything that might point us toward whoever is dealing Second Sight at McGill.

There's an ad for guitar lessons, a flyer promoting a safe sex seminar for freshmen, and an inscrutable manifesto that appears to have been handwritten and photocopied alongside some black and white photos of frogs with missing eyes or multiple limbs.

"Mutant frogs." Rene frowns.

"I wonder if fae prana in the river is what's messing them up. I've seen some messed up rats too."

Rene leans in and scans the information provided. "It says magical pollution in the waterways. According to the footnotes, this paper was written for an Environmental Studies class by someone named Bliss."

"I guess Bliss thought the best way to get people to care about the plight of the five-legged, one-eyed frogs is to make posters and stick them up everywhere."

Rene shakes his head. "College kids are weird, man."

We wander around, keeping an eye out for anyone who seems out of place. The only people who don't belong here are the two adults with no discernible purpose. I don't see any glassy-eyed students or anti-magic patches anywhere.

"Should we check the class they were taking?"

We head up to the seventh floor to the Modern Anthropology class. We don't want to interrupt, so we peer inside. A few students appear to be sleeping, but that's not a symptom of Second Sight intoxication.

It probably has more to do with what the professor is writing on the board. "Intersectional perspectives regarding hypertext communication between marginalized individuals using corporate-owned social media platforms."

Rene makes a face at me. "Are you still wondering if we missed out?"

We take the stairs down to the outside of the building. "I suppose it's interesting to the ones taking it."

"I have no idea how anyone could be interested in…what was it? Interstate porpoises and hyper-sexy convents?"

I laugh. "That does sound interesting, but they're talking about how people use the Internet and social media to talk about the stuff that makes them feel trodden down. Like our fae website."

"Well, they could say so in English," Rene grumbles.

"Or French."

"Don't get me started. Speaking of your site, how's it going? I haven't had a chance to check it out since your brother got it up and running."

"Too busy checking out sexy porpoises?"

Rene laughs. "Don't go sharing my private preferences around the precinct. Really, are people using the website?"

"The one person still alive, yes."

He sighs. "Eyes forward, Jules. We'll set things right. I promise."

"Yeah, we will. I'm just gutted that—"

I stop dead in my tracks, my mental train derailing mid-sentence. Wait. That's it. The beaver tail dessert truck is parked at the curb.

"Tad and I got beaver tails when we were here."

"Yeah? They're damned good."

"No argument, but what was in the warehouse where we rescued the two faeries?"

"Food trucks."

I hold up a finger. "Specifically dessert trucks. What was the strange contaminant in the latest batches of Second Sight?"

Rene grins at me. "Cinnamon sugar."

More thoughts and memories flood my brain. "The businessman who died of Second Sight. There was a greasy wrapper from one of these trucks at his desk, remember?"

"The strings of numbers on the map?" Rene asks.

"Identification numbers for different trucks? Coordinated routes? I'm not sure."

Rene and I step back around the corner and into the shadows. He gets out his phone and fires off rapid texts to his team. "I'll have them run the numbers again, see if they match with food truck vehicle identification or license plates."

Finally, I feel like we're putting it together.

"That's why no one's been able to find their new lab. It's because they don't have one—they're using these trucks as mini production labs, moving them around the city to make sales and avoid detection."

I peek around the corner. The truck is still there, the logo on its side reading Poor Boscoe's Beaver Tails.

Rene frowns. "Do you think Poor Boscoe sounds a little too much like Poreskoro?"

"That's circumstantial at best."

"If the Poreskoro Corporation owns them, they're going to jail."

"Demon jail," I correct. "Any humans working for this family can go in the standard pokey, but these skoro minions need to be sent back to the hell where they came from."

"We're working on ways to incarcerate and punish empowered folks. Right now, Bakkali is helping."

"Excellent."

Rene checks around the corner. "Do we take down the truck or sit on it and see where it leads us?"

"Door number two."

"I like the way you think."

Rene and I return to his car, which has a warning notice for parking in the student lot without the appropriate sticker. He crumples it up with an eye roll.

With the headlights off, we pull around the campus lot until we're at the back of the next lot with a full view of our truck.

"Now we wait," I say.

"Are you one of those cops who loves a good long stakeout, or do you find them excruciatingly boring?"

I shrug. "I used to hate them, but now I think it's nice to be still and have time to sit and think."

"Too bad we can't treat ourselves to some beaver tails," Rene jokes.

"I can't believe Tad and I ate food from that truck last time, and it didn't click."

"I wouldn't worry about it. It was part of everyday life. It didn't stick out until it did."

Rene's right, but we don't dwell.

We're quiet for a long while, watching as a delivery guy on a bike rides past, then circles back to buy himself a pastry. Students wearing heavy backpacks trickle out of the building, most stopping at the truck for a late-night treat.

Rene has pulled his camera with a long lens from the trunk, and he's clicking photos of everything. "I only see one guy inside."

"I can't tell if he's dealing. He gives everyone the same white paper sack."

"Some kids are talking with him longer than others."

"Could be a complicated beaver tail order."

"I'm sure that's what their lawyers would say."

We're not here to catch college kids buying a few pills. Busting them might confirm our suspicions, but it would also alert the truck's operator that we're on to him.

"What's your favorite flavor?" Rene asks.

"I'm a traditionalist. Apple with cinnamon or hazelnut spread with almonds."

"You've got a sweet tooth."

"Yeah, you?"

"I like banana chocolate all the way."

We chat for a while about our families and lives outside the force. One of us watches the white truck while the other checks around us.

The night classes end at eight-thirty and students stream out. A crowd clusters around the truck. We watch as the guy inside sells what must be over three hundred bucks worth of pastries before the students disperse and the area around this section of campus goes quiet and dark.

"That's his last big rush. We should leave soon."

Within minutes of the last student leaving, the dessert truck putters into gear and pulls away. We wait long enough to give us a good surveillance distance, then follow.

"Now lead us home, asshole. Take us to your leader."

CHAPTER TWENTY-FIVE

The dessert truck drives for a bit, and I record our route on the map we found in the warehouse. It makes a couple of stops along the highlighted routes, and I mark those too.

The truck parks outside a club called the Kissing Killer, and a few guys in work shirts come out to haul cardboard boxes out of the back of the truck.

"I've never known a dance club to offer freshly baked pastries," Rene notes.

"Maybe they're opening a new market base. Or maybe they ordered a nice new batch of party drugs."

At the next stop, the truck idles on a residential corner near Nakey Kid's old apartment for a while. We park under a tree down the block, watching various people come out from their homes or wander up the streets. The paper bags they buy look heavier than the ones the college kids were carrying off.

After another hour of watching the truck make deliveries, we eventually follow it to a large industrial property. It's a big asphalt lot where off-season carnival equipment is stored.

I wince when I see the giant clown billboards. "This place is uber creepy. Look at that horrifying thing."

Rene follows my finger and grimaces at the giant plastic slide with a huge clown head on top, its long tongue lolling out of its mouth to form the slide. "If I ever had kids, no way would I let them on something like that."

"I'm an adult, and I'll be having nightmares."

With both of us of the same mind, we resume stalking the dessert truck.

We find our object of interest idling at a gate leading inside a fence to the carnival storage lot. The man at the gate opens it and waves the truck through, then glances around before shutting things up and returning to his guard post.

"It's a smart location," Rene notes. "It's in the middle of fucking nowhere, so there are no nosy neighbors to notice trucks coming and going in the night. Even if they did, it makes sense to store a dessert truck with carnival equipment."

"Not to mention if you're a nasty ass demon summoned from hell to serve your evil overlords, you'd love to set up shop around all this creepy shit."

"That too."

We do a lap around the perimeter with our headlights off. A handful of guys stand around keeping guard, and with our windows rolled down, we can smell the telltale odor of burned cookies.

Yep. This is it.

"You ready to end this thing?" Rene asks.

"More than ready."

"Then I'll call it in and get the warrant."

"How long will that take?"

Rene grins. "Mayor Tremblay has a judge on standby, and I have a guy stationed outside her home for such an occasion."

"Good thinking, Michaud."

Rene winks and shoots messages to his task force. I wonder briefly about calling in my squad from the Twenty-Third.

As capable as the guys are as cops, there's no way for them to be ready to take on skoro assholes without training and knowing what they're up against.

Instead, I text the family chat, giving them an update on the situation and the address.

Replies pop in faster than Onyx when he sees a dried liver treat. Azland, Tad, and my siblings will all be here as soon as possible. According to Kenzie, it will be about fifteen or twenty minutes.

Tad's never been here, so they have to drive.

The wait is fine, despite my general impatience, because that's the amount of time it will take for Rene's team to get here with the warrant.

Until then, Rene and I will sit and wait.

We keep the windows rolled down in case we hear anything, but all is quiet.

Rene's team arrives first. Two nondescript undercover cars pull up, and Rene introduces me to the squad. "This isn't everyone on the fae task force, but this is the empowered side of the team, the ones with the chops to bust in after some demonic thugs."

"Pleasure to meet you," I say.

"This is Carlo." Rene gestures at an older man with olive skin wearing round, silver-rimmed glasses. "He has magic eyes."

Carlo grimaces. "Really? That's the way you put it?"

"Am I wrong?"

Carlo looks at me and frowns. "I see through walls and can send out streams of lasers."

Rene turns to another guy with a huge curly Afro and laugh lines around his eyes. "This is Tomie. They're a shapeshifter."

As if to demonstrate, Tomie reaches out to shake my hand while transforming into a tall, elegant woman wearing a floor-length gown.

"That's not very practical battle wear," I tease as I shake Tomie's hand.

"This is Hannah, our resident elemental."

"Earth," she says simply as she greets me. Hannah is short and petite, with closely cropped brown hair and wide shoulders. Her arms are crossed, and she gives the impression that getting through a brick wall would be easier than getting past her.

"This is Bellarmine and Gonzaga, our warriors."

Bellarmine and Gonzaga are very obviously siblings—most likely twins. They have the same round green eyes, shaggy auburn hair, and crooked grin.

Bellarmine has her hair in a long braid and carries a huge sword at her hip, while Gonzaga's hair falls just above his ears. He has a crossbow strapped to his back. Other than those minor differences, they'd be impossible to tell apart.

"Can we get this party started?" Bellarmine says, one hand resting on the hilt of her sword.

Rene accepts a folded paper from Carlo, which I assume is our warrant. He checks it and nods at me. "We're waiting on Jules' team, but let's get a perimeter worked out."

They disappear into the night, leaving me waiting until Kenzie's blue car pulls up and everyone piles out.

"Did you find their headquarters?" Kenzie asks.

"We think so," I confirm.

"How did we never find this place before?" Zephyr looks around at the powered-down carnival equipment. "It's so creepy. It might as well have a giant neon sign advertising evil shenanigans afoot."

I blink and chuckle. "Why thank you, Sherlock."

He makes a face at me. "What? A guy should be able to use interesting words and not get ridiculed."

Hilarious. "Anyway, we found them, and it's time to bust in and take them down."

Rene's team returns from their perimeter check, and we put our heads together to devise a plan. "My task force will work from the perimeter into the center of the property. There are a few guards and a few exits, and we don't want people sneaking through the cracks. Your team is the direct assault. Tad can portal you inside the locked gates so you can be in the middle of the action when things go down."

I love this plan. "Direct assault works for me. Good luck, my friend." I knuckle bump with Rene, and he jogs off to join his team.

"What's Rene's power?" Kenzie asks.

I shrug. "It's the weirdest thing. I've asked him, and he's told me, but I can never remember. I think it's some kind of memory wipe or amnesia thing."

Kenzie chuckles. "That is a weird superpower."

"Handy to keep things from spilling into the public," Briar notes.

I nod. "I guess."

Azland pegs me with a serious look. "Maintain a fluid balance between offense and defense."

"And keep track of each other," Tad reminds us. "Your powers are stronger when combined."

"Got it." Briar cracks his knuckles, then summons his shield and hammer. Zephyr brandishes his staff, and Kenzie calls her jeweled bracelet into action.

My hands go to the handle of my whip. Heat rises within me as we get ready to rush in and finish this. "All right, let's go."

Discarded equipment clutters the inside of the carnival storage lot. Zephyr and I climb to the top of a giant spider ride to get a better vantage point. There's a round, striped tent set up in the middle of the lot, with dessert trucks parked in a haphazard ring surrounding it.

Zephyr points his staff at it and closes his eyes. A strange wind rushes through the yard, rustling the tent's edges. It gets stronger and stronger until I have to grip the metal fang-tipped jaw of the creepy crawly to keep myself from being blown off.

The wind's force continues to build until it lifts the entire tent, sending the canvas flapping and flying and exposing the entire operation to the night air.

All attention turns toward us, and the bad guys know they've been caught.

"Now!" I drop to the ground, roll to absorb the momentum, transfer the motion, and get to my feet without effort.

With their cover blown, a dozen men scramble, grabbing folding tables and shoving baggies of pills into bins and boxes while others gear up for a fight.

Matthias is there, and something hot ignites inside me at the thought of facing him again. "Briar, you and Kenzie stay on the drugs. Zephyr and Azland, you're with me on the guy with the leather jacket. He's the most dangerous."

"On it!" Briar replies as he holds his shield before him and races into the fray.

Kenzie hops into one of the dessert trucks, turns the key, and it rumbles to life. Several skoro try to rush for her, but she slams on the gas and blows through them, driving in quick, nimble maneuvers around the increasingly chaotic compound.

A rumble in the ground underfoot has me tracking Briar. I expect to see him doing something, but it's not him. It's Tad. Our druid has opened a huge gash in the ground, exposing rich dark soil underneath.

With his lips moving, fissures are opening in the ground and snaking across the lot, stopping skoro and their human drug workers from making it to the fences for their escape.

My gawking around has cost me time. Azland and Zephyr have taken the lead with Matthias and some of his thugs. I crack my whip, releasing fire down its length as it catches Matthias around the ankles and grabs hold.

This gives Azland a chance to deliver a few strong blows to

the man's face before he's yanked away.

Azland grunts, readying for the onslaught of thugs. "I've got these assholes. Zephyr, go help Jules with Matthias."

I'm about to argue that he's the one who needs the help, but he turns the tables. One against three means nothing. Azland's kicks are perfectly placed, and he times his leaps impeccably.

That leaves us to do our part.

Matthias.

The brute glares at me with nothing but amusement in his eyes. I summon the fire within me, releasing it from my hold and freeing it to spread over my skin.

The rush of flame taking over my flesh is incredible.

I hold my hands out at my sides and embrace the surge of my true self. Fire *is* power. It consumes. It creates. It is both destruction and rebirth.

Step by step, Matthias stomps closer. His hands are in fists, and I can tell he's not used to being challenged by someone he deems so far beneath him.

"What's the matter, big guy? Did we invade your secret clubhouse? I told you I was coming for you. It's not my fault if you didn't take me seriously."

The two of us collide with a teeth-rattling blow, and I fight to hold my ground. He has me on brute force, but I like to think I have more than one skill to put into play to even the odds.

With a burst of adrenaline, I push him off and gain some distance. I send a stream of fire at him, forcing him to dive behind a large stack of crates.

Instead of him ducking and hiding, he grips a crate's edge and heaves it through the air.

Now it's me diving out of the way, dodging the projectile as he advances. My confidence wavers. My fire power wasn't enough to save me last time.

He's so freaking strong.

"You didn't think I'd go down easy, did you, little girl?" He's coming at me, swiping metal fencing and stacked framework as he closes the distance. Tossed in the air like it's weightless trash, the crashing of metal on metal is deafening.

I stand my ground and grab a metal pipe in one hand.

Off to my side, some shoots at him, releasing round after round.

Nothing hits home.

It's not like their aim is off—they have a solid line on him—but it's like there's an invisible shield stopping the incoming projectiles before they penetrate his body.

Rude.

His approach is fast and furious, and by the time he's closing in, I go back to my flame whip and pipe. The shooter stops.

The fist to my ribs hits with enough force that I double over, my breath escaping as the echo of broken ribs makes me wince.

A meaty hand closes over my throat, squeezing my windpipe as he lifts me off the ground. My vision fritzes, my focus blurred behind the need for oxygen and the pain searing my right side.

"Supernova, Jules!"

Tad's cry rings across the battlefield, and I recall his lesson. Time to advance and time to get some distance to spare my life.

Right. I could use some distance here.

I need to get this fucker away from me...to *keep* him away from me.

Calling to the flame burning in my cells, I welcome the destructive power building within me. The crackling of potential energy. The promise of a force that brute strength can't beat. It pushes at my insides like a balloon too full and stretching, ready to explode.

I embrace everything in me that will get this sadistic fuck away from me. Then I turn up the heat.

The eruption of flames feels incredible.

My body vibrates with pleasure, with the joy of accepting my truest self.

I vaguely register as I fall that the hold on my neck is gone, and the life-giving pathway of my throat is open so I can breathe again.

When I hear the groaning this time, I'm not worried or upset. No. This time, such sadistic pride fills me that it's almost scary because I'm glad this fucker is hurt.

For Keith.

And Sean.

And Nazim.

And Morgan.

I'm glad Matthias' skin is smoking, and his hair melted and scorched. I'm glad he no longer has eyebrows and looks like something out of a horror movie.

He laughed when his skoro friends sucked the life out of me. Now it's my turn. "Looks like I get the last laugh, asshole. Enjoy the burn unit."

I wave at Tad, who's finishing off the final skoro of his battle. He *poofs* out and back to me a moment later holding Gareth's black T-shirt. "I see ye've learned to follow instruction."

I nod in thanks, turn my back, and release my flames. The moment they no longer encase me, I try to slide into the T-shirt but gasp as the pain of my cracked ribs takes the triumph out of my win. "I might be thick-headed, but still teachable."

Kenzie rushes over to help me. "Somewhat like a lab chimp. Tad, can you give us a little privacy for a moment, please?"

"Aye, I cast the spell before she dropped her flames."

"You're a good man, Tad McNiff."

Kenzie rolls her eyes and swings her hands gracefully before me so her orb of water dances in the air and kisses my bare ribs and side. "If you keep telling him that his ego will take it to heart, and he'll be impossible to live with."

The cool, healing energy washes against my skin and I exhale a sigh of relief. "I don't know. I think he's pretty easy to live with. I enjoy having him around."

"Thank you, Jules." Tad's back is still turned toward me, and I appreciate it as I cover up with Gareth's T-shirt. "What would ye like me to do with this heap of smoldering flesh?"

I pull the shirt's hem over my thighs and wrinkle my nose at Matthias rolling on the ground. His burns are gross and oozy, with bits of dirt and storage lot debris sticking in them. That isn't even mentioning the stench of burned flesh and hair. "Rene said Bakkali accepts empowered criminals for the fae liaison squad until they get a handle on containment facilities."

Tad knows that's his cue. "All right. I'll deliver him and be back. Don't start anything fun without me."

When he *poofs* out, I giggle and bump shoulders with my sister. "He's a good one."

"Yeah, he is."

The two of us scan our surroundings and assess where we're needed.

Zephyr has a couple of skoro caught up in a small cyclone and tosses them backward into an industrial-size cotton candy machine. The metal drum spins with the impact, and Zephyr grins.

He raises his staff and makes the machine spin faster and faster. Its mechanical parts rattle. A few of them fly off, *pinging* with metallic noises against the rest of the carnival equipment.

"Oh my. He's crazy." Kenzie laughs.

The two of us watch as the spinning drum with the two skoro *bangs* and *clunks* around while Zephyr plays puppet master, making his marionettes dance.

It explodes with a loud *crack*, sending the two skoro flying. They crash into a pile of metal rebar and lie dazed, groaning as they press their heads to the ground.

"Nice one, dude!" I'd give Zephyr a high five, but it hasn't been long enough since I was on fire, so we join forces to find Briar and Azland.

It doesn't take long to find our brother. We follow the earth tremors until we locate him at the base of a huge pit where he's pounding skoro who can't escape because the sides are too steep.

Briar's gone full stone and looks like the Michelin Man...if he were chiseled out of granite.

We stand at the top of the ridge and Briar grins up at us until he pinches his eyes shut and turns the other way. "Get my sister some fucking pants."

I take a very quick few steps back from the edge.

Kenzie busts up laughing. "Briar, did she burn out your retinas?"

"Yes, and may we never bring it up again."

Thankfully, Tad *poofs* back with a pair of Kenzie's yoga pants and sneakers. "I didn't want to go into yer room. I hope this is okay."

"It's great, thanks." I pull the stretchy cotton up my thighs before pulling on her shoes.

"You can keep those pants because we both know you don't have undies on." Kenzie makes a face at me.

"Whatevs. Looks like I have to make an emergency travel outfit readily available for pick up."

"Looks like it, yeah."

When the onslaught ends, Kenzie heals everyone the best she can, and we scan the battlefield. Rene and Tad work on cleanup, deciding who goes to regular jail and who goes to empowered prison.

"Who is behind all this?" I ask Rene. "There were no Poreskoro siblings here and nothing to tell us who is in charge."

"Second Sight was Lamech's doing. You took care of him, but maybe what he set in motion didn't end with his death."

"Or maybe one of the others took up the mantle, and we've shut down the operation, but the person in charge never got caught on our radar."

Rene shrugs. "It wouldn't be the first time."

"It has to be one of the others, right?" Kenzie interjects.

"Because if this were only about Lamech and his plans to make money while mutating humanity, the skoro forces working the streets and distributing the product would've died when he did."

I nod. "Good point, Kenz. Right, when Lamech died, so did his sired line of skoro assholes."

Rene frowns and glances at some of the men Bellarmine and Gonzaga have hog-tied. "Maybe they'll tell us?"

"Maybe. I can't imagine loyalty is much of a moral compass for these guys. Let's see what he knows."

Rene moves to grab the front of his shirt, and the asshole spits black ichor at him. The goo lands on his jacket and eats through the fabric like acid.

"Whoa, not cool, dude." I rush forward with my hand alight, and the guy's eyes flare wide. "Tell us which of the Poreskoro sired you and it doesn't have to get nasty."

"Fuck you!"

I frown. "Or maybe it does have to get nasty."

He wriggles forward and lunges at me with his teeth bared.

I smack him with a fiery hand and singe his cheek. "How stupid are you? I'm the one with flames dancing on my hand, and you're tied up. In what world do you think you're attacking me?"

"Which of the Poreskoro siblings are you from?" Rene demands, now minus his jacket. "Tell us, and we ship you off somewhere dark but cozy. Keep it to yourself and Jules here will give you a five-star on your cheek."

I am? Oh, yeah. I nod and take a step closer, holding up my flaming hand to prove my point.

"Like I said, fuck you. You're cops. You're not going to burn me."

I grin. "You're only partly right. We are cops, but we're cops of a squad tasked to take down empowered scum. We get to play by different rules." To prove my point, I press my palm flat on the right side of his face and brand my hand into his skin.

The scream that tears from him makes my stomach churn but

not half as much as the stench of burning flesh. "I can't. She'll kill me…"

I straighten and grin at Rene. "She. That means it's either Sasobek or Zissa."

The guy throws a panicked glance at the love tunnel and screams, "I didn't tell them. I didn't tell them anything!"

I straighten and meet Rene's gaze. "Are you thinking what I'm thinking?"

He waggles his brows. "If you're thinking of getting me alone in the tunnel of love to have your way with me, I have to decline."

I roll my eyes and laugh. "You wish. Now, let's catch this bitch and end this. Azland and Zephyr, you're with us. Kenzie, watch your back."

A plastic tarp covers the entrance to the love tunnel, but the dust at the edge has recently been disturbed. I creep forward and use the tip of my gun to pull back the curtain. The space is dark, a hollowed-out tunnel sculpted to look like the inside of a stone cave.

The five of us make quick work of moving forward. I have my arm up, my hand aflame to light the way. The little train that used to run people through here has long since expired. We pass the eight heart-shaped cars with cracked pleather seats.

We jog the length of the tunnel, but there's no sign of anyone hiding. Since the other end of the tunnel lets out on the back of the lot, I assume whichever Poreskoro it was, she's long gone.

By the time we get back to the others, Tad has deposited all the bad guys where they needed to go, Kenzie has fixed up Rene's team, and Carlo is pulling bags and bags of Second Sight from the dessert trucks and piling them on tables to be inventoried.

"We did it." I grin as Rene and I scan the ruins of this drug operation. "Let's hope this is finally over."

CHAPTER TWENTY-SIX

We stay a while after the battle to brief the local cops and walk Bakkali through things. Once that's taken care of, Kenzie drives our brothers home. Tad portals me back to the firehouse after I wrap up a few more details. Onyx is thrilled that we're all covered with powdered sugar and cinnamon and licks us from head to toe before we can extricate ourselves to change and shower.

As usual, the water isn't nearly hot enough to replenish the energy I've expended, especially after going supernova. I'm drained and daydream about Gareth's fireplace sanctuary.

The daydream morphs and now it's only about Gareth.

I dry off and pull on comfy clothes before following the delicious scent of sizzling meat and pasta sauce. *Score!* Briar is making Sloppy Joes, with Onyx begging at his feet.

"Briar? Are you feeding my dog raw ground beef?" I'm toweling my hair in a way that makes Kenzie grimace and roll her eyes.

"Yep. He loves it. Don't you, hell dog?"

I laugh at how Onyx wags his tail as if supporting Briar's statement.

"Hey, do you want me to treat your hair with healing waters?" Kenzie watches me towel my head.

"Nah, I'm good. The last time you magicked my hair, people complimented me for days. Pass."

Kenzie opens her mouth to argue with me, likely to point out that getting complimented on one's hair isn't a bad thing, but Briar interrupts her.

"Jules. You look pale."

I nod. "Yeah. I'm a little low on fuel. Going supernova to take out Matthias drained me."

"Why don't you go try your new magma pit?"

I stop toweling. "Wait. What? Is it ready?"

"Only one way to find out." Briar grins.

I'm not sure who is coming out for the grand opening of my elemental sanctuary, but I don't care. I grab the brass pole, slide down without pause, and book it into the back yard.

I'm not going to lie. It's damn sexy.

The pool is dug into the ground with a stone retaining wall around it so I'm at eye level with anyone sitting on the porch when I'm inside. The purple-hued volcanic stone is glossy and smooth, and the magma inside is bubbling and glowing invitingly.

There's even a screened-in area, complete with orange fabric embroidered in an intricate flame pattern, where I can go to get undressed without burning my brothers' retinas out again.

"Sweet." I step behind the privacy screen and see a fluffy black robe. It's nearly identical to the one I borrowed at Gareth's house, but this one is my size, with a J embroidered on it.

I run my hand down the soft fabric and smile.

Gareth is too much.

Eager to try out my new elemental spa, I undress, step into the little screened-off access cove, and lower myself into the magma.

Every skin cell I possess tingles to life.

"Oh, my God. It feels heavenly."

The intense heat feeds my cells, filling my emotional well and refreshing my elemental energy. As I settle in, I find the molded seat where I can soak and bask with only my head and the tops of my shoulders peeking out from the pool of molten lava.

"So, you're happy?" There's a hint of worry in Briar's deep voice.

Zephyr's standing beside him, biting his bottom lip. How did I get so lucky?

"I'm in heaven. There's no way I can thank you, boys. You went above and beyond on this one. Consider this my birthday and Christmas present for the rest of my life. You are officially off the hook forever."

"Sweet." Zephyr grins. "I'm going to hold you to that, Jules."

"Sounds good. I mean it."

"Then we'll leave you to it," Kenzie says.

"You don't have to go." I lift my arm and beckon them over. Gobs of fire drip off my hand. "Come on in. The magma's fine."

Kenzie laughs. "Hard pass. I might not love my skin being blue, but I appreciate it being there."

"Then feel free to pull up a chair."

The boys decline and head back inside, but Kenzie keeps me company. She collects one of the patio chairs and brings it over. When she settles, she lifts her feet and sets them on the stone retaining wall, well back from the heat.

As she's settling in, a metallic glint on her hand catches my eye. Lurching up, I try to process the silver band on her ring finger.

Despite being in the most relaxing place I've ever been, I nearly have a heart attack.

"Kenzie!" I shout, pointing at the ring. "What on earth is that—you're engaged?"

Kenzie shakes her head. "Don't be ridiculous. Tad didn't buy this for me. Well, I guess technically he did, but he bought them for everyone."

"Huh?"

"Emerald Moon and Luc...your dead guy doctor knows his stuff. His research idea worked, and the white witch seductress came through for us. These little bands are shields to prevent our fae energy from being detectable, even to those using Second Sight or other magical methods to ferret us out."

I'm still recovering from the shock of thinking my baby sister had gotten engaged after a month of dating a guy. As my heart rate begins to regulate, I sit back and think about how much of a game-changer these rings might be. "Will they work with fire and ice and everything we'll put them through?"

"Only one way to find out."

Kenzie reaches into her pocket and pulls out another silver band. Hers has a small blue jewel set into it, while mine has a glittering garnet. She sets mine on the edge of the pool. I don't reach for it until she's back at a safe distance.

After picking it up, I wait a beat to see if the metal melts in my hand.

It doesn't.

I slide it onto my ring finger, but it's too loose. I twirl it around a few times, then try it on my middle finger, where it fits perfectly.

Ha. It's like a magical way of giving the bird to anyone trying to track me down.

I let my hand sink under the surface of the magma and swish it around. The ring doesn't dissolve or loosen.

"It's perfect."

"Glad to hear it." Tad waves from where he's setting a couple of drinks out at the patio table. "I heard ye were out here enjoyin' yer new toy."

I sink back into the depths of the magma and sigh. "It's not a toy. This is a very important magical medicinal device."

"Aye, that it is." Tad smiles.

Then Aurora descends to land on Tad's shoulder with a dead rat hanging from her beak.

"Oh, yuck." Kenzie wrinkles her nose.

"Och, aren't ye the most cunnin' girl. Well done, lass." He strokes a loving caress over her head and then points at the shadow in the yard. "Enjoy yer dinner, little one."

Thankfully for Kenzie, Aurora follows his instruction and flies her deceased vermin dinner over to eat it on the ground. She barely gets started eating it when Onyx scampers over and makes her squawk.

"Och, no, lad. Don't fight her for her rat."

I groan and push to the front of my pool. "Oh, no, come on. If he eats that, there's no telling what it'll be like coming out the other end. Onyx, no. Drop it!"

Onyx ignores me, barking and jumping around as he enjoys his fun new game of keep-away with his tasty new treat.

"Onyx! Come here, boy! Come!"

The prospect of joining me in the magma spa is enough to convince him to give Aurora back her dead rat. He drops it and runs wildly toward me, ready to jump in.

Kenzie squeals and runs away, which is a good call, given how wide the splash zone would have been if I hadn't caught him before he hit the pool's surface.

Still, there are now a few burned-out patches glowing in the grass.

"We've gotta teach yer pup to climb in gracefully," Tad notes. "Or yer entire backyard will need to be paved in obsidian."

"We'll work on that training," I promise.

Tad's the one who can commune with animals, so I'm sure he'll be a big help.

Kenzie checks the hem of her dress for singed patches. "On that note, I'm heading in and heading to bed. You have a nice night."

"You have a better one," I reply.

She grabs the drinks off the table, Tad's hand in hers, and pulls him behind her, grinning. "Oh, I intend to."

I roll my eyes, but I'm super happy for both of them.

I stay in the spa for a while, eventually getting out and tugging on my new heatproof robe. I play with Onyx in the backyard while we both cool off enough to go inside safely.

At the table, Briar and Zephyr are bent over Zephyr's laptop, laughing at the new fae-themed jokes being shared on the website.

Hannah, the earth girl from Rene's team, has been added to the Discord channel and apparently she's hella funny.

They're completely preoccupied, but I hug both from behind and press a sisterly kiss on the tops of their heads. "Thank you, boys, for your hard work on my pool, for backing me up today, and for being awesome. You rock socks."

"Yeah, we do," Briar agrees.

Zephyr chuckles and winks at me. "You're welcome. You're pretty all right too, I guess."

I laugh and turn in for the night with my puppy trotting behind me. Once I'm washed up and snuggled in bed, I text Gareth to thank him for the magma pit, and Onyx, and the rest of his efforts to support me as I figure out how to navigate this weird new world of being a fire elemental.

He doesn't respond, but I'm not worried. It's late. Anyway, I have another call to make.

I dial Rene's number, and he answers in a sleep-thick voice. "Jules? Is everything all right?"

"Yeah, sorry. I know it's late. I just wanted to say I'm in. I'll join your team."

"Seriously?"

"Yeah."

"Excellent. I'll make it happen. Thanks, Jules. You're going to be a great addition to the team. I'm thrilled to have you on board."

I chuckle and close my eyes, my body ebbing with blissful relaxation. "Yeah, I recorded that. I'll play it back for you when I'm driving you nuts."

He chuckles on the other end. "Which will probably be tomorrow."

"Sounds about right."

I hear the smile in Rene's voice. "I'll risk it. Go into the precinct tomorrow like always, and I'll be in touch mid-morning. That should give you time to talk to your boys and get sorted."

I don't want to think about saying goodbye to the guys, but they'll understand. "Tomorrow, then. Thanks, Rene. I look forward to seeing what good we can do together."

"Me too, Gagne. It's going to be magical."

ENDNOTE

Thank you for reading *Magicae: Power Dawning*, book two in the Chronicles of an Urban Elemental series. While the story is fresh in your mind, and as a favor to Michael and me, please click HERE and tell other readers what you thought.

A quick star rating and/or one sentence can mean so much to readers deciding whether to try a book, series, or a new-to-them author.

Thank you.

If you want more of the Quebec Quint, you can find book three in the series, *Potentia: Bonds Forged*, on Amazon.

THE STORY CONTINUES

The story continues with book three, *Potentia: Bonds Forged*, available at Amazon.

Claim your copy today!

AUTHOR NOTES - AUBURN TEMPEST

WRITTEN JANUARY 26, 2023

Thank you for reading book two of the Chronicles of the Urban Elementals and since you're reading this, for sticking with me right until the end.

At the time of publication, book three is written and book four is well underway. A lot of fun adventures are coming your way. I hope you enjoy them all.

If the reviews are anything to go by, readers love the character crossovers from the Urban Druid series. In truth, I love that too.

It makes sense to me that Fi and Sloan would make themselves available to Jules, especially because Tad is becoming rooted in their lives. I'm so happy he's finding his footing with people who need him and value the bond of family by choice.

As always, thank you for your support, comments, and reviews, and for entrusting your time to my characters and the stories they have to tell.

If you enjoyed it and want to keep your finger on the pulse, feel free to join the Facebook Fan page.

Or drop us a line: UrbanDruid@lmbpn.com

Blessed be,
Auburn Tempest

AUTHOR NOTES - MICHAEL ANDERLE

WRITTEN FEBRUARY 10, 2023

Thank you for not only reading this book but these author notes as well!

I'm going to share some dirt on someone I really appreciate and believe is a hoot to be with, talk to, and to find out what the @#%@# she is up to.

Auburn Tempest.

Yes, that's right. I'm going to drop some dirt on my collaborator. Why? Because I think it's funny. I'm not being ugly, I promise!

You see, Auburn is a VERY serious introvert. When COVID shut all of us in the house, she just thought, "This is grand!"

Seriously, if Auburn doesn't have to leave her comfy house, she is not bothered at all. In comparison, I ended up renting out the condo, and my wife and I bought a house to get away from the Las Vegas Strip (where we lived at the time) because I could not handle the four walls of our condo after a month.

I went stark raving mad. Huh, maybe these author notes are more about me.

Want to ask Auburn questions about the stories? She's at

her keyboard, honest. Just drop ~~us~~ *her* a line: UrbanDruid@lmbpn.com

While Auburn is fine when she travels (as evidenced by her coming to Vegas for 20Booksto50K™ and London for a romance conference in a couple of months), travel isn't something she plans all the time.

If you catch her in the wild, she will have bright eyes and a huge smile. She will MAKE you smile just because she seems so damned happy.

In fact, you know what I think will make her smile? YOU GOT IT! An email ;-)

Tell her Mike sent you. I can't wait to hear the comments she makes since she won't realize I am helping her deal with boredom. She has to be bored if she is at home all the time, right?

(Probably not, but even if you send a short email saying which character is your favorite, I chuckle thinking of how many emails she might get.)

Chat with you in the next book.

Ad Aeternitatem,

Michael Anderle

MORE STORIES with Michael newsletter HERE:
https://michael.beehiiv.com/

BOOKS BY AUBURN TEMPEST

Join us on the Facebook page: https://www.facebook.com/groups/167165864237006

Or feel free to drop us a line: UrbanDruid@lmbpn.com

Find Me

Amazon, Facebook, Newsletter,

Web page – www.auburntempest.com

Email – AuburnTempestWrites@gmail.com

Auburn Tempest - Urban Fantasy Action/Adventure

Chronicles of an Urban Druid

Book 1 – A Gilded Cage

Book 2 – A Sacred Grove

Book 3 – A Family Oath

Book 4 – A Witch's Revenge

Book 5 – A Broken Vow

Book 6 – A Druid Hexed

Book 7 – An Immortal's Pain

Book 8 – A Shaman's Power

Book 9 – A Fated Bond

Book 10 – A Dragon's Dare

Book 11 – A God's Mistake

Book 12 – A Destiny Unlocked

Book 13 – A United Front

Book 14 – A Culling Tide

Book 15 – A Danger Destroyed

Case Files of an Urban Druid

Book 1 – Mayhem in Montreal

Book 2 – Sorcery in San Francisco

Book 3 – Necromancy in New Orleans

Book 4 – Hazards in the Hidden City

Book 5 - Hexes in Texas

Book 6 - Wendigos in Washington

Chronicles of an Urban Elemental

Book 1 – Incendio: Fire Born

Book 2 – Magicae: Powers Dawning

Book 3 - Potentia: Bonds Forged

If you enjoy my writing and read sexy/steamy romance, my pen name for the books I write in Paranormal and Fantasy Romance is JL Madore.

You can find me on Amazon.

BOOKS BY MICHAEL ANDERLE

Sign up for the LMBPN email list to be notified of new releases and special deals!

https://lmbpn.com/email/

For a complete list of books by Michael Anderle, please visit:

www.lmbpn.com/ma-books/

CONNECT WITH THE AUTHORS

Connect with Auburn

Amazon, Facebook, Newsletter

Web page – www.jlmadore.com

Email – AuburnTempestWrites@gmail.com

Connect with Michael Anderle and sign up for his email list here:

Website: http://lmbpn.com

Email List: http://lmbpn.com/email/

https://www.facebook.com/LMBPNPublishing

https://twitter.com/lmbpn

https://www.instagram.com/lmbpn_publishing/

https://www.bookbub.com/authors/michael-anderle

www.ingramcontent.com/pod-product-compliance
Lightning Source LLC
LaVergne TN
LVHW091719070526
838199LV00050B/2461